# EXTRAORDINARY

# RENDITION

# Also by Paul Batista

*Death's Witness*
*The Borzoi Killings*

# EXTRAORDINARY
# RENDITION

*A novel by*

## PAUL BATISTA

Oceanview Publishing
Longboat Key, Florida

ISBN 978-1-60809-210-9

Published in the United States of America by Oceanview Publishing
Longboat Key, Florida

www.oceanviewpub.com

10 9 8 7 6 5 4 3 2 1

PRINTED IN THE UNITED STATES OF AMERICA

# DEDICATION

*For*
*Iris Gerber Damson*

# 1

THE PLANE WAS BANKING over Florida's Atlantic coast when Byron Carlos Johnson felt the first tug of the landing process beginning eighty miles from Miami. He raised the plastic window shade to his left and, for the first time in two hours, looked out at the sky and the dazzling ocean. He put the book he'd been reading—Wilkie Collins's *The Moonstone*—into the elasticized pouch in front of him. He'd last read the intricate nineteenth-century mystery when he was in college, and his concentrated passage through the Gothic prose had been a welcome reprieve from his incessant thinking about Ali Hussein, the Syrian who had already spent two months in the Federal Detention Center in Miami after years in foreign prisons not yet disclosed to Byron—mystery places somewhere in the world.

Since he carried only a slim briefcase for this one-day visit to Miami, Byron didn't have to wait for baggage. He left the terminal before any other passenger on the flight and was in a barely air-conditioned taxi fifteen minutes after leaving the plane. The driver was a talkative Jamaican who seemed intrigued by the destination Byron gave him: "The prison on Southwest 137th Avenue."

The driver repeatedly glanced into the rearview mirror at Byron. In that familiar Jamaican lilt, he asked, "You a lawyer, man? You look like a lawyer."

2 | PAUL BATISTA

"What does a lawyer look like, Jacques?" His name was on a plastic license taped to the dashboard.

"A dude in a suit, man. Down here anybody in a suit is a lawyer."

Byron, who could see the driver's face in the rearview mirror just as the driver could see Byron's face, smiled. "Only crazy men wear suits, Jacques."

"You don't look crazy, man."

"You never know, Jacques."

The Miami skyline had changed in the thirty years since Byron first saw it. Then, Miami was a city with the low, smoky skyline of a Latin American capital. Byron remembered enjoying the streets in the heart of the city with small Cuban grocery stores and colorful, hole-in-the-wall bars. He spoke fluent Spanish—his mother was a Mexican who had given him the middle name Carlos and his father, who was the United States Ambassador to Mexico in the early 1960s, during the Kennedy Administration, was also fluent. Byron still had vivid early recollections of Mexico City and the black Packards with gaudily uniformed chauffeurs who drove him around the city, the slowly rotating ceiling fans, the parties on the leafy grounds of the Presidential Palace, and the sweet grammar school where he had only five classmates, all of them children of men who worked for his father at the grand embassy.

Now Miami's skyline was dominated by high towers of flashing glass and steel. As the taxi sped along the causeway toward the city, Byron stared at the modern office buildings that reflected all the light of this brilliant day. Since Byron believed that taxi drivers knew everything, he asked Jacques, "Are there any tenants in those new buildings?"

Jacques whistled. "Empty, man. I never pick anybody up there, never drop anybody off. Somebody's not making too much money."

Byron gave Jacques a big tip, and in exchange Jacques gave Byron a big smile. "You my man," Jacques said.

As soon as Byron stepped out of the taxi at the prison's security gate, he was submerged in heat and humidity. He walked as quickly as he could across the football field–sized parking lot, his suit jacket slung over his shoulder. The Federal Detention Center, built in the 1970s, rose like a Soviet fortress over the warehouses on the waterfront. In the wide Miami harbor, tall cranes stood against the tropical sky in which cumulus clouds towered. Tankers and cargo ships, pleasure craft and sailboats moved on the water.

After thirty minutes of security checks in the ammonia-smelling entrance to the prison, where the air conditioning was so minimal that Byron continued to sweat as much as he had during the long walk, he was led by a heavy-set Hispanic prison guard to a locked room. When the guard left, the iron door resonated briefly as the magnetic lock engaged itself. Byron sat on a steel folding chair. Directly in front of him was a narrow ledge under a multi-layered, almost opaque plastic window, in the middle of which was a metal circle.

Ali Hussein seemed to just materialize in the small space behind the partition. Dressed in a yellow jumpsuit printed with the initials "FDC" for "Federal Detention Center," Hussein, who had been described to Byron as an accountant trained at Seton Hall, in Newark, was a slender man who appeared far more mild-mannered than Byron expected. He wore cloth slippers with no shoelaces. The waistband of his jumpsuit was elasticized—not even a cloth belt. He had as little access to hard objects as possible.

He waited for Byron to speak first. Leaning toward the metal speaker in the partition and raising his voice, Byron said, "You are Mr. Hussein, aren't you?"

The lawyers at the Civil Liberties Union who had first contacted Byron told him that, in their limited experience with accused terrorists, it sometimes wasn't clear what their real names were. There were often no fingerprints or DNA samples that could confirm their identities. The name *Ali Hussein* was as common as a coin. It was as though genetic markers and their histories began only at the moment of their arrest.

"I am." He spoke perfect, unaccented English. "I don't know what your name is."

The circular speaker in the window, although it created a tinny sound, worked well. Byron lowered his voice. "I'm Byron Johnson. I'm a lawyer from New York. I met your brother. Did he tell you to expect me?"

"I haven't heard from my brother in years. He has no idea how to reach me, I can't reach him."

"Has anyone told you why you're here?"

"Someone on the airplane—I don't know who he was, I was blindfolded—said I was being brought here because I'd been charged with a crime. He said I could have a lawyer. Are you that lawyer?"

"I am. If you want me, and if I want to do this."

All that Ali's more abrasive, more aggressive brother had told Byron was that Ali was born in Syria, moved as a child with his family to Lebanon during the civil war in the 1980s, and then came to the United States. Ali never became a

United States citizen. Five months after the invasion of Iraq, he traveled to Germany to do freelance accounting work for an American corporation for what was scheduled to be a ten-day visit. While Ali was in Germany, his brother said, he had simply disappeared, as if waved out of existence. His family had written repeatedly to the State Department, the CIA, and the local congressman. They were letters sent into a vacuum. Nobody ever answered.

Byron asked, "Do you know where you've come from?"

"How do I know who you are?"

Byron began to reach for his wallet, where he stored his business cards. He caught himself because of the absurdity of that: he could have any number of fake business cards. Engraved with gold lettering, his real business card had his name and the name of his law firm, one of the oldest and largest in the country. Ali Hussein was obviously too intelligent, too alert, and too suspicious to be convinced by a name on a business card or a license or a credit card.

"I don't have any way of proving who I am. I can just tell you that I'm Byron Johnson, I've been a lawyer for years, I live in New York, and I was asked by your brother and others to represent you."

Almost unblinking, Ali just stared at Byron, who tried to hold his gaze, but failed.

At last Ali asked, "And you want to know what's happened to me?"

"We can start there. I'm only allowed thirty minutes to visit you this week. Tell me what you feel you want to tell me, or can tell me. And then we'll see where we go. You don't have to tell me everything about who you are, what you did before you were arrested, who you know in the outside world. Or you don't have to tell me anything. I want nothing from you other than to help you."

Ali leaned close to the metallic hole in the smoky window. The skin around his eyes was far darker than the rest of his face, almost as if he wore a Zorro-style mask. Byron took no notes, because to do so might make Ali Hussein even more mistrustful.

"Today don't ask me any questions. People have asked me lots of questions over the years. I'm sick of questions." It was like listening to a voice from a world other than the one in which Byron lived. There was nothing angry or abusive in his tone: just a matter-of-fact directness, as though he was describing to Byron a computation he had made on one of Byron's tax returns. "One morning five Americans in suits stopped me at a red light. I was in Bonn. I drove a rented Toyota. I had a briefcase. They got out of their cars. They had earpieces. Guns, too. They told me to get out of the car. I did. They told me to show them my hands. I did. They lifted me into an SUV, tied my hands, and put a blindfold on me. I asked who they were and what was happening."

He paused. Byron, who had been in the business of asking questions since he graduated from law school at Harvard, couldn't resist the embedded instinct to ask, "What did they say?"

"They said shut up."

"Has anyone given you any papers since you've come here?"

"I haven't had anything in my hands to read in years. Not a newspaper, not a magazine, not a book. Not even the *Koran.*"

"Has anyone told you what crimes you're charged with?"

"Don't you know?"

"No. All that I've been told is that you were moved to Miami from a foreign jail so that you could be indicted and tried in an American court."

There was another pause. "How exactly did you come to me?" Even though he kept returning to the same subject—who exactly was Byron Johnson?—there was still no hostility or anger in Ali Hussein's tone. "Why are you here?"

In the stifling room, Byron began to sweat almost as profusely as he had on the walk from the security gate to the prison entrance. He recognized that he was very tense. And he was certain that the thirty-minute rule would be enforced, that time was running out. He didn't want to lose his chance to gain the confidence of this ghostly man who had just emerged into a semblance of life after years in solitary limbo. "A lawyer for a civil rights group called me. I had let people know that I wanted to represent a person arrested for terrorism. I was told that you were one of four prisoners being transferred out of some detention center, maybe at Guantanamo, to a mainland prison, and that you'd be charged by an American grand jury rather than held overseas indefinitely. When I got the call I said I would help, but only if you and I met, and only if you wanted me to help, and only if I thought I could do that."

"How do I know any of this is true?"

Byron Johnson prided himself on being a realist. Wealthy clients sought him out not to tell them what they wanted to hear but for advice about the facts, the law, and the likely real-world outcomes of whatever problems they faced. But it hadn't occurred to him that this man, imprisoned for years, would doubt him and would be direct enough to tell him that. Byron had become accustomed to deference, not to challenge. And this frail man was suggesting that Byron might be a stalking horse, a plant, a shill, a human recording device.

"I met your brother Khalid."

"Where?"

"At a diner in Union City."

"What diner?"

"He said it was his favorite, and that you used to eat there with him: the Plaza Diner on Kennedy Boulevard."

Byron, who for years had practiced law in areas where a detailed memory was essential, was relieved that he remembered the name and location of the diner just across the Hudson River in New Jersey. He couldn't assess whether the man behind the thick, scratched glass was now more persuaded to believe him. Byron asked, "How have you been treated?"

"I've been treated like an animal."

"In what ways?"

As if briskly covering the topics on an agenda, Ali Hussein said, "Months in one room, no contact with other people. Shifted from place to place, never knowing what country or city I was in, never knowing what month of the year, day of the week. Punched. Kicked."

"Do you have any marks on your body?"

"I'm not sure yet what your name really is, or who you really are, but you seem naive. Marks? Are you asking me if they've left bruises or scars on my body?"

Byron felt the rebuke. Over the years he'd learned that there was often value in saying nothing. Silence sometimes changed the direction of a conversation and revealed more. He waited.

Hussein asked, "How much more time do we have?"

"Only a few minutes."

"A few minutes? I've been locked away for years, never in touch for a second with anyone who meant to do kind things to me, and now I have a total of thirty minutes with you. Mr. Bush created a beautiful world."

"There's another president." Byron paused, and, with the silly thought of giving this man some hope, he said, "His name is Barack Hussein Obama."

Ali Hussein almost smiled. "And I'm still here? How did that happen?"

Byron didn't answer, feeling foolish that he'd thought the news that an American president's middle name was Hussein would somehow brighten this man's mind. Byron had pandered to him, and he hated pandering.

Ali Hussein then asked, "My wife and children?"

No one—not the ACLU lawyer, not the CIA agent with whom Byron had briefly talked to arrange this visit, not even Hussein's heavy-faced, brooding brother—had said a single thing about Hussein other than that he had been brought into the United States after years away and that he was an accountant. Nothing about a wife and children.

"I don't know. I didn't know you had a wife and children. Nobody said anything about them. I should have asked."

It was unsettling even to Byron, who had dealt under tense circumstances with thousands of people in courtrooms, that this man could stare at him for so long with no change of expression. Hussein finally asked, "Are you going to come back?"

"If you want me to."

"I was an accountant, you know. I always liked numbers, and I believed in the American system that money moves everything, that he who pays the piper gets to call the tune. Who's paying you?"

"No one, Mr. Hussein. Anything I do for you will be free. I won't get paid by anybody."

"Now I really wonder who you are." There was just a trace of humor in his voice and his expression.

As swiftly as Ali Hussein had appeared in the interview room, he disappeared when two guards in Army uniforms reached in from the rear door and literally yanked him from his chair. It was like watching a magician make a man disappear.

# 2

It WAS AN INTERNAL conference room. Beige walls and fluorescent lighting made the faces of the other people in the room sallow or haggard or both. The makeup of the only woman appeared to be flaking in the unforgiving light. Plastic chairs surrounded a utilitarian wooden table. There were photographs of Barack Obama and the Attorney General on the wall, both men posed next to American flags. The photographs had the quality of high school graduation pictures. The men were eager to please, wholesome, and highlighted with flesh-colored tints.

Over the years Byron had rarely attended meetings with other lawyers alone. He once heard that large firms like his always sent at least two lawyers to even insignificant meetings because lawyers, like nuns, travel in groups. Now, on the other side of the table, were four people: two lawyers, one agent from the CIA, and another from Homeland Security. Byron was the only one on his side of the table. Only the lawyers mentioned their names. Byron wasn't introduced to the agents.

His attention was immediately captured by the presence of the lead government lawyer. Hamerindapal Rana was a Sikh. He was well over six feet tall. He wore a deep brown turban of elegant fabric. His suit was beautifully tailored. Byron, himself a careful dresser, recognized that Rana's suit was handmade, possibly in London. The other men on Rana's side of the table were bulky and blond, like former college football players, and wore off-the-rack suits with American flag lapel pins.

Rana said, "Mr. Johnson, you must understand we will indict Mr. Hussein at a time and in a place of our own choosing. It may be an hour from now. It may be six months from now. And it may be in Miami and it may be Juneau, Alaska, with Sarah Palin as the judge."

In the five minutes since the start of the conference, Byron had let go of any pretense that this would be what he liked to describe as a "good, cordial meeting." He said, "Mr. Rana, the man is now in jail in the United States. He's been in detention more than nine years by my count. I don't think you have the right to delay indicting him indefinitely."

"You think so, Mr. Johnson?" Like his clothes, Hal Rana's voice was elegant, almost British-accented. Byron, who had the sense that Rana must have spent time in an English boarding school, was intrigued. Rana continued, "The Congress and the president don't see it your way. We have an anti-terrorism bill that gives us the option to decide when to indict and where to indict. We don't need to be concerned about whatever speedy trial rights your client may have, because he has none. And, in this kind of case, we can indict him anywhere in the country, and he can't complain that it's the wrong place."

"So you're going to pick a state where the jury is most likely to convict, right?"

"We've been thinking about Oklahoma, Mr. Johnson. We relish the idea of putting a terrorist on trial in front of an Oklahoma jury near the site where McVeigh blew up the federal building."

"I don't think that's fair."

"You don't? Then you have to complain to Congress. I'm just a simple country lawyer."

Byron knew he had few options since new laws gave lawyers little leeway to do what they ordinarily did when they represented accused people. He couldn't insist on a quick indictment, couldn't seek bail, and couldn't demand a speedy trial. Judges for the most part were timid and unwilling to disturb whatever the Justice Department, the CIA, and Homeland Security decided to do.

"My client and I don't even know what the charges are, Mr. Rana."

"We don't know either yet. We can take our time to decide what the charges are."

"Listen, I asked for this meeting so that I could develop at least *some* information to defend this man."

"Information? You want information? I have a suggestion for you: Ask your client what he knows."

"Ask my client? Don't you think it might be fair at some point to let him know whether he's accused of killing Kennedy or driving bin Laden around?"

"We don't think he killed Kennedy. You don't have to ask him about that. As for bin Laden, he's left the planet and doesn't need drivers any more, except for celestial chariots."

"I don't particularly want to go to the newspapers and tell them that the United States government is stonewalling. Reporters are dying to hear about this case, Mr. Rana. The Attorney General saw to it that this story was all over CNN, FOX, all the networks."

"It hasn't been our experience that there's really a public outcry when we hold a terrorist in jail. And we are being nice to you by having this meeting. We can stop having meetings if you don't work with us."

"Work with you? What does that mean?"

"In my world, Mr. Johnson, a lot of the work involves information. Information is hard currency here."

"Information about what?"

"I can't tell you how to do your job. But you might want to connect the dots for your client. He's an accountant. He's far better versed in numbers than most people are. Also, we know he's a wizard in the wonders of money transfers—cash, wires, checks, computers, virtual accounts, human mules carrying cash taped to their bodies." Rana paused. "I assume you're following me? As they say in the mobster movies, *capiche?*"

"All I know, Mr. Rana, is that he's an accountant. And so far I've had exactly thirty minutes to talk to him."

Rana smiled almost benignly. "What does your client's brother have to say?"

Byron was instantly unsettled. He had made no attempt to conceal the meeting at the diner in gritty Union City with Ali Hussein's brother, but it had never occurred to him that the government would know about it.

"All his brother could tell me was what a nice man Mr. Hussein is, and how long he'd been gone."

"You know what, Mr. Johnson? We do want to help you and your client. You probably haven't done much of this kind of criminal work, and I can tell you're a nice man just trying to do the world a favor by representing the oppressed. But you might want to talk with Mr. Hussein about the people he did accounting work for, what cash they had, where they got it, how they gave it to him, where he sent it, who gave him instructions about where to send it, the names of the people he dealt with on both ends of the transactions—the collection of the money and the distribution of it, what the accountants call 'first in, first out.'" Rana waited. "And, most important, ask him where he put the money just before he joined us and where it is now."

Byron wanted to restrain himself, as he had throughout the conference, from responding to the condescending message that he was walking into dangerous and unfamiliar territory where he knew nothing about the pitfalls. He also resented that cultured edge of British superciliousness in Rana's tone. "I appreciate that you're trying to help my client. The government has been a great help to him over these last years. But, so that I don't just grope around in the dark, tell me what you think he might know."

"We don't know what he knows."

"You've had many years to chat pleasantly with him about his background and his work. Most marriages don't last that long."

"You know better than I do, Mr. Johnson, that creativity is the lifeblood of the law, as Oliver Wendell Holmes wrote and we all heard in our first year at law school. Maybe once you get to know your client better you may want to think creatively and then call us if there's anything that we might do for him in exchange for information. Your client knows a great deal about the value of exchange—he can apply the skills he learned about exchanging money to the exchange of information. We've found that Syrians are very effective in the workings of trades, exchanges, and bargains. The skill dates back to long before Biblical times."

"Syrians? I thought the Justice Department wasn't supposed to discriminate on the basis of national origin or religion."

"You might also ask Mr. Ali about religion, now that you mention it. Nine years ago he was a devoted member of the Al Sunni Mosque in Newark, on Raymond Boulevard. He was particularly impressed, we've learned, by the teachings and wisdom of the Imam of the mosque, Sheik Naveed al Haq. Over the last few years Sheik al Haq has told a few of his congregants that he is particularly concerned about the fate and the soul of your client. Maybe your client can favor us with a little bit of information about the teachings of the Imam and what happened to the mosque's collection boxes."

"Now that's useful information at last, Mr. Rana." Byron still instinctively felt uncomfortable engaging this exotic man in any kind of cynical banter but found it hard to resist. "Now I know about the Imam. That's a start. Are there any other people you can tell me about who I can call for information?"

"Maybe as we go along, Mr. Johnson, I can give you a boost on that. Maybe when you make your client understand that if he wants to help himself we might be able to help him, by someday letting him have the hope of seeing Damascus again, where he can enjoy the blessings of a true democracy, and in this life, not the next."

# 3

THREE BANDS WERE PERFORMING at the firm's party in the Central Park Zoo. One was a reggae group near the pool in which the seals lived. Another band, more remote, up in the rocky area where the polar bears were kept, was a rock group playing music from U2 and Guns N' Roses. More sedate, and far more popular with the older partners and their wives, was a band playing Motown music near the trees and mossy boulders where the monkeys lived.

Byron's firm had rented the entire zoo for the night and invited not only the three hundred partners and associates who worked in the firm's New York office but also the lawyers from the satellite offices in Chicago, Los Angeles, and Miami. They had come with their husbands, wives, partners, and children. The party, which was held once each year in the summer, started in the late afternoon and would run on until ten.

Byron looked forward to the day when he would never have to go to one of these parties again. He had attended the firm's summer outings—at country clubs, in the Met, at the zoo—for years. Although the people had changed from year to year as lawyers joined the firm, left the firm, retired, died, or were forced out, with more and more new lawyers always replacing them, the core nature of the firm never changed—hundreds of lawyers celebrating their wealth, their success, and the firm's longevity. In many ways, SpencerBlake was like a baseball team: it had a name, and that name remained the same despite the fact that the lawyers who worked for the firm were constantly in flux. That nebulous thing—the firm—survived the specific identities of the lawyers who made up the firm. Not one of the players on the Boston Red Sox this year had been a player in 2007, yet the identity of the team survived its human parts.

Drink in hand, Byron walked around the zoo. He had arrived alone, six hours after his meeting at the U.S. Attorney's Office in lower Manhattan. Byron was divorced, against his will, six years earlier.

"Mr. Johnson, I've been wanting to say hi to you." The young woman—tall, slim, black-haired, beautiful—touched his elbow while he watched the seals leap into the air and clamber on the boulders as two zookeepers, young women in knee-high green waders and safari-style clothes, tossed fish into the air. The kids clapped each time the seals caught the fish in midair, as they always did, with the unerring accuracy of major league infielders. Even the adults applauded.

In the dusk, Byron faced her. He no longer made any effort to know the names of every lawyer in the firm and never looked at the pictures in the firm's ever-changing, yearbook-size directory or on its splashy promotional website. He did what he always did when he encountered someone whose name he didn't know or couldn't remember. "I'm sorry," he said, "but you have to tell me who you are."

"Christina Rosario."

"Christina, hello."

She shifted the drink she'd been carrying in her right hand to her left. When he touched her now free right hand it was chilly and wet, electrifying. From years of meeting thousands of people at parties, at conventions, and in the ordinary course of his busy life, Byron instinctively knew how to engage a new person, even one as distractingly good-looking as Christina Rosario, in conversation. "Are you in the New York office? Chicago? LA?"

"I'm a summer associate, here." Her voice was warm and calm, appealing.

"Welcome, Christina." Byron asked the natural next question. "Where do you go to law school?"

"Columbia."

She stood closer to him than he would have expected. She wore a red summer dress. In the steadily deepening dark, with the tinkle of glasses and laughter and the partying voices all around him, he saw that the dress was cut low enough to reveal the lovely shape of her neck and her shoulders, all that flawless young skin, and the swell of her large breasts.

"I've been hoping to work in the litigation department with you."

Until five years ago—when his involvement in the work he had done for years began to wane—Byron had been the head of the firm's litigation department. "We still have a rotation system, Christina, I'm sure you'll get there."

Christina made him uncomfortable, that mix of desire and concern. The desire was understandable: a long time had passed since Joan divorced him, he had spent several years essentially alone except for the fewer and fewer people with whom he had contact at work, and, although a handsome man, he had dated only seven or eight women. He had spent a few nights with only three of them. His sons, Hunter (his father's middle name) and Tomas (the first name of his mother's father), lived in distant cities; they were in their early thirties, born just a year apart, probably the same age as this gorgeous woman, and they were starting their own careers. They were always popular, always engaged with friends and with life, more like Joan in that way than like him.

And the concern he felt, as he stood close to Christina in the dusk that gradually filled the zoo, was understandable, too. Male partners in the firm routinely received email reminders from the executive committee that alerted them to the absolute prohibitions against what was called "unwelcome" contact with the junior women and men in the firm. Two years earlier, the firm had been sued when a fifty-year-old corporate partner told a twenty-eight-year-old associate that she had a great ass. Byron barely knew the partner, but at a closed meeting among dozens of the partners, he was impressed by the man's sincerity when he described the flirty conversation in which he had used those words. "I never even touched her hand," he kept repeating, completely bewildered by what was engulfing him as a result of uttering one sentence. "I meant nothing by it." The firm had settled the case swiftly with a payment of half a million dollars to the woman, who left the firm, complete with a six-month paid leave of absence, to join a firm in Houston. The partner had been forced to resign. Privately Byron considered the punishment too swift and too total.

Faced with this alluring young woman with her unsettling presence, Byron heeded the danger signals. She made him feel awkward, somewhat like a teenager at his first party. He raised the glass he was holding in a kind of mock salute. "Maybe we will get a chance to work together," he said. "We'll leave that up to the hidden hand of the powers on the assignment committee."

She stared directly into his eyes and smiled. "I hope so, Byron."

Even as he turned from her, her presence continued to jar and stimulate him. *Byron*? There was a daring in her sudden, unexpected use of his first name. Should he avoid her for the rest of the summer? Or did he want to see to it that she worked for him for a week or two? Did he want to follow the temptation that she clearly knew she was presenting? Or did he want to concentrate on that enigmatic man in the prison in Miami?

Almost involuntarily, he glanced over his shoulder. She was in profile, talking to the wife of another partner. Byron registered her entire body—the black hair, the perfect profile, the simple dress draped alluringly over her, and her slender legs. Around her slim left ankle was the distinct tattoo of a bracelet.

Sandy's real first name wasn't Sandy. It was Halliburton. He was Halliburton Spencer IV. He was the chairman of the firm. Tall, slender, sandy-haired, and impeccably dressed, he was the grandson of one of the founders of the firm. Although Sandy was to the manor born—his parents had an apartment on Fifth Avenue overlooking the Met and Central Park, he had spent the first seven years of his schooling at Collegiate in Manhattan before he graduated from Phillips Exeter, Yale, and Yale Law School—he was charming, easygoing, almost impossible to dislike. He had been able over the last three years to tell Byron that his share of the partnership profits was declining—from three million each year to one and a half million—so soothingly that Byron, who had done nothing to resist the cutting of the percentages that accounted for a partner's pay, had simply told Sandy that of course he understood. "It's part of the arc of a partner's career," Byron had said, although Sandy, who was only four years older than Byron, had a career arc that continued to increase his pay every year.

Sandy disengaged himself from a group of people near the festive archway where clowns were entertaining the children. Multi-colored balloons swayed in the air. Sandy was a master of working any crowd, but there was nothing unctuous about him. "Byron," he said, "I didn't expect to see you here."

Sandy was as tall as Byron, and they were among the tallest men in the firm. They had known each other for twenty-five years. "I'm not that much of a recluse yet," Byron said.

"Even Thoreau left Walden every day to visit Emerson in Concord."

"I think the firm would really benefit, Sandy, if the next lecture was on Thoreau and Emerson instead of marketing and networking."

"Networking." Sandy paused. "Awful word, isn't it?"

Byron said, "It's an even more atrocious concept."

Effortlessly Sandy turned to a new topic. "How was your escapade in Miami?"

"Frustrating. I had a total of thirty minutes with him."

Five days earlier Byron had sent an email to Sandy and the six other members of the executive committee simply announcing that he'd been approached to represent an accused terrorist brought from a foreign prison to the United States to be indicted and tried. He wrote that he had decided that he would represent the man, if the man in fact asked him. Byron didn't request that this be treated as a *pro bono* assignment, which would have required him to get approval from yet a different committee so that he could list the hours he spent as though they were time devoted to a paying client. Part of his annual income depended on the number of hours he billed to paying clients or to approved *pro bono* cases. No one had responded to his email.

"What's he charged with?" Sandy asked as casually as if asking what Byron's golf handicap was.

"I don't know yet. This new regime fascinates me. A man is held in limbo in detention for years. Now he's been in a United States prison for weeks. Publicity about it everywhere. Even the president commenting on it. And the man still doesn't know what he's charged with."

"What's his name again?"

"Ali Hussein."

"Doesn't sound real. It's a name right out of *A Thousand and One Arabian Nights*."

"Sandy, he's not living a fairy tale. He's real."

Dozens of small birds, black against the deepening blue-black screen of the evening sky, swept over the zoo. Sandy said, "I think you can assume that he's not charged with littering the sidewalk."

"That didn't appear to be what the CIA and the Justice Department had in mind when they called me into the U.S. Attorney's Office so they could do a ranting-and-raving routine today."

"So that's where you were this afternoon? How did it go?"

Byron was annoyed that someone had taken account of his absence. But he masked his annoyance. "It wasn't exactly a dialogue. It was a classic Mussolini-on-the-balcony scene."

"It's been a long time, Byron, since you did any criminal work."

Byron's first job out of law school was a two-year stint at the Justice Department. He had been assigned to criminal cases as an assistant to more senior lawyers. It was an era when a short tenure at the Department was considered a credential that, for the chosen few, followed graduation from certain New England prep schools, prestigious colleges, and elite law schools and preceded the passage to big law firms. It was exactly the trajectory Byron's career had followed, and until now he'd never resisted it.

"Cases are cases, Sandy. There's one side, there's the other side. There's one version of the facts, there is another version of the facts. Or several versions, sometimes all true, more or less. The law that applies is usually pretty simple, certainly the law's no Jesuitical mystery, no matter how hard we want people outside of this business to believe it is. Cases start, they move forward, and they come to an end, all in the fullness of time."

"Speaking of time, Byron, have you thought about how much time you'll spend on this?"

"Not at all. It's like any other case in that way, too, Sandy. It takes whatever time it takes. It may take no more time than the hours I've already put into it. Ali Hussein may decide he doesn't want me to represent him."

"I doubt that, Byron. You're skillful, you're dedicated, you're respected all around the country—"

"And I'm free, Sandy."

Streams of multi-colored rockets began to rise, hissing, from reedy poles placed all around the zoo. It was a dazzling display. The firm had all the resources in the world: it could spend thousands of dollars to rent the Central Park Zoo; it could bring together popular bands; it could assemble caterers, magicians, and entertainers; and it could stage fireworks.

Sandy waved his glass at the display of sparks, the expanse of the zoo, the skyline of the grand buildings along Fifth Avenue. "Nothing is free, Byron. You know that."

Not answering, Byron looked up at the fireworks and, beyond them, the black heights of the park's ancient trees. During the years he was married to Joan, he had lived in an apartment three blocks from the zoo, at Fifth Avenue and 65th Street. He had never lived as long anywhere else in the world: his father was a career officer in the Foreign Service who never stayed more than four years in any post, and as a child Byron Carlos Johnson had lived in New York City, Mexico City, West Berlin, and Washington, DC. At thirteen he was sent to Groton and, during the four years he spent there, he saw his patrician father and aristocratic Mexican mother eight times, never for more than three weeks each time. He knew even then that there was no real relationship between him and his parents; they were acquaintances, and something about the world in which he grew up—an all boys' prep school, an all-male college, and law school in the sixties and early seventies—made him believe there was nothing unusual about a family in which a boy visited his parents once or twice each year in whatever city in the world they lived at the time and spent three weeks each summer with them on Monhegan Island, just off the coast of Maine, in the sprawling, shingled house that had been in his father's family for ninety years. If he had ever been asked if he felt lonely, if he often wondered what his mother and his father were doing in their lives at the lonely moments he was thinking of them, he would have said *no*, and would have believed it.

Raising his martini glass as if making a toast at a wedding, Sandy said, "I'm glad you're here, Byron. It's important for the younger lawyers to see that the old guard is still involved."

"When did we get to be the old guard?"

"When the young Turks started wondering what we really do."

"What is it you think we do, Sandy?"

"We make money so that we can have these parties."

# 4

DECADES HAD PASSED SINCE the 1967 and 1968 riots in Newark, yet the corner of Broad Street and Raymond Boulevard still looked devastated. Byron remembered the grainy televised images from 1968 when, at a hamburger joint on Nassau Street while he was still at Princeton, he watched news footage of burning storefronts and overturned cars in Newark during the days after Martin Luther King, Jr. was assassinated. In the fuzzy, black-and-white images on the screen, National Guard troops ran chaotically back and forth. Black men stood on the sidewalks and streets, apparently unconcerned with the presence of the tense, obviously frightened soldiers. There were trash fires, smashed store fronts, and burning police cars.

Byron traveled to Newark on the PATH train from Penn Station in Manhattan to Penn Station in this old, eternally decaying city. From the station, he walked to the intersection of Broad Street and Raymond Boulevard. The Al Sunni Mosque glowed brilliantly in the early afternoon sunlight. The crescent-moon symbol fixed at the top of the dome glinted like a curved sword, dazzling.

He saw Khalid Hussein standing near the wrought-iron fence that surrounded the mosque. Just above Khalid was a horizontal screen, at least twenty feet long, on which sentences in English were electronically displayed, moving from left to right like a zipper-message strip in Times Square. The words *All are welcome to worship Allah* slid across the display board again and again.

Khalid was in a business suit, a somber, heavy-set man noticeably different in appearance and presence from his brother. Now that Byron had seen Ali Hussein three times, he believed there was a possibility that these two men were half-brothers.

Byron knew from his first meeting with Khalid in the diner in Union City that he didn't shake hands. So Byron didn't offer his hand as he said, "It's good to see you, Khalid."

"How is my brother?"

Byron had also learned that Khalid had zero interest in pleasantries. "Your brother's a very unhappy man."

Khalid's voice was much heavier, far more determined than his brother's. "Wait until we go inside to tell me more. I want the Imam to hear this."

Without speaking, Byron walked at Khalid's side toward the ornate entrance to the mosque. Khalid slipped an identity card through a slot on the fence, and the gate made a magnetic clicking noise as it disengaged from the frame. Between the fence and the mosque's circular wall was a lush lawn, totally unique in this area of the city, where every bleak surface was either cement or tar. There were fresh, newly planted weeping willows on the lawn. As he walked, Byron touched in his pocket the piece of paper on which the night before he had written words from the ninth chapter of the *Koran*, words he had found himself reading several times on the train from Manhattan here: *Those who were left behind rejoiced at sitting still behind the messenger of Allah, and were averse to striving with their wealth and their lives in Allah's way. And they said:*

*Go not forth in the heat! Say: The heat of hell is more intense of heat, if they but understood.*

Every night for the past several weeks Byron had steadily read three pages of the *Koran*, and from time to time he wrote down passages for no particular reason. Ali Hussein had recently been allowed, because Byron had persisted in asking permission for it, to have a paperback copy of the *Koran*, in English only because the government wanted to know precisely what its prisoner was reading. Byron wasn't interested in books that interpreted or explained Islam, a subject to which he had never paid attention beyond what he'd read from time to time over the years in newspapers and magazines. Always with the instincts of a genuine student, he decided to read the *Koran* itself, without guidance, without preparation for what he might expect, and without any external explanation. What was it, he wanted to know, that this book said? More than two hundred pages into the text, he was baffled. He kept returning to earlier pages, reading out loud, underlining passages, and sometimes putting question marks in the margin. And now he had taken to writing down sentences and paragraphs. What did the words mean? *The heat of hell is more intense of heat, if they but understood.* In the two hours Byron was now allowed to spend with Ali Hussein on his trips to Miami, Ali had quoted the passage from memory, and it had taken Byron two days to find it. When he did, it was precisely as Ali Hussein had recited. Ali had even recalled the numbers of the separate books of the *Koran*, the chapter numbers within each book, and the numbers of the verse lines within each chapter that he repeated from memory.

The mosque's interior was not as ornate as the outside walls and the bronzed, glinting dome. The inside was plain, almost utilitarian, with cinderblock walls, like a public high school cafeteria. Byron, carrying nothing, followed Hussein down a hallway. There seemed to be no other men in the building. Byron, when he had asked Hussein to make arrangements for a visit to the Imam, imagined for some reason that there would be as many guards protecting the Imam as Louis Farrakhan always seemed to have. Certainly Byron never imagined that he could simply walk through a door into the almost bare room in which the Imam sat at a simple wooden desk.

He was smaller and younger than Byron expected, probably no older than thirty-five. When Ali Hussein, at their meeting a week earlier in Miami, told Byron that he was certain his brother could arrange a meeting with the Imam ("Please do this for me, see him and convey my respects to him," Ali had said), Byron had cruised through the miraculous Internet to search for more information about him. He easily located many entries, mainly copies of news articles and pictures of the man. The photographs were not posted by the Imam or anyone around him; instead, they were pictures posted by people Byron assumed were right-wing American men, who added messages such as "Is this bin Laden's brother?" and "Put a hole-a-in-the-Ayatollah."

The man was in a robe. He wore heavy glasses. He had a beard. Somehow he had the look and demeanor, Byron thought, of an Orthodox Jewish rabbi. Byron nodded slightly, respectfully, not knowing if this was the proper way to greet a Muslim holy man. He waited for some signal that he should sit. Khalid translated the words the Imam spoke, "Why don't you sit down, Mr. Johnson?"

Byron was surprised that Khalid translated. On one of the Internet sites devoted to the Imam, Byron had seen and heard a video, obviously surreptitiously made, of him speaking in clear English to an audience. In that Internet video, the Arabic translation of what he was saying ran across the lower screen.

Although his face was somber, his voice almost had a lilt, was almost in fact effeminate. Khalid translated, "You have seen our brother Ali?"

Byron was uncomfortable. This was a strange setting—a bare room in a mosque. These men were also strange: a brooding man in typical American clothes and an Arabic-speaking Imam in a robe. This mosque, too, was for Byron otherworldly. He tried to convey nothing of his discomfort, but he was aware of the quaver in his voice. He wondered whether the other men detected it.

"Ali isn't happy. And I can't say that he looks healthy."

And then the soft voice spoke, followed immediately by Khalid's abrupt-sounding, harsh translation. "The people who did this to our brother are not good people."

"It's not those people who concern him," Byron said. "Ali is very concerned about his wife and children."

It was Khalid who answered, not the Imam. "They are well taken care of." Khalid seemed to resent the question.

"But he wants to know where they live, what they're doing, what's happened to them."

Khalid translated Byron's words, listened to the Imam, and then translated. "You can tell Ali that they have been well cared for."

"Ali isn't asking that. He wants to know where they are, what their health is, what schools his children are in."

Khalid didn't translate. There was silence in the room. The Imam spoke, and then Khalid said, "What has our brother told you?"

Byron knew that he would confront this problem: he had explained to Ali, when Ali asked that he visit the Imam, that there was very little he could say to him about what Byron and Ali had discussed. Byron had tried to make Ali understand that there was an attorney-client privilege that made it impossible for Byron to tell anyone the words that he and Ali had exchanged. And Byron had explained that, if Ali gave him permission to tell his brother and the Imam what their conversations were, then the attorney-client privilege would be lost and Byron might be required to tell other people as well. He was certain that Ali, an intelligent man who had worked as an accountant, understood. But Ali simply said, "Please, just speak to my brother and the Imam. I want them to know that I'm here, I want them to tell you about my wife and kids, I want you to let them know that you are a life-giver, and that you were able to bring me the holy *Koran*."

Byron spoke slowly: "I can't tell you everything we've talked about."

Again Khalid translated: "What has our brother said to you?"

"I can tell you this: that he was in prisons in Europe, or so he thinks, for two years, and then for years in a hot place, probably Guantanamo, in Cuba; that he has been very badly treated; that he doesn't know what he's accused of. And that he now has a copy of the *Koran*."

The Imam spoke. Khalid translated: "What did he tell you about the *Koran*?"

"He said that it was life-giving water to read it again."

Khalid said, "My brother was always very devout."

"And he also wanted me to let the Imam know that he has read and understands at last the words of book nine."

"What words in book nine?"

Byron removed from his pocket the yellow sheet of paper. He read aloud: "*Those who were left behind rejoiced at sitting still behind the messenger of Allah, and were averse to striving with their wealth and their lives in Allah's way. And they said, Go not forth in the heat! Say: the heat of hell is more intense of heat, if they but understood.*"

Suddenly the Imam, his voice sibilant and rapt, began reciting words in Arabic. It took almost a minute for him to finish. At the end, Khalid said, "The Imam asks that you let our brother know that the next lesson he must understand is in book eight, chapter six, the verses 55 through 62. Ali's strength is in Allah, in the *Glorious Koran*."

Byron had read enough about the *Koran* to know that its title was properly translated as the *Glorious Koran*, not just the *Koran*. He wrote down the reference that the Imam had given him. *Book, chapter, lines of verse. 8, 6, 55, 56, 57, 58, 59, 60, 61, 62.* He knew also that almost every edition of the *Koran*, no matter who the translator was, had the same chapter, verse and line number so that readers could all find the same text, just as the Bible and Shakespeare's plays had common chapter, verse, and line numbers.

Then, somewhere outside the room, a bell sounded. Byron had seen a sign indicating that there were classes for children in the building, and the bell, although muffled, sounded like a school bell. There were no children in the building, no sound of children's voices anywhere.

Khalid stood. Byron did as well. The Imam remained seated. "The Sheik sends his blessings to our brother," Khalid said.

Three hours later, in his apartment, Byron turned to the passage of the *Koran* the Imam had mentioned. He had an old translation by a long-dead man who wrote in his preening introduction that he was Marmaduke Pickthall, the first Englishman who had himself become a Muslim to translate the holy text.

Byron read aloud: *Lo! The worst of beasts in Allah's sight are the ungrateful who will not believe. Those of them with whom thou madest a treaty, and then at every opportunity they break their treaty, and they keep not duty to Allah. If thou comest on them in the war, deal with them so as to strike fear in those who are behind them, that haply they may remember. And if thou fearest treachery from any folk, then throw back to them their treaty fairly. Lo! Allah loveth not the treacherous. And let not those who disbelieve suppose that they can outstrip Allah's purpose. Lo! They cannot escape. Make ready for them all thou canst of armed force and of horses tethered, that thereby ye may dismay the enemy of Allah and your enemy, and others beside them whom ye know not. Allah knoweth them. Whatsoever ye spend in the way of Allah it will be repaid to you in full, and ye will not be wronged.*

Byron typed these words into his computer. He had developed a habit of typing notes and sending them through the ether by email to himself, so that he had them in both his *Sent* column and his *Old* column. He printed out the passage. He planned to take the sheet of paper on his next trip to Miami to read to Ali. He felt it was part of his task to give this man, isolated for so many years from his family, his neighborhood, his surroundings, and his religion, some link to the world he once knew. And Byron believed he could never assess another person's religion—life had taught him enough about the mysteries of religion that he long ago gave up considering Roman Catholicism, Islam, Buddhism, even the Episcopal formalities of his youth, absurd or misguided or useless. They all mattered to billions of people in the world, and sometimes they mattered to him.

From the privacy of his loft apartment on Laight Street in Tribeca, where the sounds of huge garbage trucks and tractor trailers still rumbled at night on the cobblestone pavements of the old warehouse district, he gazed at the top of the Empire State Building. Shimmering red and blue lights were draped over its heights. He then read again: *Lo! Allah loveth not the treacherous. And let not those who disbelieve suppose that they can outstrip Allah's purpose.*

"What the hell," he said aloud, "can this mean?"

# 5

TOM NASHATKA WAS WELL over six feet tall and, at thirty-nine, still weighed less than two hundred pounds. He was blond and blue-eyed, the son of a Polish immigrant family that had settled in Pittsburgh two years before he was born. He went through the Pittsburgh public school system and graduated from Penn State, where he played football and was the captain of the Greco-Roman varsity wrestling team. He had even contended in the 1996 Olympic trials. Tom enlisted in the Navy after he graduated and trained as a Navy Seal. He spent six years in the Navy and was then accepted for a rare slot as a special agent of the Secret Service. After September 11, he asked for a transfer to the new Department of Homeland Security and got it.

His head was completely shaven. For years he had worn an earring, a golden circle in his right earlobe. It gave him, he said, deep cover. "I look like Mr. Clean—bald head and earring, ready to take care of the kitchen and bathroom."

He was friendly and engaging. After his transfer to New York, he developed many friendships in the upscale, gentrified Cobble Hill neighborhood in Brooklyn. He had girlfriends—not one of them knew he was a federal agent—and he enjoyed several nights out each week at the coffee bars and the real bars of his neighborhood. By eleven he was usually in his small, neat apartment on the third floor of a renovated brownstone.

His friends thought he worked at a brokerage firm. Although they found it odd for someone in the sales business, Tom let his friends know he didn't want to take them on as clients because he thought there might be some kind of conflict of interest. There were times, too—and his young friends thought this was strange for a broker—when he was out of town, without explanation, for two or three weeks at a time.

As soon as Byron Carlos Johnson sent the email to himself with the quotation from the *Koran*, Tom Nashatka's own computer screen was filled with the same words. He immediately knew they were from the eighth book of the *Koran*, a chapter entitled "Spoils of War." And he immediately recognized the strange translation, first published in 1930, by Marmaduke Pickthall, that bizarre Englishman with the look and mannerisms of Oscar Wilde.

As he re-read the two quotations from the *Koran* that Byron had so carefully typed and then emailed to himself, Tom Nashatka was grateful that Byron had abandoned his old practice of writing longhand notes to himself. It had been time-consuming for Tom's agents to copy every page of Byron Johnson's loose-leaf notebooks; the agents spent hours on many nights in Byron's twenty-seventh floor office in the quiet of the Seagram Building on Fifth Avenue, copying all those handwritten pages. Byron's use of emails to himself made it easy for Tom to intercept and review Byron's thoughts and actions in real time.

This was the second fragment of the *Koran* Byron Carlos Johnson had typed into his computer. He had sent the first quote to himself from his laptop as he sat in the Jet Blue terminal in Miami after a visit to the devout Ali Hussein. It had been Tom Nashatka's idea to grant Byron's request to allow Hussein to have a copy of the *Koran*, and to have it in English even though Hussein had asked for the original Arabic text. Tom had collected enough information about Byron Johnson to know that Byron, who was slow to learn the mysteries of email and the Internet, had gradually developed the habit of writing notes on his computer and emailing them to himself, a neater, more modern extension of Byron's old practice of jotting messages to himself. The email notes had only recently started to replace the handwritten notes dating back to 1980, all kept in loose-leaf binders on a shelf in Byron's office, which he had accumulated each year, a kind of diary, business calendar, and personal message system. And it was no longer necessary to arrange with Sandy Spencer for the agents' late-night access to the office.

Tom Nashatka forwarded the email to Kimberly Smith, the professor at Stanford who still worked undercover for the CIA and who probably had studied the intricacies of Islam even more carefully than he had. But she was the one who wrote the articles that appeared in scholarly journals, as well as places like the editorial page of the *Wall Street Journal*, because her academic credentials as a writer and teacher gave her even deeper undercover protection than he had. Tom was anonymous, Kimberly was famous.

She was the one—blonde, edgy, striking—who appeared again and again on shows on CNN with Anderson Cooper and Wolf Blitzer and on Fox with Bill O'Reilly. On television she was known as the "Islamic expert from Stanford." The computers she and Tom used to communicate were as secure as any computers in the world; and the messages about the *business*, as they called it, were veiled, and indecipherable to anyone who might have, through some extraordinary feat of computer expertise and intuition, intercepted them.

Just seconds after he forwarded Byron's email, Tom's computer screen flashed a red star that registered an incoming message from Kimberly's BlackBerry.

"Quite the student, isn't he?" Kimberly wrote.

For the thousandth time, he thought about the two nights he had spent with her, first in San Francisco and then at the Essex House on Central Park South where she stayed when she came to New York for her television appearances. "This is strange," she had said the first night they were together. "I never fucked a man with an earring."

Tom wrote, "Are you naked, Professor Smith?"

There was a twenty-second gap as she typed. Then the message arrived: "I'm on a stationary bike at the gym. Almost naked. The old faculty letches are staring at my ass."

"I have a hard-on."

"That's standard issue weaponry, right?"

"Fuck you, lady."

"In your dreams, fella."

"When are you coming out here?"

"Check the CNN listings."

# 6

BYRON JOHNSON WAITED MORE than a week after Christina Rosario left the firm in mid-August to send her a tentative email. He had a right as a partner to ask the personnel office for information about her—partners, after all, owned the intangible entity known as SpencerBlake. Byron learned that Christina was in fact older than the fifty other young eager summer associates; she was thirty-four. Her appearance, her qualities—gestures, glances, reactions, her aura—were too developed for a woman in her twenties. According to the firm's records, she'd worked in advertising at one of the very large, now lost-through-merger firms that was, when Byron was early in his own career, the archetype of the Madison Avenue advertising firm. She had graduated Phi Beta Kappa from Bowdoin, that college in Maine not far from where he spent parts of his summer on Monhegan Island, where no cars or trucks were allowed and people pulled their groceries and luggage on red children's wagons from the ferry boats to their big, wood-shingled and weather-beaten homes. When he was young, Bowdoin was an all-male school. He'd considered attending it because he was attracted by the idea that it was the college from which both Hawthorne and Longfellow graduated in 1825; but his father was a Princeton graduate and the social forces that made Byron follow him there were as profound as the tides.

Christina's email address was in the firm directory. So was her apartment address—405 West 116th Street, an immense, curved building that faced Riverside Park just two blocks from the Columbia campus. Byron found himself thinking that the building was a quick uptown drive from his apartment in Tribeca—there was no need to make the difficult passage across the island from the east side to the west. The thought was, he realized, a fantasy, a projection, a desire.

His first email message, which he sent at eleven-forty-five on a Wednesday night, wasn't answered for a week. During that week he was often embarrassed by the note, and he tried to "unsend" it. He was mystified by that word on the computer screen: it was like reclaiming and eliminating an event, canceling a moment in the past. But he learned that since she was on a different Internet service it wasn't possible to unsend the note. In that way, the sending of the note was like the sending of a letter in the time before the Internet—once dropped in an iron mailbox, the letter couldn't be retrieved.

Byron's note was simple enough: "This is Byron Johnson. I'm sorry we weren't able to work together this summer. I guess the gods on the summer associate committee decided otherwise. Hope you enjoyed your summer with us. And that you have a good last year of law school."

That was it, he thought, a valedictory, just a polite note from a senior partner that could easily have been sent to all of the summer associates as part of the firm's vigorous policy of generating good relations with all these summer associates and the famous schools to which they returned for their third year of law school—Harvard, Yale, Columbia, Penn, Berkeley, Cornell (all of the schools from which all of the older partners had graduated) and NYU, Northwestern, Michigan, even Hofstra (the more diverse law schools from which, in the less elitist years of the last two decades, more and more of the associates and partners came).

During the week in which his email to Christina was out there, unanswered and irretrievable, Byron wondered whether his sending it violated the firm's policy on contact between male partners and women associates. He had never given any attention to any of those proliferating personnel policies, because, he felt, they reflected only the common sense and respect by which he had instinctively lived for so long—there had never been a time when he thought it was appropriate for a male partner to have sex with a female associate (there were many years when there were very few female lawyers at SpencerBlake), and he had always believed that a lawyer should not be hired, or should be hired, because he or she was black or Jewish or Asian or gay or, as he now thought after meeting Hamerindapal Rana, a Sikh. What mattered, he had always said, was the person's ability and the willingness to learn and not color or gender or religion or sexual preference. Three of the younger partners were gay males, and he had heard rumors, to which he paid no attention, that one of the new female partners was a lesbian.

During the week without a response from Christina, Byron felt nervous, offended, dissed. There was also at times a sense of jealousy. Who was the other guy? There had to be another guy, for the lady was so gorgeous. A Columbia professor? A writer? A hedge fund billionaire? A professional athlete? He had made a fool of himself even by making this simple overture. At one point he even thought of sending her an email claiming that his earlier one had been sent inadvertently and asking her to ignore it.

And he knew he was smitten. It had been years since he found himself with such an intense and uncontrollable crush, imagining her virtually all the time, her name resonating constantly in his mind. Once a man with very methodical habits—including the ability to get to sleep no later than eleven and sleep soundly until seven—Byron over the last several months had become restless at night. He kept his computer on all night long, and, at various times in the quiet overnight, checked the screen. At three one morning, under the *New Mail* heading on his computer screen, he saw the screen name "ChristinaBrighteyes." He almost lunged at the laptop glowing brightly in his home library. He clicked the mouse. He was so excited that the first click missed its target. Then he put the arrow more securely on the target and hit it. The hourglass image lingered over the line on the screen that bore the word "ChristinaBrighteyes," and then, as if by miracle, the screen opened to the text of the message.

"So good to hear from you, Byron. I've been away. I had a great summer. Only regret is that we didn't get to work together."

Byron was naked as he read the message. He hadn't read any words so avidly in years. *My God*, he thought, *she wrote back*. He checked the date line and saw that she had written her note only an hour earlier, 2 a.m. He imagined that she had returned from wherever it was in the world she had been traveling, saw an email from him, and, even before she started unpacking, wrote to him. That had to mean she was not with another man, at least not now. Byron thought it would be cool and appropriate if he waited a day or two before responding to her, but at three in the morning in his big apartment, he realized he wasn't interested in being cool.

He wrote: "So glad to hear from you, and happy you enjoyed your summer with us. I do have some work that I might ask you to help me with, a kind of special project. Would you like to talk about it?"

Before sending it, he read the message six times, adding sentences, altering words, and even changing the typeface. Finally he pressed the *Send* button; in an instant the screen told him that his message had been sent.

He went to the bathroom. His spacious apartment—the ceilings in this converted warehouse building were fifteen feet high—was always suffused with light from the outside even at night, since the tall industrial windows were at the same level as the street lamps and Byron rarely drew the shades. As soon as he finished in the bathroom, he found himself drawn again to the glowing computer screen, yearning like a teenager for a response. On it was another message from Christina: "I'd love to, Byron. Why don't you come up to the Three Guys diner at 115th and Broadway tonight at 7 and I'll buy you a cup of coffee."

Without hesitating, Byron wrote: "Will do."

Dressed only in his jockey shorts, Byron felt the erection that just reading her note gave him. It strained against his underwear. *Miraculous*, he thought, *I'm a teenager again.*

Soon he slept, without once waking until eight in the morning.

In his quiet apartment in Cobble Hill, Tom Nashatka heard his computer emit that blip of a noise that signaled the lodging of new emails. He opened the screen, and there were the emails he had expected to see during the week since the lonely, driven Byron Carlos Johnson had, like a love-possessed college kid, written to Christina Rosario.

When the new emails arrived, he immediately forwarded them to Kimberly Smith. He had been speaking to her on his regular cell phone, since they didn't use their secure cell phones when they spoke late at night. Even for Kimberly, in Palo Alto, it was late, as it usually was when they had their nightly conversations. At night, they never talked about their intriguing, deeply secret work. Those talks happened during the day, and were invariably about business—the decoding of the mysteries of intercepted messages, many of them in Arabic, a language they had both fully mastered.

Tom interrupted their long conversation. "Well, well, well, will you look at this." He had kept his laptop computer near him in bed while speaking to Kimberly. "The Eagle has landed."

"What is it?"

"Lord Byron is lovesick."

"Really?"

"Sure, look at this." He forwarded the emails to her.

She read them. "Aw, ain't that sweet?"

"Can you believe it? They already have a date."

"He doesn't have a chance," she said. "The lady is a maneater."

"That's right," Tom said, "he doesn't have a chance."

# 7

IN THE TWO WEEKS after the hot night when they met at the diner at 115th Street and Broadway, Byron Johnson fell more deeply into that exciting mixture of infatuation and love. He found that he could establish a direct connection with her—a connection he craved and that was suddenly at the center of his life—by asking her to research issues relating to Ali Hussein and prepare drafts of papers. He soon dropped the pretense of acting solely as her mentor and assignment-giver. Within two days they were in touch with each other many times by email, cell phone calls, and face-to-face encounters at diners, his apartment, her apartment, and the squash courts.

Byron in fact needed the information she researched and the papers she drafted for him. He no longer had the free use of the younger lawyers at the firm. She was a fully formed lawyer even though she was still in law school. Byron was struck by the fluency of her legal writing. Ordinarily it took years for a new lawyer to develop the style of writing that was the rare currency of the leading lawyers in the country—the fluent, well-crafted, slightly supercilious language that most federal judges, themselves products of major law firms and major federal agencies, used and in turn wanted to see from lawyers. Christina Rosario had it from the outset, and it only reinforced Byron's ardor.

And there were those three squash matches they played soon after the meeting at the diner. She had casually mentioned she played squash, and he suggested they play. Christina was a powerful and experienced player, driving fast rail shots from just above the tin on the front wall of the court that, almost skimming the side walls, raced to the deep corners of the rear wall. The shots forced Byron to sprint backwards to reach the speeding black ball.

Byron was more skillful. He rarely relied on a hard shot. Instead he used the front wall to hit feathery drop shots. Racket drawn back, Christina raced forward, frequently reaching the ball just as it grazed down from the wall, but just as often not reaching it as it fell to the floor without a bounce.

Christina was strong and perfectly built, and it was an exciting pleasure to watch her as she ran, stretched, and hit the ball. But more fascinating and exciting to Byron was the nape of her neck. She wore her black hair in a tight knot. Loose tendrils of hair fell to the sweating skin on the back of her neck. That sight overpowered him. His lust was intense.


Byron Johnson had never felt as uneasy in a courtroom as he did now. It was late on a Friday afternoon in Miami. The hearing had already lasted more than an hour, and the visible impatience of United States District Judge Ursula Betancourt was dripping from every haughty, weary-sounding word she uttered.

"Mr. Johnson, you still haven't given me a single statute, rule, or precedent for the order you're now requesting."

For years, Byron, as a lawyer for clients in big corporate cases had on his side what he knew was the competitive advantage in a legal system weighted heavily in favor of the interests he represented. He had spent a career defending corporations accused of antitrust violations in an era when more and more federal judges rejected antitrust claims more and more often. And he had also spent years defending companies accused of securities fraud when rule after rule steadily undermined the pursuit of those claims. In the fields of Byron Johnson's expertise, it was simply the case that laws passed over the last three decades and the conservative judges appointed since Reagan became president—even the judges appointed by Clinton and Obama—made it easy for Byron Johnson and other big-firm lawyers to protect the companies and executives they represented. The law, as it had come to exist, simply operated in their favor. The conservatives had gradually occupied the field.

Byron Johnson was standing at the podium. "Judge, there are constitutional issues that make these new laws on detention suspect."

"Detention, Mr. Johnson? Do you mean the new laws on terrorism?"

"I don't want to debate semantics, Judge."

"Semantics? I'm looking at the title of the new law. It says 'terrorism,' doesn't it?"

"That word isn't used in the Constitution, Judge."

Judge Betancourt was forty-two years old, appointed to her lifetime position by the second Bush. She had very black hair and that aristocratic Hispanic look that Byron Carlos Johnson's own mother had. Byron thought that she could easily have been one of the associates or young partners in his firm; in fact, he knew from what Christina Rosario had reported to him after an Internet search that this young judge had worked as a lawyer in a Republican law firm in Miami, a firm to which SpencerBlake had often referred clients. The anonymous Internet entries by lawyers who knew her said she was smart, autocratic, often courteous to lawyers who practiced the same kind of law she had spent her career in but icily skeptical of lawyers who represented plaintiffs or criminal defendants.

"Mr. Johnson, what is it that makes you think your client is even entitled to constitutional protection?"

He had been waiting for this question since the day he first decided to file a challenge to Ali Hussein's interminable imprisonment, his solitary confinement, his claims of torture during his years overseas, and the strict time limits imposed on his meetings with Byron. He had asked Christina to research precisely the question Ursula Betancourt was now asking: did the Constitution give Ali Hussein as a foreign national arrested overseas the right to a speedy trial, to effective representation by a lawyer, to freedom from cruel and unusual punishment and to other constitutional guarantees? Christina reported back to him that there were no decisions at any point in the last hundred years that definitively answered that question.

Byron was evasive, hoping to re-frame the conversation. He said, "Mr. Hussein was a legal resident of the United States."

"Don't you think I know that? I did read your papers. Now get back to my question."

"Anyone arrested in the United States has a right to due process."

"But he was arrested in Germany, wasn't he?"

"He had a right to return to the United States."

"But he didn't, right?"

"He was arrested in Bonn before he could do that."

"What's the significance of that? He was carrying a Syrian passport. He could have intended to use it. He could have seamlessly gotten back to Syria."

Byron had been involved in hundreds of these jousting contests with judges. Many of them enjoyed the back-and-forth and the sophisticated spontaneity of the game. Even Byron often enjoyed it. But this judge, he sensed, had a stinger in her tail.

"There's absolutely no evidence in the record that he intended to leave the U.S. permanently," Byron said.

"He wasn't just arrested out of thin air because the agents enjoyed the sport of seizing people in Bonn, Germany. Perhaps your client had wind of the posse chasing him and left here under the guise of going for a business trip to Europe."

"Judge, he has a wife and children in this country."

"He does, Mr. Johnson? And how do I know that? Because you tell me so?"

"He told me that. I see that as a reliable source of information."

Her expression conveyed her skepticism. "Really?" She changed the subject. "He's been designated an enemy combatant, hasn't he?"

"He could have easily been designated Attila the Hun."

She sharply slapped the wood on her bench. "I would expect more from you, Mr. Johnson, than a facetious comment."

When was the last time, Byron wondered, that a judge had scolded him? He couldn't remember. It may never have happened.

"It's a strange constitutional world, Judge, in which the United States Government has the right to hold a person indefinitely, without charges, in what have been intolerable conditions of confinement, just by giving him a label."

"But Congress decided to pass a law that gave the government the right to do that, and the president signed that law."

"Judge, let's face reality here. This is a regime in which the government has in effect suspended habeas corpus and negated the constitutional rights to trial, due process, and freedom from cruel punishment."

"There you go again, Mr. Johnson. Those are grand sentiments. I don't see any decree from the president suspending habeas corpus. And you haven't shown me why Congress and the president are not entitled to treat this person you say is your client in precisely the way it is treating him."

"Judge, the chair beside me—the chair in which every federal prisoner has a right to sit during a vital hearing—is empty."

"It's empty, Mr. Johnson, because the law says the government doesn't have to bring him to court if the government decides that it's a risk to security to have him here."

"Where does this all end, Judge? We are in entirely new and dangerous territory. What if the government simply issues an order saying that Mr. Hussein is guilty and has been sentenced by the Justice Department to life in prison?"

She waved a dismissive hand. "Keep yourself to why you forced us to be here, Mr. Johnson. You filed a motion that frankly I consider frivolous. Don't waste my time with what could be or might be in a world that might have been or may never come to be." She paused. The air conditioning in this windowless, wood-paneled courtroom in Miami was cold. "I have to tell you, Mr. Johnson, that for a lawyer of your long experience I frankly think that these motions you've filed are frivolous."

*Frivolous.* It had become a loaded word over the last twenty years in the world of federal litigation. Calling a lawyer's motion frivolous often led to imposing big money penalties on the lawyer as well as the professional stigma of having been sanctioned for what was called frivolous conduct. Byron flushed at the use of the word, which he had sometimes in the past invoked against an opposing lawyer but which had never been turned on him. Ursula Betancourt was threatening him, and even in the artificially cold courtroom he experienced a sweaty sense of frustration and now, with the use of the word frivolous, a sharp pang of resentment. For the first time in his career, he was no longer, he realized, a select member of the choir.

Byron Johnson simply stared at her, declining her challenge. When Ursula Betancourt realized that he wasn't going to rise to what she knew was a taunt, she posed a question that was meant to test him, and it did. "One issue you've not addressed at all in your papers, Mr. Johnson, is the impact of the SAMs designation of your client. Do you want to address that now before I rule?"

Byron Johnson was speechless. Even a mind as fast as his failed to frame an answer to a question about which he knew nothing. "I'm not familiar with that term."

Ursula Betancourt glanced at Hamerindapal Rana, who had not said a word at the conference after announcing at the outset who he was. It was as if they shared a secret, for they both knew the term.

"Special Administrative Measures," Judge Betancourt said. "SAMs, Mr. Johnson. Are you not familiar with them?"

The tone of her voice bore the mocking disbelief of a seventh-grade teacher asking a student why he was not familiar with the answer to three times eight. After waiting precisely five seconds without an answer from Byron, she became brusque, business-like. "The motion for the release of the defendant, for dismissal, for change of conditions of confinement, for an expansion of the hours of attorney-client meetings, and for permission for family visits to the detainee are all denied. Among other things, Mr. Johnson has failed to note that his client is subject to a SAMs designation and, as a result, his client is committed to the custody of the Justice Department, is expressly not allowed bail, and is explicitly prohibited from contact with all outsiders other than a lawyer."

She turned off the reading light in front of her face. And finally she said, "I think it's only fair to Mr. Johnson to give him warning that, if he again asks for relief that new federal law makes clear he can't get for his client, the court will consider imposing substantial financial sanctions on Mr. Johnson personally. I can't tolerate a waste of Mr. Rana's time, not to mention the court's time."

Hal Rana remained silent at the prosecution table. He didn't even glance at Byron Carlos Johnson.


Christina Rosario had waited for Byron on a bench outside the locked courtroom. Only lawyers, the judge, and three armed United States Marshals had been allowed inside. When Byron emerged, she stood up. He saw her expectant, questioning look. He said, "Bad day in Black Rock."

She frowned.

As they stepped out onto the bleak sun-drenched stone plaza in front of the courthouse, three news cameras focused on them. Reporters pressed forward, vying for his attention. Byron looked stunned. It had never occurred to him that reporters knew about the court appearance or that they had simply followed him to Miami and the courthouse. The motion he had filed had been sealed, hidden from the public computerized court files. No notice had appeared anywhere of the scheduling of the hearing. Plainclothes guards had locked the entrance to the courtroom.

Byron didn't speak. The taxi he had hired to bring him and Christina to the courthouse was waiting. He let Christina step inside before he did. Voices outside the locked door continued their insistent clamor. Cameras were pointed at the tinted windows. The car moved steadily forward through people who stepped to the side only as the front bumper came within inches of them.

# 8

SANDY SPENCER—GREGARIOUS, GENTLEMANLY, always at ease—often passed Byron Johnson's light-filled corner office on the twenty-seventh floor overlooking Park Avenue and the urban landscape of midtown office towers. As the lead partner of the firm, Sandy made it a point to walk at least once each week through the five floors the firm occupied in the Seagram Building to make his presence known. On these tours he spoke with the firm's other partners, the associates, the secretaries, and the messengers. Byron, who was always respectful and friendly to people on the staff, thought Sandy's tours through the office were a form of politicking, as if, Byron once told a bitter, now retired partner who had been removed from the firm in a campaign Sandy orchestrated, he were running for Mayor of Park Avenue.

Byron was making notes on a yellow legal pad when Sandy knocked on the edge of his open office door. Sandy, his suit jacket off, wore a regimental striped tie. His initials were woven into the cuffs of his crisp white shirt. "Byron," he said, "when are we going to get you to stop using those yellow legal pads? I thought Nixon was the last man to use them."

"Sandy, the beauty of these is that I can burn them and nobody can ever know what was in my mind. That's why Nixon used them. They tell me that what you type on a computer lives forever."

Sandy had worked as a young lawyer on the staff of the Watergate Committee for its Republican members. Sandy said, "Hell, Byron, I still have Nixon's notes."

Bright light from the late morning sun flooded Byron's sparely furnished office. He still had enough sense of attachment to the firm that he thought it was best for him to sit and banter for a few minutes with Sandy Spencer.

"Sandy, you're the man who keeps the secrets. That's why Nixon loved you."

Sandy sat in the visitor's chair in front of the desk. He crossed his elegant legs, the relaxed posture of Rex Harrison in *My Fair Lady*. As if announcing good news, he said, "I just got a call from Jack Andrews. They have a new case they're sending over. Securities fraud, he said, with a sprinkle of racketeering claims to spice it up."

Jack Andrews was the chief inside counsel at American Express, a client of SpencerBlake for all the years both Byron and Sandy had worked there. Jack Andrews had once been a junior partner at the law firm, which long ago had managed the brilliant tactic of placing him in the in-house counsel's office of a major client. Jack had soon become the ultimate decision-maker in selecting outside lawyers to represent American Express. Jack Andrews "spread the jewels around," as Sandy Spencer often said, but he usually saved the "crown jewels" of legal work for his old law firm.

Smiling, Byron said, "Sandy, is there a bank in America big enough to hold all your money?"

Sandy returned Byron's smile. "I've moved the excess to the Channel Isles."

"Now that Switzerland is giving up information right and left," Byron said, "there are all these other countries racing into the growth industry of tax havens. Or are they islands, dukedoms, principalities?"

"Where there's money there's always a way to hide it," Sandy said, laughing. He then looked at Byron as if, Byron thought, he was about to cajole a boy. "Jack specifically said he wanted you to be the lead litigation partner on this case. It's important enough to Amex that he wants to be sure you handle it. Even at your $950 hourly rate."

Byron clicked the tip of his pencil on the top of his desk. "When did clients get the privilege of deciding who's assigned to what cases? Isn't that our decision?"

Sandy's expression changed from its usual urbanity to that wintry look his father used when he was unhappy with another lawyer in the firm. Sandy's father was still working at SpencerBlake in the first three years Byron was there. He was "Mr. Spencer" to everyone, including his son. There were times when, if he wasn't satisfied with the research of a young lawyer, he'd throw a book across the desk at him. It was a different world then, austere, aristocratic, and arbitrary.

"Byron, work with us. I don't want to discuss when clients can and can't pick the lawyers they want on particular cases. Jack asked for you. He rarely does that."

"Jack can't have me," Byron said.

"Why not?"

"I'm fully tied up."

"Really, Byron? I looked at your time sheets for the last six weeks. Either you forgot to write down your time or you don't have more than three billable hours."

Byron found himself drawing, in pencil, the shape of a house crowned by two triangles meant to represent a sloping roof. It was precisely the kind of drawing he had made in grammar school. "Sandy, I expect my client in Miami to be indicted next week. When he's indicted I'll have to put everything and anything else aside to deal with it."

"Come on, Byron."

"Come on? I took on a client, Sandy, for better or worse. And for better or worse he wants me to represent him. He's just like any other client: he's entitled to loyalty, attention, respect."

"And so is Jack Andrews. And so is his company. You should be flattered that he asked for you."

"I'm way beyond flattery."

"I guess so, Byron, I guess so. You certainly aren't getting much these days."

Byron finished the carbon pencil streaks that represented the roof of his childlike drawing. Then he made little rectangular boxes and a door on the front of the house: the drawing had assumed the style of a colonial saltbox in New England. "There's a charm," he said, "in being on the wrong side of a genuinely unpopular case."

"Really? Who remembers the name of the lawyer who represented Bruno Hauptmann in the Lindbergh case? Or the lawyer who represented Ted Bundy?"

Byron looked up from the drawing in front of him. "You know what? Nobody remembers the name Byron Carlos Johnson in any of the cases where I've represented American Express, or Microsoft, or Goldman Sachs. It might be that that is what a lawyer is all about—working for a client so that the client is important, not the lawyer."

Sandy shrugged. He had lived in New York for so long that even he had adopted the New York Jewish shrug—weary, expressive, and frustrated. He stood, and Byron remained seated, relieved that the conversation was about to end.

But it wasn't. "Byron," Sandy said, "you are going to take the American Express case. And something else: you are embarrassing yourself and this firm. Everybody has seen the pictures of you leaving that courthouse in Miami. You looked like a deer caught in the headlights."

"It wasn't the most flattering picture I've ever seen."

Sandy waved his hand. As he watched the abrupt wave—so uncharacteristic of the patrician Sandy Spencer, as was the New York shrug—he had a sense that Sandy meant to wave him into another world. "You know what else wasn't flattering, Byron? What else is an embarrassment for the firm?"

Byron now stood. They were separated by the gleaming top of Byron's desk. He managed to control the antagonism he had held against this man for years. "What else?"

"It's very bad form, Byron, to take an associate of this firm with you to Miami and have the world witness you acting dumbfounded in front of a camera and then stumbling into a cab with her. We were trying to recruit her as a lawyer, not recruit her as your travel companion."

"She doesn't work here, Sandy. She certainly hasn't got any intention of coming back."

"You're tone deaf, Byron. You're a relic, even worse than I am. I had a call less than an hour ago from the dean at Columbia to ask the firm for an explanation as to why a partner here would travel with a law student, especially one who spent the summer working here as an associate. And one who must be decades younger than the partner."

Byron spoke slowly in an effort to take any angry edge off the tone of his voice. "Sandy, isn't it time for you to continue your captain's tour of the decks of your luxury cruiser?"

Shaking his head, exaggerating the motion, Sandy Spencer left Byron's office. And Byron knew that he was racing, no longer just drifting, toward the end of his long career at SpencerBlake.

# 9

CHRISTINA ROSARIO'S CHEEK RESTED on Byron's chest. A sheet was draped over her hips. Uncovered and naked, Byron was on top of the sheets, slowly cooling down, relaxing deeply, and utterly content. Christina looked up at the handsome ridges of his face—the taut cheeks, the sloping forehead that reminded her of Cary Grant's, the hazel eyes, the high cheekbones—as he in turn stared down at the beauty of her unblemished face and shoulders, the alluring contours of her breasts, and the tautness of her young stomach. And then, too, the swell of her womanly hips under the white sheet, still damp from their love-making. As she stroked the slightly graying hair on his chest, he felt himself get aroused again.

It was the middle of the afternoon. The windows of Christina's apartment were ten stories above Riverside Park. A breeze stirred the gauzy beige curtains. Although the weather was hot—almost, Byron had said before they began to undress each other, like "miserable Miami"—the wind was refreshing. The breeze came from New Jersey, from the high cliffs of the Palisades, over the sultry expanse of the Hudson River and Riverside Park. The old-world apartment had no air conditioning. Standing fans, rotating, stirred the air.

For the third time she whispered, "That was so, so good."

He turned slightly to kiss her forehead. "You are a sweetheart, Brighteyes." Over the last several weeks, and especially since the first glorious evening when they made love, he sometimes called her Brighteyes. She called him Carlos.

There was almost complete stillness in the bedroom. The traffic noises from Riverside Drive were muffled. Byron couldn't remember a time in his life when he'd experienced such satisfying lassitude, such contentment, as he slowly and lightly moved his fingers along the unblemished skin of her upper arm. *Why have I waited so long for this?* he wondered. This was happiness, he thought, a feeling always possible, never realized.

Christina sensed that Byron's stillness had passed into the realm of sleep. Gradually his breathing deepened. She stopped moving her hand gently across his chest. She, too, felt drowsy—more than two hours had passed since she kissed him, said, "Hey, lover boy," and, naked, led him to her bedroom. During the two weeks in which, like an uncertain schoolboy from an earlier generation, he hadn't done more than touch her hand, she had wondered what kind of lover Byron would be. Arrogant, indifferent, devoted, caring, self-absorbed, athletic, timid, quick, potent, impotent? She had been certain, from the moment she sought him out at the evening party in the Central Park Zoo, that he would become her lover. She saw the beginning of his enthrallment in the artificial bantering they exchanged in that first conversation. So she was certain he would pursue her—the week's delay after she left SpencerBlake in August and his sending her that first email didn't shake her confidence—but she could never predict how he or any other man would be as a lover.

As she lay on his chest, with the afternoon light all around them, she realized she was surprised: Byron, that handsome, polite, and at times awkward guy, was a devoted and passionate lover. In the courtroom, he was cogent and self-possessed but restrained, even when he was being battered and baited by a judge, as in Miami. But there was little restraint in the way he undressed her and helped her undress him. There was no uncertainty or prep school mannerism in the way he kissed her, stroked her, licked her, and entered her. And stayed in her, in position after position. She was young, athletic, and supple. He was lithe and strong. If he took Viagra, he didn't tell her that. But she imagined that his long endurance, his steady erection, and his intensity probably came from that magical blue pill. Even teenagers were using it: the age of the universal stud had arrived.

It was just after sunset when they both woke up. A breeze from the Hudson and Riverside Park lifted and then dropped the gauzy curtains. In all the time she had spent with him over the last few weeks—in diners, libraries, courts, airports, even in taxis—she'd been puzzled about whether Byron Johnson was a happy or unhappy person. There was that demeanor she could only describe to others as "equable"—unflustered, patient, tenacious, and at times self-deprecating. There was also what she thought of as old-world kindness. Byron let other people leave an elevator before he took a step to enter it, he held doors open for people who followed them into a restaurant, and he said thank you to taxi drivers as he paid them. She had once imagined that, if she ever met a man who behaved like that, he'd drive her crazy. But nothing about Carlos annoyed or distracted her.

She admired his focused mind. As soon as he came out of the shower, toweling his thick, subtly graying hair, he said,

"Listen, my little lovely, I need to look at these documents before I head downtown tomorrow morning. Let's order up some Chinese food."

"Or," she said, "do we want falafel from the Moroccan place on 104th Street?"

"I think it's enough that I'm learning how to read the *Koran* in Arabic. I don't need genuine Arabic food."

In Christina's experience, other men in the wake of an afternoon like this would have suggested the quiet recuperation of a movie or supper in a small restaurant. And maybe, she thought, she and Byron might later do that, but as soon as Byron put on his pants he sat down at the dining room table on which he had earlier placed two manila envelopes given to him that morning by Hal Rana. The envelopes contained two documents he had not yet read.

One of the documents was the indictment of Ali Hussein. As soon as Byron arrived at his office that morning, his telephone rang and he picked it up himself because his secretary was not yet there. It was Rana. He said that Ali Hussein had been moved the day before from the detention center in Miami to the bleak federal prison in lower Manhattan. Hussein would be indicted, Rana said, "tomorrow, for money laundering, racketeering, terrorism, and conspiracy to murder."

When he heard those words, Byron felt his body flush, that system-wide pulse of blood that was the result of sudden anxiety. This had last happened to him seven years earlier, when his wife simply looked at him during supper at their apartment and said, "I don't want to be married to you any longer. Not for one more day."

Hal Rana dispassionately said, "I'll contact you tomorrow morning, early, and let you know what courtroom to meet us in. We're going to allow your client to be in court for the arraignment. Judge Goldberg has already been designated. The indictment was filed under seal today. Only we know about it and now you know about it. Your client hasn't been told why he's been brought here. Once the arraignment is over, the indictment will be released to the media and posted on the Internet, probably before you even leave the courthouse."

"Why are you telling me all this, Mr. Rana?"

"We're not monsters, Mr. Johnson. We did start a dialogue with you a little while back, when you were down here meeting with us. You didn't continue the dialogue, but now we're showing you the courtesy of giving you a heads up."

"Don't misunderstand me, I appreciate that."

"Good. It's always good to be appreciated, Mr. Johnson. You're about to appreciate us even more because we've decided to give you a copy of the indictment today, rather than wait to hand it to you when you and your client appear in court tomorrow. That way you can spend the night with it. It might help you."

Byron said, "I appreciate that, too."

"And we are also going to give you something else, if you can guarantee me that you'll keep it to yourself and your client only, not share it with anyone else."

Byron painfully remembered the steps of the courthouse in Miami when he had been taken aback by the reporters and cameras on the scorching plaza. He felt at the time that he had been exposed as an amateur. "Maybe before we go any further,

Mr. Rana, you should tell me what you want me to keep so confidential."

"Fair enough. It's a highly classified report we've prepared explaining in detail the allegations about money laundering and money transfers that are mentioned in the indictment. It provides details ordinarily not seen in an indictment."

"Such as?"

"Account numbers your client may have used. Wiring instructions he might be familiar with."

"Why give me that?"

"We want to make sure that in the long run no one will accuse us of having been unfair to you or your client. We know how very rare this case is, so we're taking the unusual step of giving you and your client the kind of blueprint of our case you would expect to see at trial, not now, so that we can't be accused of having held onto the company secrets and taken advantage of you by springing information for the first time at trial."

"It sounds interesting."

"And maybe once your client sees what we know—as well as what we believe he knows—he'll see the wisdom in pleading guilty and cooperating with us."

Byron paused, uncertain about whether to accept the offer. Rana, a skillful man, waited. And then Byron said, "Sure."

"No one other than you and your client sees it, at least for now. Agreed?"

"Agreed."

"And we'll make it even fairer for you: if there comes a point in time when you feel you want to share it with other people, like accountants, you can file a motion, under seal, with the judge for permission to release it to other specific people. But you can't release it without a court order. Fair enough?"

"Fair enough."

"We'll need to have you come downtown to pick up these two envelopes yourself. We don't want to risk emails, pdfs, or messengers. This is hand-to-hand contact, Mr. Johnson."

Byron had been waiting for a lighthearted tone from the steady Hamerindapal Rana. Maybe, he thought, that last sentence was it. "Did you say contact or combat, Mr. Rana?"

Rana didn't respond to that. "There is one last thing, Mr. Johnson, so that you're not surprised."

"What?"

"The death penalty, Mr. Johnson. The government is seeking the death penalty."

Christina was dressed in Byron's comfortable button-down Brooks Brothers shirt and nothing else. He saw below the tapered edge of the shirt's hem the alluring curve of her ass and glimpses of the hair surrounding her vagina.

As he slipped the documents out of both envelopes Hal Rana had given him, she said, "Want some coffee, Carlos?"

"What would Gloria Steinem say about a smart modern woman making coffee for a guy?

"Baby, do you know how *over* Gloria Steinem is?"

He smiled at her. "Black, no sugar."

Throughout his career Byron had had an intense capacity to concentrate, a kind of trance focused entirely on the words in front of him or the face of a witness during one of the thousands of depositions he had taken over the years. That same trance happened now, that cone of silence, as he turned the pages of the indictment and the report stamped on every page with the words "Confidential—National Security Information." He never touched the mug of coffee Christina placed in front of him.

When the trance was broken, he slipped the documents back into their envelopes. Christina had turned the lights on in the kitchen while Byron was reading. It was almost entirely dark outside. Only the lights in Riverside Park and on the heights of the Palisades on the New Jersey shoreline were visible. The soft light shed by the lamp over the dining room table made his features, she thought, even more handsome. Christina really hadn't expected to have such a fast-developing affection for this man. This wasn't supposed to happen. It was not the plan.

Byron's face was absolutely calm and his voice resonantly thoughtful: "This is serious."

She lifted her face, silently conveying the question, *How so?*

"They're looking for the death penalty."

"That's a joke, isn't it?"

"This says he arranged the money for the attack on the U.S.S. Cole. The bombings at the U.S. embassies in Africa."

"Anything else?"

"And that he took part in funding the flight training for Mohammad Atta and the other pilots of the 9/11 jets."

After a pause, she asked, "What are you thinking about?"

"Mystery. How mysterious people are. I know absolutely nothing about Ali Hussein. He doesn't have the sulfur of evil about him, but here are all these powerful people insisting that he is a killer. Why would Rana and the others make this up? Why should I believe Ali Hussein and not the dozens of people in the government who must believe he's evil? I don't even know for certain that Ali Hussein is his name. Why in fact should I believe anybody?"

They stared at each other. "Can you handle this, Carlos?"

"I don't know, but I will. Except for Timothy McVeigh, the last execution by the federal government was the execution of the Rosenbergs. And nothing since McVeigh. States execute, not the U.S. government."

"You're going to let me go on working with you on this, Carlos?"

"Every brutal step of the way."

# 10

JUSTIN GOLDBERG WAS A tiny man, a perfect miniature: handsome, suave, and fast-moving. Even though he was in his black robes as he entered the courtroom, it took the beat of a moment before anyone noticed him. When he took his seat at the high bench, he put on his half-frame reading glasses and said, in his mannered voice, "This is the case of the United States against Ali Hussein." He glanced up. "Is the defendant in the courtroom?"

Hal Rana said, "He is. Standing next to Mr. Johnson."

Judge Goldberg smiled at Byron Carlos Johnson. "Good morning, Mr. Johnson. Good to see you again."

"Morning, Judge."

Even Ali Hussein, dressed in a prison jumpsuit and with his arms bound and immobilized in a bulletproof vest, seemed impressed by the judge's familiarity with Byron Johnson. It stemmed from a period several years earlier when they had served on the same bar association committee. Byron and Justin Goldberg were co-chairs of the committee, which met only once every six months. Byron was barely able to conceal his lack of interest in the committee's work—it related in some way to pre-trial discovery issues in federal civil cases—and his impatience with having been persuaded by his firm to co-chair the committee so the firm could burnish its reputation for service to the legal community. At the time, Goldberg was a junior partner at another big law firm. Two years later, at age forty-two, he was one of the many young, conservative, business-and-government friendly federal judges named over the last two decades. Goldberg had always been unfailingly polite to Byron, but Byron sensed that Goldberg's WASPish style (which he had developed, despite his origins in Queens, while in college at Amherst and law school at Yale) barely concealed a tightly wound and petulant core.

Goldberg said, "I understand the government has a sealed indictment of the defendant?"

"We do," Rana answered, holding up a copy of the indictment and waving it like a small flag.

"Have you favored Mr. Johnson with a copy?"

"Yes, Judge," Byron said, "Mr. Rana let me pick up a copy yesterday."

"Have you had a chance, Mr. Johnson, to give the indictment to your client?"

Byron hadn't been certain when he would have his first opportunity to signal to Goldberg that there were problems with the process in this case. He had decided to draw attention to everything that was unusual and unfair about the treatment of Ali Hussein. "Give, Judge?"

Goldberg peered over the upper line of his glasses, as if searching for a reason why Byron Johnson would have trouble understanding the meaning of the word "give."

Byron said, "No, I wasn't able to give Mr. Hussein the indictment because Mr. Rana instructed me that I couldn't do that. In fact, in the weeks that I've been able to visit with Mr. Hussein in Miami I haven't been allowed to hand him a piece of paper, and he hasn't been allowed to give me one."

Goldberg paused, and in that pause Byron thought again, as he had several times since learning that this fastidious little man was assigned to the case, that until now he had always been on the same side of the law as Goldberg himself. They both represented corporations, banks, and their executives, and both were far more often than not on the winning side. Goldberg continued to adhere to the same interests Byron had represented as a lawyer, ruling consistently in favor of the corporate clients Byron had represented. But he knew that in this case he and Goldberg were bound to part company and to clash—Goldberg had spent a career currying the favor of big law firms, big corporations, and big people in government. He had done that with a quick intelligence and unfailing loyalty, a modern courtier. He was not about to do anything different in this case, although Goldberg, Byron knew, was smart enough to never describe Ali Hussein as an Arab terrorist and would in fact treat Hussein with maddening decorum.

"Mr. Johnson, knowing how thorough you are, I assume you fully advised Mr. Hussein what the charges are in the indictment?"

"As well as I could in the ten minutes I had with him in the holding cell, Your Honor."

"Does your client speak English?"

"He does."

"Fluently?"

"He lived lawfully in the United States for ten years before he was detained, Judge. He was an accountant. He is very articulate."

"I'll let you have as much additional time as you want right now to speak with him further about what the indictment contains. You can let him read it. I can call a recess for that."

"The indictment is more than fifty pages long, Judge."

"Mr. Johnson, if it were three hundred pages I'd still accommodate you and Mr. Hussein."

"Frankly, Judge, what I want to do is give it to him. And I'm at a loss to understand why I can't do that."

"Let's not argue that kind of issue right now, Mr. Johnson. We can cross that bridge when we get there."

"I think we're there already, Judge."

Byron Johnson detected that acute, pained expression of annoyance he had often seen on the faces of judges like Goldberg—the suppressed antagonism, the tightening of the mouth and eyes. "I don't think so, Mr. Johnson. All that Mr. Hussein is entitled to at this moment is an understanding of the crimes with which he has been charged."

Byron interrupted: "I think Mr. Rana should be required to tell us why it is that we can't give a copy of the indictment to Mr. Hussein."

"Mr. Rana can be required to do only what I require him to do." Judge Goldberg adjusted the reading light in front of him. "And at the moment I'm not requiring that he do that. What I do require, Mr. Johnson, is some indication from you that you have reason to believe your client understands the charges against him so that he can intelligently plead guilty or not guilty."

"Let me cut this short, Judge, and simplify it. He pleads not guilty."

"Is that so, Mr. Hussein?"

In his clipped, precise English, Ali Hussein said, "Yes, it is, sir."

"Very well," Justin Goldberg said. He was efficient. "The next item is discovery. Mr. Rana, what kind of discovery do you have for Mr. Johnson? Documents? How many? Tapes? How many hours? Videos? Electronic messages? Surveillance tapes? Statements by Mr. Hussein? Give me a sense of the universe."

"Judge, all of the above. There are mountains of evidence. As the indictment shows, Mr. Hussein had many co-conspirators, there are many confidential informants."

"That gives Mr. Johnson much to work with."

Hal Rana held up his right hand, as if giving a pause signal. "Much of what the government has is national security material. There are documents and surveillance tapes, for example, that are highly confidential and not discoverable in a terrorism case."

Byron Johnson spoke into the pause after Rana's voice trailed off. "If that's the case, then how does the government ever plan to prove these complicated, very serious charges?"

Justin Goldberg said, "I imagine that the government believes it can prove its case in a more focused way than by advancing what Mr. Rana describes as not just one but many mountains of evidence."

"You know, Judge, in many ways it doesn't matter at this stage what the evidence is that Mr. Rana wants to use to prove his case at trial. What matters is, in fairness, to give Mr. Ali the opportunity to review the evidence that has already been put together and that could be used against him, not just the evidence selected by the government that it will use against him at trial. We need to look at those mountains of evidence to identify and follow leads, to go down avenues that might be useful to defending Mr. Ali, to ask questions and raise issues. Even to find material that exonerates him."

"That's a nice speech, Judge," Hal Rana said. "It would be a nice idea in the typical big civil case Mr. Johnson is a master of, but this is a criminal case, a unique one, the first of its kind in an American court, with serious consequences for the security of this country."

"Serious consequences?" Byron asked. "This is a death penalty case. That's a direct, serious consequence to Mr. Ali—death—not some nebulous possibility that national security will be jeopardized."

Justin Goldberg's voice was abrupt. "Enough speeches. Here is what we are going to do. Mr. Rana will write me a letter detailing the information the government has about Mr. Ali, the charges in the indictment, and an overview of the national security interests that might be implicated. After I review that letter, we will have another conference."

"When will I have a chance to respond to the letter?"

Justin Goldberg feigned surprise. "To respond to the letter? You've missed something, Mr. Johnson. Mr. Rana's letter is for me only, at least at this stage. It will contain, I'm sure, national security information that can't be shared with you or your client."

Byron felt angry, but he controlled the tenor of his voice. "I have to object, so the record is clear, to the procedure. One-sided communication from the prosecution to the Court? That was unfair two hundred years ago, and it's unfair today."

Justin Goldberg said, "You've made your record clear, counselor. We're adjourned."

He stood, looked at Byron Johnson as if he were an alien presence, and left the courtroom.

Ali Hussein, moving awkwardly in the bulletproof vest that encased his arms and chest, was literally hustled out of the courtroom. Five United States Marshals, all in combat-style uniforms, surrounded him so closely that the collective movement of their bodies seemed to lift Hussein off his feet and carry him into the holding area. Somewhere—probably in Herman Melville—Byron had read a description of a sudden, unexpected death as the *bundling out of life*. Those were the words that came to his mind as he followed closely behind the group of men whose large bodies almost hid Ali Hussein.

As Hussein was handcuffed to a horizontal bar that ran along one of the walls in the holding area, Byron asked, "Who said I can have only ten minutes with him?"

The oldest of the guards, a man whose name was sewn into the fabric over the left shirt pocket of his uniform, said, "It doesn't matter who said it. It's ten minutes."

Byron glanced at him, suppressing a flash of anger. He asked, "Officer, can we take off the vest?"

"Not a chance. Not until he's back in his cell."

Almost deferentially—he didn't want to lose the opportunity to spend even ten minutes with Hussein—Byron asked, "Can we at least have enough room for a private conversation?"

Still in a crescent formation around Byron and Hussein, the five guards stepped backwards, almost in military formation. The M-16s each of them carried were pointed downward. Byron could smell traces of cordite and gun grease.

When he pressed close enough to Hussein so that they could whisper to each other, Byron Johnson smelled yet another odor in the room. Ali Hussein, who had been so calm and passive in Miami during their conferences, smelled of sweat, of fear, of rancid and poorly digested food. His dark eyes rapidly darted from the five armed men to Byron.

Byron said, "You understand what happened in there?"

The precise, terse certainty with which Ali Hussein usually spoke was gone. "I'm not sure, I'm confused."

"Did you listen?"

"I thought they were talking about somebody else. Not me."

"Do you know what they're accusing you of?"

"Money, Mr. Johnson. I don't know anything about money except how to count it for other people. I'm a bookkeeper."

"Do you want me to tell you what money laundering is?"

"It's all a fantasy, Mr. Johnson. I lived in New Jersey, I took care of my family, I worked, I went to Germany for two weeks. These people are crazy, Mr. Johnson."

"These people say that huge amounts of money—cash, wires, checks—were sent to you and that you in turn arranged to send that money all over the world. Did that happen?"

"Never, no. How could I do that?"

"These people say you took instructions from clerics and sleeper terrorist agents who you knew were directing money for terrorist training and attacks. Is that true?"

Their faces were close together. Ali's breath was foul. He was sweating. So was Byron. "No."

"They say you arranged to put cash into the hands of Mohammad Atta so that he could pay flight schools for training before nine-eleven." Byron paused. "And is that true?"

"Mr. Johnson, I liked living in this country. I had friends here. My kids went to school here. I liked my work. These people are crazy."

"Is it true, Ali, that you arranged to put cash into the hands of Mohammad Atta?"

"No, never."

"Do you understand that they want to execute you? Kill you?"

Hussein's black eyes were sunk even deeper in the dark pouches that encircled them. He nodded. His lips were dry. Byron saw the tiny, moistureless cracks on the man's upper lip, like cracks in the soil in a place of drought.

Hussein whispered, "There was a man in that courtroom who used to come to see me."

"See you where?"

"Wherever I was. He followed me from place to place."

"What man?" Byron tried to recall the faces of the very few people who were in the sealed courtroom. There were five or six men, all seated in the gallery. It was clear to Byron Johnson that they were government agents, since no one else would have been allowed there. Armed guards had stood at the doors to the courtroom. Byron had barely noticed them, since when he was at work in a courtroom he was completely focused on the people in front of him—the judge, the jury, the stenographer, the witness—and not on the people behind him. Look forward, not backward.

"Older than the others."

"I wasn't paying attention to them."

"The one with the mustache and the three-piece suit."

"What do you want to tell me about him? Do you know his name?"

"I haven't known anybody's name except yours, Mr. Johnson, for years."

Byron whispered, "We don't have much time today. We need to start talking about these charges, you need to help me understand the facts so that I can defend you."

Ali Hussein said in an intense whisper: "He used to spend hours and hours with me. He asked me questions all the time. He asked me questions about the *Koran*, about where I was born, who my relatives were, and where I traveled. He asked me about the names of banks, mosques, airports, people."

"And?"

"I never said anything."

Byron stared at him. "That doesn't mean he won't swear that you told him things. You understand that, don't you?"

"He was the one who beat me."

"I know, you said that."

"He is a very strong man, Mr. Johnson."

"When was the last time he hit you?"

"Just before I was taken to Miami."

"Did he use his hands or a weapon, a stick, a baton?"

"His hands. And he used water."

*Water?* It was only after the invasion of Iraq that Byron had first read in the *New York Times* about waterboarding. He understood that it involved forcing a man's head under water so that he feared he was being drowned. There was no way, Byron thought, that this sweating, frightened man could ever have heard the word waterboarding. He had spent years in total isolation. "Tell me more."

"I was tied up and lowered into water. I started suffocating. Water filled my nose and my mouth and then my lungs. I couldn't even scream."

"Did that man do it?"

"No. He had other people do it."

"Where was he?"

"Always there. He decided when they could pull my face up out of the water."

Byron imagined that anyone near him in this fetid room could smell his own fear. The ten minutes were rapidly coming to a close. "Is any of this happening now?"

Again Hussein ignored that question, too. "There were times, Mr. Johnson, when there was a video camera in the room when this man was with me."

"What was happening?"

"He was talking, I was sitting. But the video camera was also there when I was pushed down into the water."

Abruptly the lead guard said, "That's it, fellas. The show's over for today."

The plaza at the front of the impressive new federal courthouse—a congested area of old Manhattan where the other courthouses were all constructed almost a century ago—was teeming with news vans with tall antennas, reporters, onlookers, and dozens of men and women in uniform. On the fringes of the plaza were the ancient Chinese men and women who always seemed to be there, exercising, stretching and gyrating. The warren of streets and alleys that was Chinatown was so close that it almost extended to the steps of the courthouses. The old men and women were, as ever, mute and oblivious to anything happening near them.

Given the size and closeness of all the buildings, the plaza was steeped in shadow even on a bright day. Byron had hoped to find a rear door from which he could leave the highly secure courthouse, but there wasn't one that he was authorized to use. He had to leave through the revolving doors at the main entrance, stepping out onto a slightly elevated set of steps. Every eye and camera seemed to turn instantly in his direction. He was ready for this. He had decided, remembering Sandy Spencer's harsh and critical words, that this time he wasn't going to act like a deer caught in the headlights.

As several people surged forward in his direction, he paused at the top of the stairs. Microphones were thrust up toward him, and reporters, some of whom he recognized from the television broadcasts he sometimes flipped through at night, raised their voices, asking questions. He found himself unexpectedly calm, with no tremor of the stage fright that had seized him on the steps of the courthouse in Miami.

He heard a strong voice ask: "Who are you?"

"My name is Byron Johnson," he said. "I represent Ali Hussein. Mr. Hussein has just been indicted, after years in total isolation during which he was brutalized by government agents. He is accused of serious offenses, and I'm here to do all I can to see to it that, even though all the scales of government power are weighed against him, there will be some element of fairness in his trial."

A sleek black woman extended a microphone toward him. "How long have you represented Mr. Hussein?"

"Several weeks."

A man's voice, more strident, interrupted the black woman before she could ask another question. "Does your client know he faces the death penalty?"

"He does."

"How did he find out?"

"He learned that precisely fifteen minutes ago in Judge Goldberg's courtroom."

Another voice overrode the others: "What was his reaction?"

Byron knew he had to stay composed, deliberate, and focused, despite the turmoil and noise surrounding him. "Mr. Hussein is a human being. He lived peacefully and productively for many years in this country before he was snatched up into years of confinement at various places in the world. How did he react? Quietly. But it's reasonable to assume that Mr. Hussein, as would anyone else, is very disturbed to learn that someone wants to put him to death. Particularly if that someone is a government that has held him totally incommunicado, isolated from friends, relatives, human contact."

"Is it true that your client met Osama bin Laden?"

"He's not accused of that. That claim isn't in the indictment."

There was a tumult of questions. But one rang out so decisively that Byron had to pay attention: "Why are you representing him?"

It was a question Byron had known he'd be asked at some point. He wasn't famous in the way that some lawyers were in an age of televised obsession with trials and crime, but who he was and what he did were not secrets. Google, Bing, and other search engines made it a simple exercise to pull his name and details about him from the vast storehouse of information in the ether. Anyone in his profession who looked at the twenty or so entries for him would have been impressed by his credentials and his experience, but to journalists dealing with the huge story of a terrorist accused of a crime in a United States court, Byron's credentials and experience would have mystified them. There were criminal lawyers in America who were almost household names. Byron had labored for years in a rarefied field, dealing in cases remote from the trials broadcast on Court TV or discussed at night on CNN and Fox. Until now, Byron had never once appeared on television. It had never crossed his mind to seek out an interview on television, even though the public relations firm that SpencerBlake had hired urged him to do it.

Byron answered, "I was asked to do this by civil liberties organizations, by Mr. Hussein's family, and of course by Mr. Hussein himself."

The question came back, the tenacious voice, "But why are you doing it? Why you?"

Byron decided to be playful. He smiled. "Because I'm a lawyer. This is what I do."

Then another question: "Who have your other famous clients been?"

Byron and his law firm had a client roster that was the envy of other lawyers in big law firms like SpencerBlake. But none of the names of those clients would resonate at all with the people now asking him questions. There were no names like Angelina Jolie, Lady Gaga, or Casey Anthony on the list.

"It's Mr. Hussein who is my only concern."

# 11

TOM NASHATKA AND ANDREW Hurd left the courthouse through
the rear entrance reserved for judges and some high-ranking
government employees. The area had become, since 9/11, a
Baghdad-style green zone. Huge, dirty-white New York City
garbage trucks blocked the entrance to the maze of old Manhattan streets that ran among the five nearby courthouses.
Iron grates implanted in the roadbeds rose like sharks' mouths
from the streets. And United States Marshals in combat boots
patrolled the area.

For Tom Nashatka, Andrew Hurd was an enigma, but a
heroic one. He had met Hurd two months earlier on the flight
from Guantanamo to Miami as they escorted the blindfolded,
smelly Ali Hussein. From the outset Tom knew that Andrew
Hurd was the boss, the *capo di tutti capi*, as one of Tom's mentors had described him. Tom wasn't familiar with the name,
but when he met Andrew Hurd he felt he was in the presence
of someone special. Even on sweltering nights in Cuba and
Miami, Hurd dressed in a blue suit and tie. His black shoes
were highly polished. He sported a black mustache, black hair
streaked with gray, and the look and swagger of an agent in a
James Bond movie. He smoked cigars even in the small plane.

It was a ten-minute walk from the courthouse to Juliano's,
an Italian restaurant on Mott Street with tables and chairs
from the 1950s and an even older tin ceiling from which empty

bottles of wine hung. Kimberly Smith was waiting for them at a table with a red-and-white checkered tablecloth. She raised her hand to get their attention, as if a beautiful blonde woman in a room crowded with men in suits needed to signal anyone.

For Kimberly, Andrew Hurd was not an enigma but a joke. She had first met him in a conference room at the CIA headquarters in Langley as Hurd was assembling "Team Ali" with Tom, Hamerindapal Rana, and several other agents. She saw him as cultivating the raffish look of crazy, communist-hunting G. Gordon Liddy, the leader of the Watergate break-in who claimed that he could hold the palm of his hand over a candle flame, the ultimate symbol of macho. Even in Hurd's presence she seemed to mock his eccentricities, his cigar-smoking, his taste for double-malt Scotch.

Kimberly and Tom glanced at each other over the tops of the big plastic menus. She was impatient to finish the lunch with Hurd. He was so erratic—calling meetings at strange times and unexpected places, sometimes gently asking questions and at other times screaming, and often calling Hal Rana that "fucking towelhead"—that she never really wanted to see him and, when she did, wanted to spend as little time with him as possible. Besides, she was anxious to spend the afternoon at Tom's apartment in Cobble Hill. Tom was a powerful and physically exciting lover.

"The plan," Tom Nashatka said into the din of voices in the restaurant, "is working well so far, Andy."

"Is that so? Tell me why."

"Johnson has already showed the memo to his girlfriend."

"My, my," Kimberly said, "he's a bad boy. That's a no-no. He promised not to do that."

Hurd actually had a roguish smile at times. "Love makes men blind, doesn't it?"

When the Italian-accented, raven-haired waiter stood over their table, Hurd was the first to order. "Diet Coke and a Caesar salad," he said, handing the oversize plastic menu to the waiter. "Too early for a Chivas."

Tom and Kimberly ordered a small pizza and iced tea. When the waiter left the table, Hurd picked up his glass of water. "Byron is going to have a visitor at his apartment tonight. Khalid Hussein is driving into the city to meet with him."

Kimberly said, "They're going to have a prayer meeting, don't you think, about the *Koran*?"

Hurd didn't respond to her. He asked Tom, "When did brother Khalid last talk to the Imam?"

"He was in the mosque for an hour early this morning." The mosque was wired with multiple listening and recording devices that Hurd's agents had implanted and that so far had eluded detection.

"And what about Johnson and Khalid? How are they in touch? Computer, cell phone, smoke signals?"

"Email most of the time. Khalid and Johnson have one thing in common: they don't sleep. They had an email exchange at two this morning to set up the meeting tonight."

"Christina must be keeping Byron up at all hours," Kimberly said.

Although Hurd recognized what she intended to convey by *up*, he again ignored her. "Anything else?"

"Johnson wrote—and Kimberly and I actually believe he is still this naive—that the case against Ali was complicated and that he thought Khalid might help him understand some new information he had. Mr. Johnson doesn't get it that every-body's using him."

"Did he mention the memo Rana gave him?"

"Not in the email."

Hurd sipped more water as he watched the waiter approach with a basket of plain bread and garlic rolls. "What else?"

"Johnson's so smitten that he's told Khalid that his assistant will be there, too. I guess Byron wants to introduce his *amor* to the family. *Omnia vincit amor.*"

"Love conquers all," Hurd said. Just as the waiter was placing the breadbasket on the checkered tablecloth, Hurd added, "Be careful who you love."

Kimberly was surprised that Andrew Hurd knew a Michael Jackson lyric, just as she was surprised that he knew a Latin maxim. She often thought of him as a belligerent and stupid action figure. She was bemused by him, not afraid of him.

Tom had never told her that Andrew Hurd had killed twelve men since 9/11.

"Be sure," Hurd said to Tom, "that we find out exactly what these two guys talk about tonight. Word for word, gesture for gesture."

"Don't worry, Andy. Johnson's apartment is, as they say, transparent."

# 12

KHALID HUSSEIN DROVE A gleaming Mercedes SUV through the Holland Tunnel. It was Tuesday night. Since the traffic was light, he increased the speed of the powerful car, racing between the tiled sides of the tunnel and the flexible yellow poles in the center of the roadway that divided the flow of traffic. He chased the red taillights of the car far ahead of him. Even inside the air-conditioned SUV, he heard the sustained whine of all the vehicles in the tunnel.

When he emerged onto Van Dam Street on the New York side of the tunnel, he sped eastward to the nearby streets of Tribeca. Most of the street surfaces were still old, paved with worn bricks. His Mercedes ran over them with a solid, well-built rumble.

Khalid Hussein knew these streets well. When he arrived in the United States in 1980—the first of his family to leave the Middle East—he found work on Warren Street at a huge brick warehouse. Khalid, who had earned a civil engineering degree in Lebanon before the civil war, took a job as a forklift operator. He worked at night, moving wooden pallets from the dim interior of the warehouse to unmarked trucks on the street outside. He had a sense that the warehouse operation was illegal, because there were no signs anywhere, the building was closed during the days, and the movements of large quantities of shoes in crates—or at least crates that he was told

contained shoes—into and out of the warehouse only happened at night, for the most part between midnight and four
in the morning. Never once, in the five years Khalid worked
there, did he see a single policeman or police cruiser on what
were then the largely unoccupied streets of that old industrial
and warehouse area, long before the actors and investment
bankers moved into the renovated buildings and before the
area was suddenly given the made-up name Tribeca.

Despite its transformation—there were now many people
on the cobblestone streets at all hours of the night, going to and
leaving the after-hours clubs with names like X-3 and 2inc—
the area was still familiar. Khalid had worked at the warehouse
for five years. By 1985, just as he was turning twenty-nine, he
borrowed five thousand dollars from Nick Ferrante, the handsome, engaging man who said he owned the warehouse, and
bought a delivery van. He used some of the cash to buy spices
from a Saudi who somehow always seemed to have Middle
Eastern specialty food to distribute. Khalid often spoke about
the first night he loaded bags of fragrant spices into the van and
drove his precious cargo through the Lincoln Tunnel, working his way up Bergenline Avenue, Kennedy Boulevard, and
Boulevard East in Jersey City, Hoboken, North Bergen, and
Edgewater—that string of towns along the Palisades—selling
the spices, for cash, to the Lebanese, Syrian, and Jordanian
shops that were then slowly proliferating through these old
towns. Even on that first trip, he made twice as much money
selling the spices as he had spent to buy them. He was amazed
by the reality of capitalism—you could buy something for three
dollars and sell it for six. American magic. Within a month he
had paid back Nick Ferrante all the money he had borrowed,

and, without being asked, he gave Nick another nine hundred dollars. He and Nick stayed friends eight more years, until Nick was arrested. Khalid, fluent in English, read that Nick was taken down with thirty-five other members of the Gambino family in 1993. Khalid missed Nick, who always embraced him and called him "buddy." Khalid liked that word: he still called many people "buddy."

But not Byron Johnson. Khalid didn't want this polite man to think he was anything other than a driven, narrow-minded Arab. And he didn't want Byron Johnson to know that he was wealthy, that his first trip in the fragrant, heavy-laden van along the Palisades so many years ago was the start of Khalid's assembling wealth that he never could have imagined even when, making his way out of the Middle East through Syria in the late 1970s, he glimpsed the rich men in armored Mercedes on the streets of Riyadh, surrounded by armed guards trotting along the sides of the cars.

Five blocks from Byron Johnson's apartment on Laight Street, Khalid pulled into a gleaming new garage in the basement of a renovated warehouse that was swiftly filling up with people who were spending at least three million dollars for each apartment. Khalid owned the garage, but he didn't want the cleanly dressed car jockeys who worked there to know that. He took a ticket like everyone else and told the snappy, efficient Puerto Rican garage man in a white shirt and black bowtie that he would be back around midnight.

Khalid Hussein had lived in America long enough to love American women. And he spent as much time as possible with them. There were quick-talking, sexily dressed Jersey girls who worked in the office at his immense new warehouse near the Meadowlands; the perfectly tanned, Harvard-educated lawyer at the big firm in Roseland that handled the lawsuits that seemed to swirl around business; and the twenty-five-year-old Oklahoma woman who was the hostess at the popular restaurant he and three partners had recently opened on West Broadway. Khalid no longer had to work at the business he had established and ran for so many years; he had three nephews who operated it for him and who, he was sure, were intensely loyal to him. So Khalid had time during this stage of his life to enjoy these enthralling women whenever he liked. If his wife, Benazir, knew anything about them—and she had to—it didn't matter, because she had ab-sorbed the lessons of obedience.

Khalid almost smiled when, just after Byron Johnson opened the door to his apartment, he saw the gorgeous young woman standing in the light at the end of the hallway, waiting to be introduced to him. Suddenly, putting on what he knew was his dark, brooding face, Khalid said, "And who is this?"

"She's helping with your brother's case. Christina Rosario, this is Ali's brother Khalid. This is Christina Rosario." He made no effort to shake her hand. He even succeeded in the difficult effort of barely glancing at her.

There was black coffee for the three of them at the dining room table. Byron wore a white shirt with his initials sewn into the pocket. He also wore chino pants but, to Khalid's sur-prise, no shoes or socks. Khalid took in something else that surprised him about Byron: he was not only tall but strongly built, a body constructed from a youth of playing squash, la-crosse, and tennis.

"Khalid," Byron said, "you know what an indictment is, don't you?"

When he dealt with what he often called "white men," Khalid roughened up the tone of his voice. "I read the news-papers. But tell me what it is."

"It's something in writing that tells a defendant what he's charged with, the crime. Do you want to see it?"

Khalid shrugged.

"Here," Byron said, "take it anyhow."

Christina, who rested her chin in her hand as she looked at them, noticed that Khalid dyed his thick hair black and had man-icured fingernails gleaming at the blunt ends of the back of his hairy hands. She also registered that his real voice and accent were far more polished than he made them seem. And she saw that he was a very good-looking man. Wanting to goad him just a little because of his studied annoyance about her presence, she decided to speak: "Byron's meeting with your brother tomorrow."

Khalid ignored her. He spoke to Byron. "What does Ali say about this?"

"Very little, Khalid. They only gave me ten minutes to speak to him." Byron was careful not to mention yet the thirty-page memo he had picked up the day before from the United States Attorney's Office.

"And what happens next?"

"Your brother has to explain the facts to me."

"My brother is an honest man."

"You can help him, too, Khalid. I have to start understand-ing what happened. And what didn't. I need information in order to defend him. I need to know more about his background. I hope you can help."

With his thick fingers, Khalid raised the edges of the document. He wore a gold bracelet on his right wrist. "You want me to read it tonight?"

Byron spoke quietly, pouring more of the black coffee for himself. "If you can, Khalid. Without learning as much as I can as fast as I can, I won't be able to help. There are some names of people and places and events in here—not many, but some—that you might know something about. Ali needs help if he is going to have any chance at all."

"You seem to be a nice man. But for years I've seen what's going on. My brother doesn't have any chance at all. Nobody will see him again outside, here, in this life."

"I'm not that pessimistic."

Khalid raised the document, rolled it, and tapped its bottom edge on the table, as though trying to arrange the pages even more neatly than they already were. "I'll read it."

"Can we meet tomorrow somewhere? In the evening? Maybe you can talk about this with his friends or yours and let me know."

Khalid asked, "What do you really think?"

"That your brother is in a very dangerous place."

"We visited the Imam before I came tonight, Mr. Johnson. He knows this is a dark time for Ali. Can you tell him that there is in the *Koran* a guide for courage?"

"Sure. What is it that you want me to give him?"

Khalid said from memory, "Have Ali look at book three, chapter five. The tenth through the twentieth lines. The Imam says he will be able to draw strength from that."

Byron and Christina both wrote down the reference as Khalid, with the document in his hand, abruptly got up from the table. "We'll meet tomorrow, Mr. Johnson."

He left the apartment. He didn't even look at Christina.

Three hours later, as Christina and Byron drove uptown along empty Riverside Drive, the river to their left and the dense, rustling trees of Riverside Park to their right, Christina said, "He's a scary guy, Carlos."

He glanced at her. She was in the front seat of the car he called his "toy," a silver convertible BMW sports car. The top was down. The gorgeous night air rushed over them. Byron Johnson didn't ask her what she meant.

# 13

ALI HUSSEIN, A MAN who cherished numbers and took pride in the fact that many of the great early mathematicians were from the Middle East, could compute without a pencil or paper that in the years of his imprisonment he had spent almost five million minutes in cells in at least four countries. At first, as the thousands upon thousands of hours accumulated, he was desperate and sick with the thought of how much of his life had been permanently taken from him. Over the last three years, struggling to see himself as free and vigorous, he thought of himself as a runner who covered unimaginably long distances alone.

But there were many hundreds of minutes over the interminable span of minutes when he had not been alone. Recently there were the precious ten hours he'd been with Byron Johnson. And on the flights to and from various parts of the world, including the flight to New York, there were pilots and armed men in the small jets in which he traveled.

And, for years, there had been Andrew Hurd.

When the door of his cell made that deep hum as the magnetic lock was disengaged, Ali instinctively knew that Hurd would soon enter the cell. Even though he was in the bowels of the prison, where there were no windows, Ali Hussein sensed it was the middle of the night, 2 or 3 a.m.

There was light in the hallway. Behind Hurd, two men in uniform, both with rifles, stood in the open doorway.

"Mr. Ali," Hurd said. "How the hell are you?"

Ali Hussein, sitting on his cot, didn't answer.

"You didn't look happy yesterday morning." Hurd pulled from its place near the steel sink a stool that was the only chair in the cell. Ali's copy of the *Koran* lay open on the stool. "Are you reading at this hour of the night?"

Dressed in a gray pinstripe suit, Hurd sat down and held the *Koran* open to the page at which Ali had left it. Hurd stared at the page. "You know, Mr. Ali, I love this book. It's so much more interesting than our New Testament and Old Testament they had me read as a kid. I mean, take a look at this: '*Let not the believers take disbelievers for their friends in preference to believers. Whoso doeth that hath no connection with Allah. Allah biddeth you beware only of himself. Unto Allah is the journeying. He knoweth that which is in the heavens and that which is in the earth, and Allah is able to do all things.*'"

Hurd paused, raising the book as if searching for better light. He smiled. "Mr. Ali, there's eloquence and poetry and mysticism in that. And I picked that passage randomly. You can learn to live a whole life out of those lines, can't you?"

Even Hurd was surprised when Ali, his head still bent forward into his left hand, his face in darkness, recited as if praying: "*On the day when every soul will find itself confronted with all that it hath done of good and all that it hath done of evil every soul will long that there might be a mighty space between it and that evil. Allah biddeth you beware of him.*"

"Jesus H. Christ, Mr. Ali, those are the very next words." Hurd closed the *Koran* and tossed it on the floor, in the direction of the lidless steel toilet. "There, you see, as I've been telling everybody, you're blessed with a prodigious memory."

Ali knew he would be hit. Hurd always hit him. And he knew the hitting would be painful. He always tried to pull away, but he'd never succeeded in eluding the hit. As he had told Byron Johnson only twelve hours earlier, the man whose name he didn't know—this man—was very strong.

"Now that your memory is really working overtime," Hurd said, "let me see how much you remember about this."

Rolling it into a tube, Hurd held up a copy of the indictment. "You remember all about Lashkar-e-Taiba, don't you, Mr. Ali? The LET terrorist organization? I'll bet that rings a bell."

Still seated, Ali looked up. Hurd saw the dark, almost effeminate oval of the man's face. "How did you get the money to LET?"

Ali Hussein stared straight ahead.

"Mr. Ali," Hurd said as he reached out and gripped the tender back of the man's neck, "you see we also know about the Dar al Arqam Islamic Center. You've got a great memory, Jesus, you can probably recite this whole great holy book. So tell me all you remember about the Dar al Arqam Islamic Center. Most of your brothers from there are already in prison, forever. You remember Ali Timimi? Well, he's in jail for life fifteen times over. And he says you know how the money got from the streets to the mosques to LET. We heard him say that. He now enjoys talking to us. He says he wants to help us. He can shorten his sentence to thirteen life terms."

Hurd's powerful right hand continued to stroke the tendons at the back of Ali's neck. He felt the sweat on the man's skin and the rock-hard tension of the muscles. "And you know what? Mr. Timimi's mad at you. He says that you know where the money is and you're not telling anybody about it. Are you saving it for a rainy day?"

No answer.

"Your rainy day is here, Mr. Ali. Pretty soon we're going to know where all that money comes from and where it is. Some of your other brothers are helping us, but they all say no one knows as much as you. You, they say, know everything. But we will figure it out without you if we have to. And when that happens, nobody will need you. Allah is not going to be able to help you. Your dummy lawyer sure as hell won't help you."

Hurd waited. There wasn't a sound. Ali counted the seconds, methodically, accurately. Ninety-six seconds passed.

Hurd took his hand away from Ali's neck. He stood and left the cell. The steel door slid shut, and the magnetic hum ended as soon as the lock was engaged.

Ali Hussein slid off the cot. He tried for a moment to kneel so that he wouldn't collapse completely. This time Andrew Hurd had not hit him, but it felt as if he had, like an instinctive memory of something that had happened again and again. Then he simply fell to the floor and stayed there. His body shook.

# 14

IT WAS THREE IN the morning, always a bad time of night, and a time at which Byron Johnson had regularly been waking for weeks. When he was in his own apartment, he made coffee and then, seated at his sleek glass desk, wandered through the Internet. He hunted for information about the *Koran*, torture, and Guantanamo Bay. He had also started to search the Internet for information about himself. Christina had brought this sometimes disturbing miracle of instant information to his attention almost as soon as they spent that first night together. He was absorbed by what he found. During every twenty-four hour period there were new entries in which his name appeared. There were newspaper articles, verbatim transcripts of radio and television broadcasts, blog postings (most of them hateful), and pictures of him that rose from the vast interstellar spaces of the Internet. Almost none of the steadily accumulating Internet entries was flattering. Once he ruefully said to Christina, "I preferred the anonymity of being a big-time corporate lawyer to this."

Most of his emails now were from reporters. He was intrigued by the fact that many reporters didn't seem to sleep or rest, because emails sent at one or two or three in the morning often appeared on his screen. When Byron was in Christina's apartment, as he often was, he would simply glance at the messages and never respond to them because writing would wake him for the rest of the night.

Leaving her bed—her lovely arm seemed to glow even in the dark—he went to the bathroom and then, naked, walked quietly to the computer in the alcove where Christina studied. He watched the little running cartoon figures dash across the screen as he connected to the spaces where he entered his screen name ("LordByron") and his password ("Mexico") and waited for a second as the familiar page suddenly materialized on the screen.

He typed by the glow from the screen. He had five emails that he assumed were from journalists, since each of them had abbreviations for newspapers and networks after the @ symbol.

And then, for some reason, he clicked on the *Sent* button. And there he saw an email that had been sent from his computer at 1:15 that morning, two hours earlier. The email had been sent to "SesameStar," an address to which he'd never sent anything. *SesameStar*?

He clicked on the blue bar. The vaudeville-shaped, gloved hand and fingers on the screen pulsed, and the email opened. He immediately saw that the report Hal Rana had given to him had been sent to "Sesame Star." He opened the attachment. Someone had scanned the secret thirty-five page report into the email. Byron Carlos Johnson knew he hadn't done that, since his computer skills were limited to email (he didn't even know how to create an attachment) and access to the search engines. He had only recently learned that the word "Google" was no longer just the name of a company but a verb, "to Google." He was still learning how to use the beautifully engineered BlackBerry Christina had given him.

The email to "SesameStar" consumed his attention. Who was SesameStar? How had the paper report been scanned into the computer, making it a permanently embedded part of the ether of this new world? He thought about the promise Hal Rana had extracted, and which Byron had made, to keep the document a secret.

Naked, slightly chilly even in the hot apartment, Byron walked to the bedroom. Christina, her hair spread over the pillow and her gorgeous body now completely uncovered, was asleep. He heard her steady breathing. He let her sleep. It took a full hour of fitfulness for Byron Johnson to drift into sleep as he watched the television images of bulky American soldiers walking across the shattered, moon-like surface of Afghanistan.

Christina Rosario's apartment was one of those roomy West Side apartments that Byron had always admired, even though he had never lived in one. There were intricately carved moldings along the seams where the walls and ceilings met. There were free-standing radiators from which the metallic paint was peeling. The bookcases along the walls were filled with books, thousands of them. The floors were brown and black parquet inlaid at angles to one another. The sink, shower stall, and built-in clothes hamper were from the fifties; they were white relics that still worked. There were two faucets on the sink, as in the bathtub, for hot and cold water. The sofas were deep, soft, and somewhat frayed.

Christina had told him that her father, now dead, had been a professor of engineering at Columbia. Her mother, a woman who wrote children's books under the pseudonym Raquel Rematti (Christina called it her mother's *nom de guerre*) lived in Paris with an Italian man twenty years younger than she was. Christina was raised in the apartment until she was fourteen, when she was sent to a boarding school in New England. Her mother still owned the apartment.

Wearing only underpants, Christina walked drowsily into the kitchen at first light as Byron sipped coffee. "How long have you been up, Carlos?"

"A little while. I found it hard to sleep."

"Really? I didn't hear you. I must have been out like the proverbial light."

"You slept like a baby. Glad I didn't wake you."

He poured a cup of coffee and held it aloft for her.

"It's early, Carlos. What time is it, anyway?"

"Six or so."

"My first class isn't until eleven." She draped her bare arms over his shoulders. "Why don't you come back to bed? We can mess around for a bit, and I guarantee you the sleep of the pure at heart."

"You shameless hussy. Love to do it, but I made arrangements to visit Ali this morning. I want to read that report again, more carefully this time."

She was fragrant with the sweet smell of sleep. As she continued to drape her arms over his shoulders her hair brushed his face.

Byron said, "I don't want to keep you awake, honey, but something's bothering me."

More alert and less seductively drowsy than she had been, Christina said, "What's the matter, Carlos?"

"When I got up at three I did what I always do these days. I've become as addicted to the computer as a teenager."

"Wait until you get to be a CrackBerry head. You'll be one of those zombies walking down Park Avenue never, ever looking up."

Now more serious, Byron said, "My sent screen showed an email to a screen name I've never heard of."

"What screen name?"

"Take a look."

Byron clicked on the blue line.

"SesameStar?"

"Look familiar?" he asked.

"Is it for Bert or Ernie?"

"Your generation, not mine." She was standing over his left shoulder. He turned and looked up at her. "There's an attachment."

"What is it?" she asked.

"The memo Rana gave me. The one you saw me reading last night."

"The secret one?"

Byron nodded. "And now SesameStar has it. You know more about these things than I do: is there some directory, some way to find out who SesameStar is?"

"I don't know, I don't think so."

"And how could anyone use my email account to send a message to a name I've never seen?"

"I don't know, Carlos."

Placing the leaning arrow of the cursor over the X at the upper right corner of the screen, Byron closed his email. He stood up. The robe he wore fell open. "Let's get ready for our day. I need to be down at the prison soon. And you need to go learn all about criminal procedure."

She touched his face. "Carlos, this is strange. Are you worried?"

"No. Intrigued, I think, is the right word." He patted her naked rear.

"How's about showering with me?"

"You'd tire me out. I want to be alert for my day. And you need to get ready for class."


Byron Johnson poured a cup of black coffee. His heart was racing. He listened to the water throbbing as Christina showered. He glanced out at Riverside Park from the kitchen window. It was early dawn. Two or three people, indistinct, ran along the park's pathways.

He walked down the long, book-lined hallway that led from the kitchen to the bedroom. He was possessed by that pre-dawn sense of dread that had arrived as soon as he'd woken up. Someone had said to him years ago, in a context he could not remember, "Your first thought of the day is your worst thought."

Byron had intended to do something challenging when he volunteered to represent someone charged with terrorism. He'd never anticipated—and this lack of foresight troubled him—that so many people would be so alienated, that the vicious, right-wing pandering Rush Limbaugh would incessantly call him that "candy-ass, stuck-up idiot," and that he'd fall in love with and constantly crave a beautiful woman who was the same age as his own sons.

And he began to recognize something else he hadn't fore-seen. There were times when, on the streets and in restaurants, he sensed that men were watching him. There were sometimes resonant voids when he used his cell phone. There were un-expected surprises on his computer, such as the appearance of "SesameStar."

*Have I ever*, he wondered, *been afraid*?

To distract himself from the anxiety, he glanced at the books on the crowded shelves in the hallway. What suddenly caught his attention was that the books consisted of all the usual classics—Dickens, Melville, Hawthorne, Hemingway, and some recent novels still in their shiny dust jackets. There was even a copy of the Modern Library edition of *The Moon-stone*, the book he had been reading on his trips back and forth to Miami.

And then he realized that of all the books on the floor-to-ceiling bookcases, there was not a single engineering or technical or scientific book in this apartment in which Christina's father, a Columbia engineering professor, had lived for thirty years.

# 15

TOM NASHATKA, WITH ANDREW Hurd just behind him, pressed the grimy buzzer of the storefront on the Grand Concourse in the Bronx. The neon sign on the window read *Money Orders, Etcetera*. Nashatka looked down the long, barren, and unoccupied entrance of the store. At the far end was a counter sealed off from the customer area by double layers of protective, shatter-proof glass. Three or four people stood behind the counter. One customer, an enormous black woman, was leaning toward the speaker in the glass partition. It was ten in the morning.

When the buzzer at the front door finally sounded and the magnetic lock disengaged, Tom Nashatka entered the store as Andrew Hurd pushed a city trash can between the open door and the frame. Nashatka walked steadily forward. Behind him, Hurd and seven uniformed U.S. Marshals filled the room, moving forward. The black woman turned and started to scream. And in the closed off area, the three women and one man began running toward a metal door behind them.

Calmly, Nashatka pressed a badge against the scratched security window at the counter. He shouted, "Police. Let me see your hands. Unlock the door and step out."

As if staring into a cloudy fishbowl, Nashatka watched a slender, elegant man, probably Pakistani, emerge through the rear door. He had a prematurely gray beard but absolutely black, glistening hair. He moved gracefully, deliberately. He

**106**

reached toward the counter and knocked the two laptop computers to the floor. From under the counter, as he ignored Nashatka's pounding on the glass, the man took out a hammer. He knelt over the computers and began hitting them. They fractured like plastic toys.

As though calmly painting a portrait, the man continued to smash the smaller and smaller pieces even while the battering ram, wielded by Nashatka and one of the uniformed marshals, struck the frame of the bulletproof door in the window barrier. The door fell backwards, intact, its hinges detached from the frame. The man dropped the hammer and simply stood over the pieces of the computer. Nashatka and the other men who entered the room had their pistols out. "Hands in the air, hands in the air."

The elegant man raised his hands. Nashatka hit him in the chest with his fist, a powerful blow, and the man collapsed. One of the marshals held a pistol to his head as another put plastic handcuffs on him. The man was groaning. A puffy red foam blew out of his nostrils with each breath he took.

When Nashatka saw that no piece of the laptops larger than a sliver remained, he kicked the man just below the rib cage. The women were screaming. One of the marshals touched Nashatka on the shoulder and said, "Sir," as though cautioning him.

Nashatka looked around the room with the fast, all-encompassing movement of a receiver in a football game. He said, "I want every security camera in here ripped out of the wall. Give them all to me before we leave. Don't inventory them."

"Sir?"

"Don't fucking put them on the inventory sheet. I'll secure them."

Byron's sparely furnished, high-ceilinged apartment had tall windows. His apartment was higher than most of the three or four story buildings that still dominated the old warehouse area, and he enjoyed the sense of light that filled his living room and kitchen—actually, there were no walls between the living room and kitchen areas in the huge apartment—during the day. And he loved to look out the big windows at night: there were all the sparkling lights of the city and, to the north, the immense tower that was the Empire State Building, its top always illuminated by at least three different colors. Tonight the lights on the spire were white, green, and blue.

Christina was as uninhibited as he was about walking either barely dressed or naked in the apartment at night, with the windows unobstructed by shades or curtains. They kept only dim lights on in the apartment at night. Traces of the bedroom, and of Byron and Christina, were always visible at night because the television, resonant with sound and vibrant with images, was always on. When they spent the night at Byron's apartment, they lay in bed watching Charlie Rose's interviews from eleven to twelve and then, before either making love again or falling asleep, watched the local news just after midnight. They often lay naked on top of the crisp sheets that Byron's housekeeper changed every day—a practice that was a holdover from the years when Byron had lived with his wife and sons on Fifth Avenue.

The late-night anchor was a literate, extremely precise Asian woman, no older than thirty, with an unaccented, chirpy voice. Christina focused on the woman's story before Byron did. "Federal agents and local police," the anchor said, "conducted raids today on three separate money exchange stores with links to terrorism. One of the stores is in the Bronx. Another is in Fort Lee, New Jersey. And the third, also in New Jersey, is in Irvington."

"Carlos," Christina whispered as Byron read an old Modern Library edition of *Moby Dick*, "listen to this."

Suddenly Byron Johnson was no longer drifting toward a refreshing, longed-for sleep. He stared at the televised images of the three raided store fronts. The signs bore the names that Ali Hussein had given him that morning: *Abad's Carnival Ice Cream, It's Your Money, Money Orders, Etcetera.* Hesitantly, quietly, Hussein had almost whispered and then repeated those names as part of the long process by which he seemed to gradually give up information while he became more confident in Byron. He wrote down the names on a yellow legal pad; Ali said he had done part-time accounting work for them.

*Hawala.* That, Hussein told him, was the Arabic word for money transfer stores that acted, as Western Union had for many years, as places where United States dollars could be sent by wire to family members in distant countries and converted into the local currencies. *Hawala.* Byron had never heard the word before, and he wrote it that morning in large, blocky letters next to the names of each of the stores, names that now flashed on the screen.

Christina, although she was used to the focus that Carlos could bring to certain events, was aware of the special intensity in his expression as he watched the broadcast. The spell didn't end when the report dissolved into a commercial for a cell phone service, an image of two cute, wisecracking girls talking into their phones in a restaurant as a trim, beautiful man walked by them, blessing them with an alluring glance.

"What's the matter, Carlos?"

Instinctively he let go of the thought of telling her that these were the three stores that Hussein had carefully spelled out that morning.

Later, while Christina slept, Byron roamed his apartment, repeatedly gazing out the windows at the streetlights, the cobblestoned pavement, the many dark windows of the buildings in his neighborhood, and the white, green and blue lighting at the curved height of the Empire State Building.

That seductive and welcome sensation he had had before the news broadcast—that drifting toward a restorative sleep—was shattered.

# 16

"VERY WELL," JUDGE JUSTIN Goldberg crisply said, "we have the court reporter here and we can start. As we do, I want to make the record clear that this is a special hearing in the case of United States of America against Ali Hussein. This proceeding is being held in my chambers, Room 1652, in the United States Courthouse at 500 Pearl Street, New York, New York. I have ordered that this be conducted as a sealed hearing in this case, which has been designated in the order of the president of the United States as a so-called Category 103 case under the Anti-Terror Executive Order 962."

Dressed in an expensive business suit rather than his black robes, Justin Goldberg paused politely when the court reporter signaled that he was having a problem with the equipment on which he was transcribing the judge's words. During that pause Byron Johnson leaned forward at the conference table in Justin Goldberg's richly decorated chambers. As he watched Henry Jones, the court reporter, concentrate on the expensive equipment, Byron tried to control the steadily escalating anger he had felt over the last two days, an anger that deepened as he watched Justin Goldberg relish the studied, pontificating role he was playing.

On a business-like nod from Henry Jones, Goldberg continued. "I called this conference in response to a letter I received yesterday from Mr. Byron Johnson, the attorney for the defendant, Ali Hussein. As soon as I received the government's response, which was stamped 'Confidential—National Security Material,' I scheduled this conference and imposed the Category 103 designation. Mr. Johnson has been advised that, as a Category 103 proceeding, this conference cannot be disclosed to anyone. As a result, these proceedings are being held here, in my chambers, not in open court. The transcript is to be sealed. The court reporter is not to divulge the existence of this proceeding or the transcript to anyone. Until I make a further order, only Mr. Johnson, the United States Attorney's Office, and I will have copies of the transcript. I want to make it clear that under the president's executive order anyone who violates these conditions will be subject to the punishments spelled out in the executive order."

Byron's edgy impatience was plain in his voice. "Judge, I want the record to be clear, just as you want it to be, that I have no idea what the executive order says about punishments or anything else because it's not published and not available. I'm being required to comply with something that's a secret."

"Mr. Johnson, isn't it the case that my law clerk explained to you yesterday when I agreed to schedule this conference, at your request, that there is an executive order that applies to this case, that it is sealed, and that it in turn provides for the sealing of proceedings in this case in the event the Justice Department so requests and I so determine?"

"I heard that. He said that to me. I just want the record to be clear that I find this utterly unacceptable. My client is entitled to an open process. This should happen in court, with access by the press and the public. The process should not be governed by executive orders that are not published and are not available. I should not be subjected to the threat of sanctions that apparently are spelled out in an executive order that no one other than the court and apparently some government officials are aware of." He paused. "'Kafka-esque' doesn't capture the full essence of it."

Byron knew before he spoke, and saw as he was speaking, that Justin Goldberg's fury would be intense but quiet. It was. "This conference does not need to be held at all. I have acted in response to your letter, Mr. Johnson. There are issues you want me to consider, isn't that right, Mr. Johnson?"

Without answering, Byron stared into Justin Goldberg's eyes. Goldberg, disengaging from the stare and turning to the court reporter, said, "If Mr. Johnson wants me to proceed, as he apparently does, to deal with the issues he raised, then I have to proceed, unless I am ordered by an appellate court to do otherwise, under the rules that apply in these new and unique types of cases. For the record, and I will not encourage Mr. Johnson to respond to this, he doesn't have to represent this or any other client whose case happens to fall in the category covered by the executive order. There are other free lawyers who can be appointed to do this."

"Let me say this again, Judge, so that on behalf of Ali Hussein I am as clear as you are: I have never been given a copy of this unpublished, unavailable executive order. If it provides for sealed hearings such as this, then my client and I object to it. We also object to potential sanctions for violation of an order whose terms we do not know."

"Do you want to have this hearing, Mr. Johnson, or not? I have other business I can attend to."

"Judge, my client is even now being threatened and physically harmed in prison just two blocks from this courthouse. Government agents are visiting his cell at night. I have reason

to believe my conversations with him are monitored and recorded. All of that and more is spelled out in my letter. I think
that is the kind of business the court should attend to."

Goldberg was a very smart and very adroit man. If Justin
Goldberg wanted to see to it that Ali Hussein was convicted
of terrorism and money-laundering and sentenced to death,
then Justin Goldberg knew that he had to craft a record in
this case that would appear balanced, proficient, and com-
petent enough to survive the scrutiny of appeals. So Byron
wasn't surprised when the judge said, "We'll move forward in
an orderly way, then. I can state for the record that it is clear
that Mr. Johnson has been advised that the executive order
provides among other things for the imposition of criminal
contempt on anyone who violates the terms of the confidentiality that now attaches to this particular phase of the case. I am
certain everyone else in this room is aware of the conditions
of confidentiality and the sanctions for violations. Now I want
to have everyone's appearances so that the record is clear as
to who is in this room. You go first, Mr. Johnson, since you
already have."

"Byron Carlos Johnson, for defendant Ali Hussein."

"Hamerindapal Rana, Executive Assistant U.S. Attorney
for the Southern District of New York. With me is Arlene
Berg, also an Assistant US Attorney."

Three men sat along the same side of the table with Hal
Rana. Byron glanced at them, expecting each of them to speak.
None of them did. One of the men was in a blue business suit
and had a dapper moustache. Justin Goldberg said, "Mr. Rana,
I understand that the three gentlemen with you are federal
agents, is that right?"

EXTRAORDINARY RENDITION | 115

"They are."

Goldberg nodded. "Very well."

"Judge," Byron said after a pause in which it became clear the men weren't expected to identify themselves, "what are their names and what agencies are they with?"

"Under the terms of the executive order they are entitled to be here."

"And my client and I are entitled to know their names."

"No, you're not."

Byron Johnson was steadily letting go of all the trappings, rules, customs, taboos, and tacit understandings by which he had lived his professional life. One abiding custom of the kind of big-firm, big-company corporate litigation he had practiced was that you didn't confront a judge, you didn't challenge or embarrass him or her, you acted at all times to preserve the collegial demeanor, you didn't shout, you didn't snicker, you didn't dissent, you didn't complain, you laughed when the judge laughed. Byron had often called it the "sycophant system of justice." Byron long knew that for lawyers like those he associated with, this was a channel that led to success, reputation, and prestige.

"There is a rich irony in that," Byron said. "My client isn't allowed to be here, at a conference that involves his safety, and three unidentified men can bring themselves to the table and I'm not allowed to know who in the world they are."

Even the agile, supple-minded Justin Goldberg was silent for a moment as he absorbed what Byron had just said.

"You know who they are, Mr. Johnson. They are federal agents."

Byron raised his hands, palms up, a gesture of mock understanding.

Like an acolyte, one of Justin Goldberg's law clerks placed neatly in front of him what Byron recognized was a copy of his own letter and what he assumed was Hal Rana's letter in response. He hadn't been given a copy of that letter. It was a single page and contained, Byron imagined, just a terse statement that his own letter raised national security concerns.

Byron was right.

"Let the record reflect," Justin Goldberg said, like an overly formal British actor reading a script, "that the court has in front of it a letter dated yesterday from Mr. Johnson raising issues about the conditions of his client's confinement and concerns about alleged violations of his client's confidential attorney-client relationship with him. The court has also received a letter from the United States declaring that, pursuant to Executive Order 962, the subjects raised by the Johnson letter implicate national security interests."

Into the pause Byron said, "What does that mean?"

Justin Goldberg had a neatly carved profile. Byron was able to stare at the profile because the furious judge was no longer even glancing at him. Goldberg knew that the only important part of this conference was the clarity of the printed record that would reveal itself in the typed transcript that Henry Jones, that almost invisible presence, was preparing. That typed record didn't reflect nuances, gestures, or attitudes—the elements that gave a conversation meaning. Goldberg, whose small hands were visibly trembling with anger, chose his words carefully so that the cold written transcript would later read with formal precision.

"The presidential executive order makes it crystal clear that federal judges do not have the authority to review precisely those issues the defendant wishes to bring to the court's attention. Like any federal judge, I lack the authority under the order to review the circumstances under which this defendant is held."

"Judge, we've cited cases in our letter in which federal judges have done precisely that—authorized investigations into whether the government, through agents acting at the request of federal prosecutors, have attempted to interview defendants who are in prison awaiting trial."

Justin Goldberg simply continued dictating. "I have reviewed all of the relevant executive orders, as well as orders issued by the National Security Court, and I find that any steps I might take to inquire into the matters this letter has raised would be unauthorized."

"My client has been, and I believe is now being, tortured. That can't be allowed to happen."

Still not turning to Byron, Justin Goldberg continued: "The relevant rules mandate that judges abstain from even considering where prisoners such as defendant Hussein are held, how they are confined, what they read, who observes them, who speaks to them, and even how frequently they are permitted to bathe."

Byron did not intend to stand down. "I'm raising, so that the record is clear for whoever might review this transcript in the future, issues that relate to his physical survival, to his mental well-being, and to his dignity as a human being. He has been the victim of practices like waterboarding, physical abuse, sleep deprivation, and continuous playing of loud rap music with obscene lyrics that are offensive to his religious beliefs, and these practices are continuing."

Intently, Justin Goldberg went on: "As to the other branch of Mr. Johnson's letter—an unsupported suggestion that his conferences and communications with his client are being tapped or intercepted, monitored and recorded and videotaped—this, too, under the relevant orders is beyond the court's ability to consider or evaluate. A federal prison for a defendant in Mr. Hussein's position is not a place in which he is entitled to any expectation of privacy or privileges. Mr. Johnson still has every right to meet with and speak to his client, and his client if he wishes has every right to speak with Mr. Johnson about any subject relating to Mr. Hussein's defense of these charges. Mr. Johnson and his client must decide how they wish to proceed and what they wish to say during those encounters. Only discussions between them that relate to legal advice and legal issues are protected by the attorney-client privilege. If they discuss non-legal issues, then they talk at their peril."

Byron Johnson, settling his mind on those last words, felt a chill. There was a clear threat implicit in Goldberg's words.

"For the record, Judge, Mr. Hussein has a right to speak with me in confidence about anything that he and I deem appropriate to the defense of the charges. That could include what he eats for breakfast, not just specific legal strategies. The government can't be allowed to decide what part of a lawyer's conversation with his or her client relates to the defense of the specific charges and what part of the conversation doesn't. The devil doesn't get to decide what's good and what's bad."

Justin Goldberg tensely paused. Still in profile to Byron Johnson, Goldberg raised the angle of his sight to the row of faces to his left—Rana, Berg, and the anonymous agents. "Let me say for the benefit of defense counsel that conversations he or any other lawyer might have with a client are not privileged if those conversations relate to the planning of a crime or the deliberate concealment of a crime or of an ongoing conspiracy. Lawyers do not exist for the purpose of immunizing criminals from liability. Nor do they exist for the purpose of facilitating crimes."

Byron Carlos Johnson was now in a moment of complete clarity: *They're hunting me.*

# 17

BYRON JOHNSON'S EXPENSIVE BUT austere office in the Seagram building had become over the last eight weeks less and less familiar to him. He'd occupied that corner office for more than a decade. Its windows overlooked Park Avenue and the MetLife Building, that diadem in the middle of Park Avenue, still known to him as the Pan Am Building even though the name had changed years earlier.

The office was what he had once described as his farm, an ancestral place where he made his daily bread and where he dealt with legal problems he once considered fascinating. He used to resort to it for twelve or more hours each day, often on the weekends, long before the annoying expression "24/7" became so popular in corporate America. Particularly during the painfully protracted two years that his divorce took, the office was his life's geographic center—a place of stability, a safe harbor. He relaxed there often, read there often, and often just spent the quiet hours between eight and ten at night reading and writing as he sometimes looked out on the unique combination of glittering lights and the quiet at the heart of the city.

But now he sensed the steady erosion of his connection to the office. Sometimes when he walked into it in the middle of the day, after a week spent at the prison, at home, or at Christina Rosario's apartment, he had the dislocated sense that he was visiting the rooms he'd once occupied years earlier at boarding school and college. There was an eerie sense, like a recurrent and unpleasant dream, of returning to a place where he no longer belonged. Byron had once been meticulous about maintaining the orderliness of the books and mementoes on the office bookcases, the gleam of the surface of the conference table, and the symmetry of the photographs, paintings, diplomas, and certificates on the walls. Now it seemed that time and inattention were steadily causing the decay of all that well-maintained structure, like an abandoned house. Some of the papers he had left on his desk—copies of letters to clients and memos from associates at the firm answering research questions he'd raised for corporate clients—were yellowing.

The laptop computer in his office also bore a light coating of dust. It had been weeks since he had turned it on. It had the corporate screen name *BCJohnson@spencerblake.com*, not his personal address. He hadn't checked his business mail for days. As soon as he raised the lid, the small twinkling lights came on and the screen filled with white and blue light. The only thing Byron had carried into the firm that afternoon was the piece of yellow legal paper on which he had written down notes from that morning's meeting with Ali Hussein.

Byron still addressed emails to himself. It was his way of preparing a diary, a resource for future reference, a kind of inventory of information. He entered his screen name in the *Send To* box before he began writing. Just two days earlier, Byron had suddenly stopped transferring to the computer the precise contents of the notes he had scrawled with the chapter, verse, and line numbers Ali Hussein had given him. Instead, Byron had decided to send disinformation.

He glanced at his notes with Ali Hussein's references to the *Koran*. Ali knew that Byron planned to make yet another trip to Newark the next day, to that gold-domed mosque, and that he would see the young Imam, Sheik Naveed Haq. "Tell him," Hussein had said of the sheik, "that these lines have always confused me. Ask him to explain them to you."

Hussein had developed a deferential, intelligent, and even playful demeanor at times with Byron. "I've got to rely on you now, Mr. Johnson, even for my understanding of the *Koran*." He smiled. "May Allah help me."

Byron picked at random these words from the paperback edition of Marmaduke Pickthall's translation of the *Koran* that he kept on his desk: *We sent no messenger save that he should be obeyed by Allah's leave. And if, when they had wronged themselves, they had but come unto thee and asked forgiveness of Allah, and asked forgiveness of the messenger, they would have found Allah's forgiving, merciful. But nay, by thy Lord, they will not believe in truth until they make thee judge of what is in dispute between them and find within themselves no dislike of that which thou decides, and submit with full submission.*

And then he typed in the numbers of the book, chapter, and lines for that quote. He put the numbers Ali had dictated on a slip of paper in his wallet.

When he finished, Byron glanced up at the glittering play of mid-afternoon sunlight on the surface of the MetLife building. Then he moved the leaning arrow on the computer screen to the yellow, cartoon-style envelope just above the words "Send Now." Instantly his computer screen displayed "Your mail has been sent."

He pressed down the lid of his computer and walked to the elevator, smiling and waving at the secretaries and young lawyers he passed in the carpeted, muted hallways.

Byron Johnson never again saw his office.

# 18

KIMBERLY SMITH LOVED THOSE hour-long periods when she sat alone in a small studio with the automated camera in front of her as she listened attentively to Wolf Blitzer or Anderson Cooper at CNN or Bill O'Reilly or Geraldo Rivera at Fox bring her into the live broadcast conversations. Just at the moment when a question was directed at her, or at the moment when she decided to intervene in an exchange, the red light at the top of the camera glowed, as if turned on by the sound of her voice, signaling to her that her face and voice were being broadcast to millions of people. She had been such a regular guest on these shows in the years since 9/11 that she was a celebrity people recognized in airports, on streets, and at conferences. These shows were deeply pleasurable for her, more engaging than teaching or writing or researching (although she enjoyed those parts of her life, too, just as she enjoyed other, far less visible work she did). Elegantly produced, stimulating, these broadcasts engaged her best qualities. She could exercise all the fluency, quick intelligence, and snappy, sardonic humor she had developed during her years in college at Harvard, graduate school at Yale, and teaching and writing at Stanford.

And she took pleasure, too, from the fact that she was beautiful. It was there for all the world to see. Sometimes, after a live show was broadcast at eight or nine in the evening, it would be repeated three or four times in the long interval between midnight and the start of the early morning live news shows at six. In the middle of the night, she would sometimes watch herself, proud of the ease and grace and feistiness she displayed. It pleased her deeply, too, to witness how enthralled the men with whom she was spending the night were when, at three in the morning, they watched a broadcast she had done at nine the night before.

Six months into their relationship, Tom Nashatka still thought of Kimberly Smith as his golden girl, even though he suspected she had many other lovers. He knew that from the first time they made love. It was at the end of a day of secret meetings in a nondescript but highly secure building on L Street. They went to a bar on DuPont Circle, and after two hours she asked, "So, do you want to come up to my room?"

*Want* was not the right word to describe Tom's intense desire—this unexpected invitation to her room was like the granting of the wildest wish on his life's wish list. Everything about her seemed unattainable. She was the daughter of wealthy New Yorkers; his father had spent a lifetime working in a steel foundry in Pittsburgh. She had gone to the best-known college in the world; he'd attended gritty Penn State. She went on fellowships to the most famous graduate schools in the country; he had enlisted in the Navy after college. She looked like one of the golden girls, the blessed girls, of American culture—the circle that included Christie Brinkley, Diane Sawyer, Valerie Plame. Tom, although he was a muscular football player and Navy Seal, could be easily recognized for what he was, the Polish son of a Pittsburgh steel worker. He had that flat accent and, at times, those working-class gestures. He used the words *you know* and *like* too often, the dominant idioms of most Americans under the age of forty. Kimberly never said *like* unless she was drawing an analogy.

After the first night in the room overlooking leafy, elegant DuPont Circle, Tom came to believe something extraordinary—that Kimberly Smith loved him. He certainly loved her. She was not only this extraordinary prize, she also had qualities he admired. She was a patriot. During graduate school at Yale, she was recruited by the CIA and became a deep undercover agent. She loved the intrigue. While she was taking her graduate degree, she did fellowships in Egypt, Jordan, and Syria, and in those times she learned the exciting art of acting as a covert agent. She wrote a book, published by the University of Chicago Press, on Arabic linguistics and culture. She was invited to attend seminars and give lectures on subjects such as the language and message of the *Koran* in the United States, Europe, and the Middle East. After the invasions of Iraq and Afghanistan, she had started to give secret seminars to CIA agents about Islam and the beliefs of Islamic men and women.

When Kimberly came to New York to appear on television, she stayed at the Park Lane Hotel on Central Park South, and the networks paid for her travel and her room. The hotel was only three blocks from the CNN studio in the new buildings on Columbus Circle at the southwest corner of Central Park. Her room, although small, overlooked the park. On the nights after her shows, when she and Tom Nashatka were together, they would have dinner in her room, make love, wake at around one in the morning, step out onto the quiet of Central Park South, return to the room, and continue working on the emailed notes that Byron Carlos Johnson regularly sent to himself, particularly the passages from the *Koran* that he copied out on his computer screen and sent to himself.

The white light of early dawn filled the trees of Central Park. Tom Nashatka woke from a short sleep and saw Kimberly at the computer. He had fallen asleep two hours earlier, after watching a rebroadcast of the show she had done the night before on CNN. She had been dazzling then, and she was dazzling now, too, although now she was naked and perched with her legs crossed on the desk chair.

"We underestimated him," she said.

"Say what?" Tom asked, drowsily.

"We underestimated Byron Carlos Johnson," Kimberly repeated, the clarity of her voice the same as when she was speaking on one of the television broadcasts. Even in private, she never spoke indistinctly or lazily.

Tom Nashatka sat up in the bed, the sheets wound around his waist. "Professor, you have got to give me more information than that."

"The financial people are telling me that the new numbers just don't compute. We're now getting book, chapter, and verse numbers that don't fit the paradigm."

For weeks, Tom Nashatka, Kimberly Smith, and unseen technicians at a Homeland Security office in New Mexico had evaluated the passages from the *Koran* that Ali Hussein gave to Byron Johnson. The numbers of the books, chapters, and verses had quickly assumed a pattern, one that resembled the pattern of numbers by which wire transfers were made. The identities of originating banks, the numbers of accounts, and sometimes the numbers of what appeared to be destination accounts, all seemed to depend on the book, chapter, and verse numbers of the quotes in the *Koran* from the old Marmaduke Pichtall translation. *6 8 12 13 48 52.* So far the numbers never quite fit the numerical patterns for bank codes, account numbers, and wiring routes for thousands of banks and fund transfer businesses in the United States and around the world. But they were getting closer to recognizable numbers that might lead to the locations somewhere in the world of real money. The virtual to the real.

Naked, Tom Nashatka scrambled out of the bed. He looked at the screen of the computer.

Kimberly said, "The last sets of numbers Byron sent don't resemble any bank numbers or wire routing codes in the world."

"Maybe Johnson just got it wrong."

"I don't think so. He's always correctly written down what Ali's given him in the past. Byron's one of those careful big-time lawyers. He doesn't make little mistakes like that. He's sent out the wrong passages for a reason."

Tom struck several other computer keys, searching for something. "I told Hurd and Rana two days ago, after that last time with the judge, that they were misreading Johnson. They think he'll get scared, fold, and work with them. That's not my take on Johnson."

"What makes you say that?"

"Our sweeps of his office and apartment. He reads Dickens and William Burroughs, he has subscriptions to the *New York Review of Books* and the *National Review*. He watches *Casablanca* and *Legally Blonde*. He writes letters to himself, some that he never sends."

She gave him one of those dazzling blonde smiles. "That's it. He's a Renaissance man."

Tom was serious. "I don't think so. Byron is restless, irritable, discontented. He's rebellious, even though he has that, like, you know, New England aristocrat in him."

"Why not just walk up to Byron and say, 'Hey, Byron, we're with the good guys, we'd like you to help us. Can't you get Hussein to tell you where all the money is and then let us know?' And America's been good to him. He's a lawyer, he has a license to print money. Why not just ask him to help us all out?"

"Andy told me weeks ago that that was not the way to reach Byron. Remember, Byron wanted to represent one of these guys. He asked for this. Andy and his profilers say that Byron can only be made to cooperate the old-fashioned way—scare the hell out of him. It's our job to scare the shit out of him. I'm not so sure."

"Who ever knows what a person will do? Profilers? Relying on a profile? Relying on astrological signs works as well."

"Hurd, loony as he is, has been in the business of nailing people for years and years. He's a legend."

"In his own mind." She glanced at Tom, waiting for him to join her in mocking Hurd.

The faintest traces of dawn had just spread over Central Park. There were the open spaces where the trees parted for the Sheep Meadow, that undulating and well-tended field of green, and, further north, the Great Lawn. In the far distance, even higher in the park, the dawn light glowed on the acres of water in the reservoir.

"What about Christina?" Tom asked.

"What about her?"

"What does she think? She's spent lots of time with him."

Kimberly Smith paused. "What do you want me to say to her?"

"What time are you meeting her?"

"Ten."

"Where?"

"There's a French restaurant on Madison Avenue and 83rd Street with long tables and benches where all the East Side ladies gather for breakfast, French-style, after dropping their kids at their forty-thousand-dollar-a-year private schools. Byron, she told me, hates Madison Avenue and would never walk into a French-style place."

"Just have the usual conversation, Kim. Let her tell you what Byron is saying and doing. But if you have a chance, ask her where Byron is keeping his notes of his meetings with Ali."

"Why?"

"We've done three sweeps of his office in the last week. He isn't keeping any of his notes there anymore. He must be carrying them with him and bringing them home."

Kimberly smiled. "The cagey little bastard. Under that Gary Cooper exterior beats the heart of Abbe Hoffman. He wants to throw us off. Something has gotten his attention. It's clear he's now sending out random passages from the *Koran*, not the passages Ali's giving him."

"Well, if anyone can find out where his real notes are, it's the foxy Christina Rosario."

Kimberly, naked, stood up. She was blonde, slim, shapely and, as she embraced athletic Tom Nashatka, deeply alluring and completely tantalizing. "Hey, Navy Seal, boy agents aren't supposed to say sexy things about girl agents. It's taboo."

Kimberly Smith loved every facet of Tom's size. He was a massive man, and at first he overpowered her, picking her up from the chair and carrying her around the room as she wrapped her legs around him. But gradually the tide of their love-making turned, and she finally overpowered him.

# 19

BYRON WAS NEVER COMFORTABLE when he had lunch at the Regency Hotel at 61st and Park Avenue, although he had spent many hours in the noisy and elegant room over the years. It was a favorite lunch spot for Sandy Spencer and other leading partners at SpencerBlake. Every day of the week for years, the restaurant attracted at breakfast and lunch not only the partners at SpencerBlake but a perennial cast of celebrities. Smiling, radiantly bald Ron Perelman was in the room almost every time Byron was there. Before they went to jail, Bernie Madoff and Conrad Black were constant guests. Byron had often seen Wilbur Ross and Warren Buffett, Boone Pickens and George Soros there. And there were always people in the room whom his partners called the "entertainers"—Barry Diller, Rupert Murdoch, Larry King, and, at almost every breakfast for years, wide-eyed, droll Al Sharpton, that man of the people who loved expensive restaurants and the parties of celebrities.

SpencerBlake had its own table—a curved, plush bench in the far corner of the room with a view toward the Park Avenue windows. Byron had only heard rumors of the monthly tab for the use of the table: there were jokes about the $30,000 table, "$35,000 when you throw in the chairs." Byron, who as a partner could have easily gotten the real information about the cost, never asked. He simply wasn't interested. For years, his wife and his law partners were baffled by Byron's almost casual attitude toward his share of the firm's profits and his disinterest in the firm's finances. Some of the younger partners speculated that Byron must have been the scion of one of those old money families and that he had been born into great wealth completely independent of his earnings as a lawyer. To the manor born.

Byron had paid little attention to money over the years simply because he had always earned enough to meet his needs, not because he had inherited any real wealth. His father had started his working life in the 1930s with more inherited wealth than he left to Byron when he died in 1980. The Ambassador had devoted his life to working for the State Department and never earned as much as he and his wife and son needed; for decades he had steadily drawn down on his inheritance to meet the expenses of his imperial lifestyle. When he died, he left Byron the trim, well-built, sturdy house on Monhegan Island off the coast of Maine, but little else. Byron had held onto the Maine house, although he used it only two or three weeks each year. It was the only property he now owned. The two-million-dollar Fifth Avenue apartment in which he and Joan had raised their children had been turned over to Joan as part of the divorce. Byron sometimes acknowledged to himself that, as his years of high earnings as a lawyer were coming to an end, he hadn't accumulated enough or held onto enough to retire, to buy another apartment, and to enjoy the sense of financial security that most lawyers of his age and experience appeared to have.

And yet Byron never envied the wealth or possessions or resources of other people. Sandy Spencer, who had inherited real wealth and over the years earned far more than Byron, owned a classic and tasteful mansion near the Maidstone Club in East Hampton overlooking Egypt Beach. He also had a ten-room apartment on Fifth Avenue and a smaller apartment near the Plaza Athenée in Paris. But Byron never felt any envy of the things Sandy possessed or the settled sense Sandy exuded that he would never have to worry about how well he would live for the rest of his life.

"Byron," Sandy said as he rose from the table. "I'm glad you were able to stop by."

Byron shook Sandy's hand. They had known each other for decades, but they still were oddly formal with one another. They had learned their manners in all-male New England prep schools where the boys were required to wear jackets and ties and call every teacher and coach and the headmaster "Mr." As they sat at the curved table overlooking the dining room, Byron said, "Someday we're going to have to learn how to do fist bumps, don't you think?"

Sandy laughed. "Byron, how the hell do you know what a fist bump is?"

"Hey, Sandy, I've walked around for a long time on the face of the earth, and I've always kept my eyes open. I even noticed fist bumps long before presidential candidates and their wives began doing them."

"And fist bumps are—how should I say this?—cleaner, don't you think? Less chance to pass germs through the knuckles as opposed to the palms."

"I never thought of a handshake as a sanitation issue." Byron settled himself into his seat, touching the cool surface of his water glass. "I've always tried to be a student of handshakes. I once thought you might be able to predict character through a handshake. Didn't they teach us that at school? For example, the wet handshake is the sign of the nervous and deceitful, or so I once thought. Handshake style tells you nothing about a person's character, I've learned. And the fist bump probably tells you even less."

A waiter in his sixties approached the table. "Mr. Spencer, nice to see you, sir. Diet Coke?"

"Sure, Juan. Byron?"

"Just water, thanks." When the waiter turned away, Byron said, "Remember, Sandy, when we started out in the seventies everybody ordered martinis at lunch?"

"Now we immediately send a lawyer who has a martini at lunch to rehab."

"Hell, Sandy, I'm so with it these days that I not only know what a fist bump is, but I've heard of things like 'dirty martinis.'"

"The Generation Z drink? My youngest daughter loves to just toss around the words 'dirty martini.' Better she says that than 'dirty sex.'"

Byron casually asked, "Helena is already in college?"

Sandy was surprised that Byron remembered the name of his youngest daughter—Sandy had four children, and Byron had last been among the members of Sandy's family at a Christmas party almost eight years earlier. But Sandy Spencer knew Byron was an immensely talented lawyer for many reasons, including a prodigious memory. "In fact, Byron, she just finished."

"What does she plan to do? Graduate school? One of those British gap years? The Marines?"

"Now that would be a learning experience for her."

Byron, touching the beads of water that clung to the surface of his water glass, said, "Sandy, why are we here?"

Sandy Spencer had developed the skill of gracefully adjusting to any turn in a conversation. Hearing the unexpected, abrupt edge in Byron's tone, Sandy calmly said, "I know you never liked this place, Byron. You showed real sportsmanship down through the years in getting through places like this, lunches with clients, firm parties, Christmas parties, and the box at Yankee Stadium."

"And let's not forget the long weekends at conventions for federal judges that I always attended, the judicial conferences. It still beggars my mind that these federal judges let us pick up the tabs for weekends at golf resorts and that we all expect that no one would accuse us, or them, of buying and selling favors."

Sandy smiled. "Those conferences, Byron, are for the purpose of fostering collegiality among the members of the judiciary and the lawyers who appear before them. Isn't that the fact?"

Byron laughed. "A weekend of golf and tennis at the Sagamore fosters lots of things. Collegiality might be one of them. I don't hear of many federal judges who spend collegial weekends with lawyers at the Legal Aid Society playing stickball in East Harlem."

Sandy's face, as if on cue, became serious. "Byron, I owe something to you. And that's the ability to be direct. We had a partners' meeting last night. A vote of ninety percent of the partners was needed to vote your expulsion from the firm. And at least ninety-five percent of the partners voted to do that."

A system-wide pulse of emotion throbbed through Byron. He wondered whether that surge of blood was fear, or anger, or resentment, or shame. "And you called me here to tell me this?"

"I volunteered. There were other ways we could have let you know."

"And you could have let me know this was under way, Sandy."

"It wouldn't have made a difference, Byron."

"Why not?"

"Because you wouldn't have done anything about it to stop it. You could have avoided this. You knew this was going to happen."

"I did? We've had partners who were drug addicts, tax cheats, even a pedophile. Every one of them had the option of resigning, and every one did."

"Byron, those of us who know you know you would never resign."

"Am I going to be given the reasons?"

"You know the reasons, Byron. You never got permission to do the work for Ali Hussein. You never even asked for permission. You stopped doing work for firm clients. You made public statements without first notifying the executive committee."

Byron said, "And I have a right to do all those things."

"Do you think so, Byron? Life's complicated. You have a right to have sex with any woman you choose, but you should have understood that in the real world in which we now live you didn't have a right to fuck a law student who came to work for the firm for the summer. The PC world now sees that as taking cruel advantage of the vulnerable, not as a sport and a pastime."

Byron tore a piece of bread. "She went back to school and made it clear she wouldn't come to work for the firm. Nothing happened while she was drawing a paycheck. And she's more than thirty."

"Byron, you know the rules. This one is pretty basic—at the Jewish firms they have an expression that gets to the heart of this rule—'You don't shit where you eat.'"

"Let's cut this out, Sandy. We've known each other for too long. You and all your minions, for all your liberal talk, don't want to be anywhere near an Islamic terrorist. You have too many clients who don't want to have a law firm with a partner who represents a Guantanamo Bay prisoner. This has nothing to do with my being with Christina Rosario. Jesus, even Bill Clinton survived Monica Lewinsky and the cigar."

"I'm not sure where we're going with all this, Byron. Even as we speak a press release is being circulated saying that you and the firm reached a mutual agreement that you needed to devote your full-time efforts to the representation of Mr. Hussein. The press release also recites the long list of corporate clients the firm has represented for years and says that we continue to be a prominent, business-oriented law firm. There's a statement from me wishing you well in this new phase of your career and citing your many contributions to the welfare of the firm's clients."

"You know what, Sandy? No reporter will pick up a statement from yet another big law firm. What the reporters want are statements from me. Any reporter who reads your press release will call me immediately."

"You need to think through another issue, Byron, before you call your new friends at the networks and the papers."

"Meaning what?"

"Meaning that you probably paid so little attention over the years to the firm that you don't know that the firm's partnership agreement was changed a few years ago."

"To say what?"

"To say that partners expelled from the firm had to clear every public statement through the firm or risk losing things like their partnership accounts, insurance payments—you know, all those things that ordinary lawyers need in order to avoid living on the street?"

"It's not a good idea to threaten me, Sandy."

"The only real threat in the world, Byron, is the threat you are to yourself. Be careful."

The early afternoon air on Park Avenue had that crystalline dazzle created by clear sunshine flooding over the handsome buildings, the innumerable windows, and the long and colorful median dividing the uptown and downtown lanes of traffic. Yellow taxis glinted in the sunlight. Byron had become used to these early afternoons on Park Avenue; they had been part of his life for years. He walked quickly, almost jogging, from the Regency at 61st and Park toward the black-glass Seagram Building at 49th and Park. All around him, hundreds of men and women walked, most of them gazing into their hands at cell phones and handheld electronic equipment. Byron was still surprised, even bemused at times, by the way people now moved, oblivious to other walkers and even traffic, transfixed by their gadgets.

Since 9/11 the security system in the Seagram Building had become more and more elaborate. Immediately after that September day, armed guards had been posted in the lobby, allowing only people they recognized into the elevators to reach the firm's offices, which occupied the 21st through the 30th floors. Then more and more invisible but elaborate screening mechanisms had been installed. Just two months earlier, Byron, like all the other partners in the firm, had started holding the palm of his hand in front of a small unit in a turnstile near the elevators that would allow the gates of the turnstile to open. It was a handprint identification device, and it was much faster and far less obtrusive than the plastic card he had used for several years.

When Byron passed the palm of his hand over the electronic eye, nothing happened. The arm of the turnstile didn't drop for him. He turned to the security guard stationed near the elevator, a black man who was almost as tall as a professional basketball player and who had always made friendly, knowing eye contact with Byron.

"There's something wrong with the gate," Byron said.

"No, there isn't, Mr. Johnson."

"What?"

"There's nothing wrong with the gate, Mr. Johnson."

"Say that again?"

"You can't go upstairs, sir."

Another security guard, also dressed in a blue blazer and a regimental-striped tie, walked over. He was short, beefy, and muscled-up, almost grotesquely bunched into the blue blazer he wore.

"Open this," Byron said, glancing at the name tag of the guard's jacket. "Mr. Ricciardi, open this up. My office is upstairs."

"You can't go up there," Ricciardi said. He had a Brooklyn accent.

Tall, still lithe and athletic, Byron vaulted over the turnstile. Although they were surprised, the two guards were quick. Ricciardi passed his right hand over the electronic eye with a magician's practiced wave, and the arm of the turnstile immediately fell open to let them through. The two guards ran forward, stopping three feet in front of Byron.

"We need you to turn around and leave, sir."

"And I need you to step out of my fucking way," Byron said, wondering if the quaver in his body was reflected in the tone of his voice.

The guards stepped even closer to Byron. Instinctively, he pushed at Ricciardi, who stumbled to his side and did a quick and awkward dance to regain his balance. As he recovered, he raced at Byron, who was pushing at the black guard's groping hands. It seemed to Byron that a thousand things were happening at once: he registered the fact that Ricciardi was really a street thug, stronger than Byron and enraged that Byron had deftly deflected and humiliated him. And, in the instant before Ricciardi's right shoulder burst against Byron's left ribs, he glanced at the elevator bank and saw the stunned, questioning look on the faces of two of his partners.

The burst of pain in his ribs and lungs was intense and fiery, but Byron controlled the instinct to cry out. Like a football lineman, Ricciardi pushed Byron backwards, trying to knock him off his feet, but Byron, who had been pushing at the big hands of the other guard when Ricciardi hit him, kept himself on his feet by grabbing Ricciardi's head.

Somehow Byron pulled himself away from the two men. His lungs heaving for breath, he managed to keep his balance. Ricciardi was disheveled, furious, ready for more, stunned that a man who was years older than he was had managed to shake him off. In that moment, as Byron waited for Ricciardi's next thrust, he felt his blood rushing through his entire body as if it were icy water. Ricciardi had an expression of sheer rage. *This guy's an animal*, Byron thought. *Run.*

Breaking the moment, the tall guard spoke, "You need to leave, sir." The voice was calm.

Embarrassed, outraged, and furious, Byron decided to leave. In order to make himself appear more collected, he tried to button his suit jacket. He groped for an awkward moment before realizing the button was torn off.

As Byron Johnson approached the revolving doors, he saw Sandy Spencer standing just inside the entrance. He had been watching. Byron stared at him: for the first time in all the years Byron had known him, Sandy Spencer looked confused and flustered. He glanced away from Byron, opening his cell phone as if taking an incoming business call. It was a ruse.

# 20

THEY MET MANY TIMES over the next three weeks. Simeon Black had immediately recognized the name Byron Carlos Johnson when he first heard the voicemail message late on a perfect autumn afternoon: "This is Byron Johnson. I've read several of your articles, *The Atlantic* especially, on terrorist detainees. I think we might have a common interest. My cell phone number is (917) 928-0111. Please call if you have a chance."

Ever since he had started his first job in journalism in 1964 at the *Washington Post* when it was still in the dreary building at 1515 L Street, Simeon had made it his daily life's work to know what was happening in the world. He read six newspapers each day, listened to CNN, the BBC, and even Pacifica Radio, and had mastered the art of seeking out information on the Internet. He instantly recognized Byron Carlos Johnson as the New York lawyer who had stepped out of the confines of corporate law firm practice—a rarified world—to represent a terrorist prisoner who had been taken to the United States for criminal prosecution. Just two months after the 9/11 attack, Simeon Black, who had won his first Pulitzer Prize in 1971 for articles about the secret invasion of Cambodia, published his first article on arrests of Arabic men in the United States and Europe on suspicion of terrorism. He had steadily and slowly published other articles over the years of the endless wars in Iraq and Afghanistan on the subject of imprisoned Islamic men.

But he could never gain access to anyone held in Guantanamo or Bagram or the other places around the world rumored to hold men arrested overseas by the United States and transferred, by extraordinary rendition, to other countries. The lawsuits Simeon filed under the freedom of information laws were all dismissed on national security grounds without yielding anything. His stories for the *New Yorker*, the *New York Review of Books*, and the *Atlantic* were based on thirdhand and even more remote sources, such as two former private government contractors who gave him what he believed was reliable information about the dark prisons around the world where Islamic men were held. He knew these were "weakly sourced" stories. Had he not been Simeon Black, had he not been proved absolutely right in the Pulitzer Prize stories about the Cambodian invasion also based on weak, attenuated sources, and had he not been given the benefit of every possible editorial doubt, the magazines in which his stories appeared since 9/11 would never have published any of them.

Simeon recognized that the most he could ever expect was to get information through the conduit of a lawyer representing one of these men. Lawyers, he knew, had the incalculable advantage of face-to-face contact with the ultimate source of information, the detainee himself. A lawyer would have been in the presence of the prisoner, would have heard his words, would have seen his clothes, and would have looked at his client's hands and face.

But until Byron Carlos Johnson left a message for him, Simeon had not succeeded in speaking to a single lawyer who had represented any of these men. Most of the defense lawyers, including those who represented prisoners at Guantanamo, were JAG officers. And JAG officers had never, in all of his years of experience starting in Vietnam, changed: they were the keepers of the secrets, they formed a green wall of secrecy, a cone of silence. Simeon had approached three former Army lawyers over the last seven years. Not one word from any of them, except "no comment" in one case and simple silence in the others. These were men to whom the name Simeon Black probably meant nothing or was associated with someone who had done damage in the past.

It was Byron who suggested that they have their first meeting in the old Viand Diner at the busy corner of 86th Street and Second Avenue. Simeon had met people for interviews in so many places over the decades in which he had been writing stories—from luxurious rooms in the Brown Hotel in London to a Motel 6 in New Mexico for a recent story for the *New Yorker* on a violent polygamist sect—that he didn't find Byron's choice strange or surprising. He was focused on the fact that Byron Johnson, who was at the center of a story that fascinated Simeon, apparently wanted to establish some sort of arrangement with him. "I want to explore," Byron had said when they spoke by cell phone to arrange this meeting, "whether we can help each other."

When he entered the coffee shop, Simeon recognized Byron from pictures that appeared on the Internet, on television, in the *New York Times*, and in the *New York Post*. In turn, Byron recognized Simeon from photographs on the dust jackets of his books. In the day between the first telephone call and the meeting, Simeon, a tireless worker even though he was now in his early seventies and could have simply lived out his long and illustrious career teaching journalism somewhere like Columbia or Missouri, had navigated through all the Yahoo and Google entries for Byron. Most were dated after the announcement that Byron was representing an indicted detainee facing the death penalty. Simeon knew scores of people. He was able to call lawyers at prominent firms to ask about Byron Carlos Johnson, and the word he got back from that very self-protective world was that Byron was a hard worker, a stand-up guy, a straight-shooter. Two of the partners he spoke to—one at Shearman & Sterling and the other at Sullivan & Cromwell (two of the whitest white-shoe firms)—let drop a note of bewilderment that Byron would have elected to represent an accused terrorist. "If Byron Johnson was out to change the world," one of Simeon's contacts said, "he managed to do a good job not letting on about that for years." The partner at the other law firm said, "Word has gone around for years that Byron was next in line for a federal judgeship whenever those openings came up, as they do three or four times a year in New York. But he never got the nod. Now that'll never happen."

Dressed in a white shirt open at the neck, Byron ordered a coffee and a slice of apple pie from the hairy, harried Greek waiter. He said, "I read your articles about Cambodia and the war as they were coming out in the early seventies."

"That was a scene. The bar at the Intercontinental in Saigon. Every thrill-seeker in the world—generals, gun-runners, spooks, diplomats, writers, drunks, mercenaries, hookers, picture-takers, senators on junkets—all in one place. It was like the bar in *Star Wars*, every improbable character in the world."

Simeon Black had that look Byron associated with David Halberstam—receding hairline, domed forehead, glasses, and handsome eyes, nose, mouth, and chin. The air of academic elegance, New York intellectual aristocracy. Byron also sensed something dedicated, engaging, and honest about Simeon Black.

Byron said, "I haven't spent a great deal of time in my life with journalists. Until recently, at least."

"I like to think of myself as a reporter, not a journalist. One of those gumshoe reporters who walks around with a felt hat and a Humphrey Bogart trench coat. Hard-drinker, gruff, seen-it-all exterior. But I don't drink, never wear a hat, and am always amazed by everything I see, day after day."

"I think," Byron said, "that I have amazing things for you."

And he did. Simeon listened, taking notes in the compact flip-up reporter's notebooks he had started using in the early 1960s, as Byron at the diner and then over the course of many days described the arrest of Ali Hussein in Bonn, his years in locked rooms in still unknown countries, the time at Guantanamo, the waterboarding, the hundreds of hours of interrogation, the hitting, and Ali's elusive reaction to the fact that he faced the death penalty. Simeon knew—because, like all old-fashioned reporters, he was wedded to the need for skepticism—that there was information that Byron simply omitted, and he suspected that Byron might not make available documents that might help give authenticity, or the appearance of authenticity, to the long article he was writing for the *New Yorker* and planned to develop into a book.

And Byron also told Simeon in detail about his conversations with Hamerindapal Rana, that imposing Sikh, and the government's approach to prosecuting the case. There were also Byron's almost verbatim descriptions of the hearings before Judge Justin Goldberg, those hearings during which Goldberg repeatedly said that everything that was discussed was confidential. "He reminds me," Byron said, "of that little mandarin Irving Kaufman, the judge who sentenced the Rosenbergs to death."

"I remember him," Simeon said. "He was a member of the Harmonie Club and a friend of my parents."

"I don't mean to offend the memory of your parents," Byron answered, "but Kaufman was one of those ambitious Jewish boys who was absolutely devoted to serving the interests of the privileged WASP class. After Kaufman sentenced that pitiful couple to death, he was rewarded with a promotion to the appeals court, where he acted like a hopped-up vigilante for the next forty years. Justin Goldberg is following the same career path."

Simeon smiled, his writing hand poised over his notebook. "The WASP ruling class?" Simeon asked. "Isn't that you?"

During their hours of conversations, Simeon began to consider Byron a friend. He was urbane and well-spoken and sincere; there were times when Byron effortlessly quoted Francis Bacon, Camus, and Seneca, references that Simeon readily understood and appreciated. And yet, of course, there were aspects of these long, on-the-record conversations that Simeon detected were not complete. Byron never, for example, let Simeon know where he lived or whether he was married or had children or held political views. Over his long career, Simeon had learned that he needed to cultivate important sources over extended periods of time to build up confidence and elicit more information, just as an interrogator over time gradually induces someone to disclose more and more. And just as a lawyer gradually develops the confidence of a client.

It was only after seven meetings that Byron mentioned the *Koran*.

# 21

"AND EXPLAIN THAT TO the Grand Jury, Agent Hurd, what these numbers mean?"

Andrew Hurd used the small silver wand to project a narrow, precise beam of light at the rows of numbers displayed on the big white chart. "These are numbers that our experts have told us are, and in some cases were, actual bank account numbers at banks in the US, Iceland, Ireland, London, Yemen, and Venezuela."

"How did you and your agents develop these numbers?" Hamerindapal Rana asked.

"Over time, a pattern emerged that correlated to the book, chapter, and verse numbers of the passages from the *Koran* that the prisoner was giving to Byron Johnson for transmittal to people outside the prison."

It had been years since Rana had presented a witness to a grand jury. That work was almost invariably done by younger and less experienced lawyers because it was easy to question witnesses who were in front of a grand jury. No judge was present to supervise what was happening; there were no defense lawyers and no spectators in the courtroom. For centuries, the process of presenting witnesses and evidence to the grand jury was secret, and the secrecy and the absence of any critical eyes made the job a vehicle for the training of young lawyers. The twenty-four people who now sat in the sealed courtroom had been gathering once a week for many months, and Rana and the other government lawyers who were managing the grand jury had come to know the members by name, to joke and banter with them, and even to ask some of them how their children were. Something verging on workplace camaraderie had developed over time. There were coffee cups everywhere after just a few minutes together.

Even though this was easy work, and despite the relaxed relationship he had developed with almost all the people in the courtroom, it still irked Hal Rana that Hurd had insisted that he and not some junior lawyer in the prosecutor's office ask the prepared questions and listen to the scripted answers. But in all his fifteen years in the Justice Department, he had never had to deal with an agent with as much authority, influence, and power as Andrew Hurd. Every other investigating agent in the FBI, the Secret Service, and the NSC and those elite officers in the criminal enforcement division of the Postal Service were subservient to attorneys at Hal Rana's level. Not so Hurd. Hurd spoke, you jumped.

"What can you tell the grand jurors about these numbers?"

"Our experts call them ideograms. They're drawn from innocuous, sometimes mundane and unpredictable sources. They could be the sequence of numbers you see etched in black on cereal containers. Or barcodes on a magazine cover. We have seen those numbers used to provide guides to counterfeit hundred dollar bills, for example. It's a matter of detecting a pattern."

"What was the pattern here?"

"During our monitoring of the detainee Hussein we noticed that he had developed a special attachment to the *Koran*, which is organized with a fairly elaborate set of numbers—both

Arabic and Roman numeral—for its books, chapters, and verses. We had some information on the detainee that in the late 1990s and early 2000s he'd become a wizard at collecting cash, money orders, and cashier checks from various sources—such as cash collections at mosques, check-cashing stores, independent benefactors, and others—and then channeling enormous quantities of cash through domestic and foreign banks and money transfer companies. He was not at that time particularly devoted to the *Koran*, in the religious sense, although our informants told us he was skilled at quoting certain passages. And he has a prodigious memory for numbers and an uncanny aptitude for mathematics. He's also, we believe, a zealot, a jihadist in a suit."

Hal Rana asked, because Hurd gave him a cue to do so, "What was it about those passages?"

"The *Koran* has coherent, cohesive messages that to the initiated and to the students of the text form patterns of meaning and storytelling. They appear in scattered sections of the text. This is because the *Koran* was written by many people and minds over a period of years, much as the New Testament was."

"And?"

"And Ali Hussein's study of the *Koran* could never lead to an integrated understanding of these themes. He was a dabbler, not a scholar. It takes years of study to draw the religious themes together. But he does know numbers."

"How do you know that?"

"Through an informant."

One of the grand jurors, a thin, sarcastic, spunky woman with orange hair, raised her hand to get attention and asked, "And who was that informant?"

Hurd, through a glance from his blue eyes, conveyed the message *no* to Rana, who said: "That's not information you need to know."

Rana was hard-working, devoted to his cases and the Justice Department, intelligent, and experienced, but he was not the kind of lawyer who could make people on juries like him. It may have been his height, his turban, or the overly formal manner he had developed at the English language schools he attended in Sri Lanka. That was a problem when he was involved in an actual jury trial, and he knew that he'd never succeeded in developing the appealing style of the best trial lawyers. But there was a difference between an actual jury trial and a grand jury. In a grand jury room, it didn't matter whether there were people who were put off, offended, or antagonized by his style, words, glances, or gestures, or people who were instinctively biased against his race and origin. In his years as a prosecutor, he had never known a grand jury not to indict someone when he asked for an indictment. Unhappy with the rebuff of Rana's refusal to answer her question, the sardonic woman who had raised her hand gave him a look as if to say, *Come off it, Hal.*

"What else," Hal Rana asked, "has this informant told you?"

"That the detainee Hussein is communicating with outside people to alert them as to what accounts and in what countries money is located."

"Isn't it true, Agent Hurd, that Hussein is held in solitary confinement?"

"He is."

"For how long?"

"Years. He's a dangerous, very high-value prisoner."

"Why is he dangerous? Is he violent?"

"Not personally. He is a small man. He's had no training with weapons or martial arts. He's dangerous, and important, because of what he knows."

"What does it mean to be in solitary confinement?"

"In Hussein's case, he is never allowed among other prisoners. Food is brought to him. He has a cot, a wash basin, a toilet. He has one book, the *Koran*. Three times a week he is allowed to walk fifteen feet to a shower room. He's accompanied by three guards when he does that. He's observed while showering."

"Is he allowed to exercise?"

"Not in the prison gym. He can exercise if he wishes in his cell. There is room for sit-ups, push-ups, isometric exercises, things like that. He is not a very athletic man."

"Can he have conversations?"

"He can speak to the guards. He doesn't avail himself of that privilege."

"Does he have visitors?"

"Only his lawyer."

"Does he have more than one lawyer?"

"Only one."

"And is that Byron Carlos Johnson?"

"It is."

"Do they meet in his cell?"

"No, never."

"Where?"

"A special room is reserved for them when they meet."

"Is anyone else present when they meet?"

"No. It would violate the attorney-client privilege if someone else could hear what they were saying to each other. So the guard stands on the other side of the closed door. There is a large window in that door through which the guard can observe."

"Why?"

"Several reasons. The prisoner cannot give anything to Mr. Johnson. Not a piece of paper, not an article of clothing. They can't even shake hands."

"What else?"

"Mr. Johnson can't give anything to the prisoner."

"Can Mr. Johnson have paper?"

"Sure. And pens. He always makes notes."

"And he can take those away with him, correct?"

"Sure."

"What does Johnson do with those notes?"

"We don't know everything, but we do know that after his meetings with Hussein he contacts another person, sometimes in person and sometimes by cell phone."

"Who is that person?"

"A man named Khalid Hussein. A Syrian immigrant who owns a big trucking company in New Jersey."

"Do you know anything else about Khalid Hussein?"

"He claims to be Ali Hussein's brother."

"Is he?"

"No."

"Does Johnson know that?"

"He has reason to suspect that they're not brothers."

"Why?"

"Khalid Hussein looks as much like Ali Hussein as Cinderella looks like Mike Tyson."

Laughter swept the room. When it subsided, Hal Rana—focusing again on how surprising and erratic Hurd could be—asked, "What do they say to each other?"

"Johnson reads the *Koran*'s book, chapter, and verse numbers to him, saying that they are the sections of the *Koran* that Ali Hussein has been studying."

"What does Khalid Hussein say to Johnson?"

"He reads out book, chapter, and verse numbers to Johnson. He says they are from the Imam, part of the religious education of Ali Hussein."

"How often do Johnson and Khalid Hussein speak?"

"As often as Johnson visits the prisoner."

"How do you know these conversations between Johnson and Khalid Hussein happen?"

"A federal judge authorized us to wiretap and intercept Mr. Johnson's conversations with Khalid Hussein. We're also authorized to intercept his emails and other electronic communications."

"Does Johnson know that?"

"No. The interceptions are secret."

"Why are Mr. Johnson's conversations being monitored?"

"Because we believe he's involved in a conspiracy to pass messages from Ali Hussein to the Imam."

"What's the purpose?"

"We think to assist terrorist organizations to locate millions of dollars of cash in secret accounts around the world."


There was a broad plaza outside the grim, fortress-like building that housed the U.S. Attorney's Office in lower Manhattan. At one side of the plaza was St. Andrew's Church. Across from the attractive brick church was the Municipal Building, and next to the church was the old federal courthouse. Scattered over the plaza were food trucks with open sides through which an astonishing variety of foods was served: Italian sandwiches, falafel, Chinese food, pastries. There were metal chairs and tables all over the plaza, and in the summer umbrellas made the outdoor space colorful. For more than fifteen years, through hundreds of different cases and investigations and trials, Hal Rana had often treated the plaza as his outdoor office. He had met there with other lawyers, government witnesses, Secret Service agents, and even journalists.

Hal Rana didn't enjoy seeing or speaking with Andrew Hurd. In the months they had been dealing with each other, Hurd had never asked him whether he was married or had children or whether he played or was interested in sports. For his part, Hal was profoundly wary of Hurd. Although he had trained himself to make few assumptions about other people, he was certain that Hurd harbored contempt for him because of his background and his manners—once he had overheard Hurd refer to him as a "towelhead."

The session in front of the grand jury had made Hal Rana even more uneasy than the earlier sessions Hurd had attended. On those days when Hurd was himself a witness, Rana didn't like the instructions Hurd gave him as to what to ask and what answers to elicit.

And it troubled Hal Rana that he had participated with Hurd in lying to the grand jury that morning.

"What next, Mr. Hurd?" There was an edgy, impatient contempt in his tone. He knew his voice had adopted that haughty inflection of a British aristocrat.

"You cut a grand jury subpoena for Christina Rosario."

"Who is Christina Rosario?"

"She's Byron Johnson's girlfriend."

"What do you think she knows?"

A slim Latino man with a gold stud through his left nostril put a slice of pizza on the table at which Hal Rana and Andrew Hurd sat. The plaza was crowded, and there were only a few open seats.

"Hey, fella," Andrew Hurd said.

The man, his hand on the metal chair as he prepared to sit, looked surprised. "Excuse me?"

"You can't sit here."

Hal wondered what the source of Andrew Hurd's personal power was. He had an unnerving way of looking right into people's eyes. He wore gray suits even in hot weather; he had a mustache. He was, simply, different, in an old-fashioned, authoritative way. The slender man picked up the paper plate that the slice of pizza had already drenched and walked away.

Hal Rana repeated: "And what does she know?"

"She knows what I tell her she knows."

Hal paused, looking out at the colorful lunchtime crowd in the sunny plaza. A hot breeze blew, stirring fragments of paper and plastic cups. "You know, Mr. Hurd, it's one thing to ask me to have a government agent—you—mislead a Grand Jury. It's another thing for me to put a civilian witness in the room if I've got a reason to believe she's lying."

"Don't worry, Mr. Rana. That won't be a problem."

"Why?"

"She works for me."

# 22

MID-AUTUMN SUNSHINE GLITTERED all over Washington Square Park. Byron walked toward the beautiful northern border of the park, where the landmark nineteenth-century arch stood. To his left were the gated small homes, so rare in New York, that looked like Victorian homes in London. Byron had always wondered, ever since his parents first took him to this cozy part of the city for an afternoon party in the early 1960s, who lived in the Mews, as the small, elegantly crafted houses were called. Professors at NYU? Writers? The city version of the landed gentry? So many years later, on this brilliant, chilly afternoon, Byron wondered the same thing: he had never seen anyone inside the gates, except once, in 1975, a beautiful woman in a mini-skirt and high, supple boots.

Byron was early for his meeting with Khalid Hussein. During their quick telephone call to arrange this meeting, Khalid sounded surprised when Byron abruptly said, "We'll meet at one tomorrow afternoon in Washington Square Park, in the Village."

Byron envisioned the expression that must have settled quickly on Khalid's heavy, belligerent face, the expression that conveyed, *Nobody tells me where to go and when.* But by this time Byron knew that Khalid needed him.

The park echoed sharply with the sounds of children and playful screams. NYU was in session, and in the sunlight hundreds young men and women sat on the benches or the patches of lawn in the recently renovated park. Frisbees—which Byron had first seen spinning through the fall air in Harvard Yard in 1967—flashed nearby. The smell of marijuana, faint but unmistakable, mixed with the stronger odors of roasting meat and chestnuts from the food carts in the park. The colorful umbrellas above the carts glinted in the clean light. Byron noticed, as he often had, that the men who worked at the food carts were all from places like Iraq, Afghanistan, and Syria. They never looked happy, and they never released anything from their hands—hot dogs, salted pretzels, or bottled water—without first taking cash from their customers. That instinctive distrust.

Byron scanned the park. For ten minutes there was no sign of Khalid, who would have stood out in the crowds of young mothers and students. Byron walked south, toward the attractive collegiate buildings of NYU at the southern end of the park. He did something he had only recently started to do, almost as obsessively as everyone else in the world did—he glanced at his BlackBerry. On the colorful screen he saw the red star over his message icon that signaled an unread email. He pressed the track ball, and the email opened.

It was from Christina Rosario. He still felt the thrill that, even after months, her presence in whatever form brought him. The message, in graphically clear script, read: "Hey, Carlos. I'm at your apartment, cooking and reading. Come home as soon as you can. I have something special for you."

What she had for him—just her presence—was always special. He often felt foolish about how attached to her he had become, in fact, how attached to her he had been since that first dusky night at the Central Park Zoo, at the firm party, when she simply started the conversation with the word "Hi." She had sought him out, and his heart, his body, and his instincts had immediately been attracted to her. In the past, when he had known or heard about men his age who were involved with women as young as or younger than Christina, he'd thought they were foolish or cynical men—foolish if they believed the young women loved them, cynical if they simply sought the buzz of being seen with women so young. Byron came to believe that his relationship with Christina was different. He also developed more sympathy for older men who had become involved with much younger women—it was possible, he thought, that they loved them as much as he loved Christina Rosario.

*Something special for you.* What had been special for Byron was the easy grace of Christina Rosario, and the fact that for months his only real desire—despite all that he now did and all the radical, frightening changes that had happened in his life—was to be with her, whether at one of their apartments, a movie, or even the desks at Columbia Law School where she told him the results of her legal research on genuinely complicated subjects and he told her almost everything that Ali Hussein said.

And another *something special* that Christina Rosario had blessed him with was sex. Byron, although confident about his ability to make love, had slept with relatively few women in his life. Despite periodic temptations during his marriage— even once with a female judge in California who later married one of the wealthiest men in America—he had been faithful. Before his marriage he had had affairs with five or six women; and after his divorce, in the six or so years in which he had wandered through his new life with little direction other than the direction his work provided him, there had been three women, all divorced from other lawyers and all very attractive, who had invited him into their homes and their worlds. None of those affairs had lasted longer than six weeks; the women were needy, they were conventional although bright, and they each made it clear that to them, Byron—handsome, courteous, well-spoken Byron with his great job and fascinating pedigree as the son of a famous ambassador—was their chance to have a second life very similar to their lives with their first husbands. But Byron had no desire to renew his old life.

Khalid Hussein suddenly materialized. He stood near a green park bench. He saw Byron before Byron saw him. He was dressed in a blue track suit. For a moment Byron saw in his face the sinister weight of the face of Saddam Hussein: the heavy eyebrows, the alert black eyes that looked as though they were scanning the crowds for signals of danger, and the thick mustache. As always happened, Byron explored the face and the contour of the body for any resemblance between Khalid and his brother, the slender Ali, whose face had the sincere and shy expression of a foreign graduate student.

If Khalid was curious or irritated at Byron's summoning him to a meeting, he didn't display it. Byron had long since abandoned any effort to shake Khalid's hand. Instead he walked by him, and Khalid followed. Nearby a derelict black man with a saxophone played a loud semblance of Duke Ellington and Billy Strayhorn's *Daydream, Why Do You Haunt Me So?* Further away, someone played on a snare drum the theme song of *The Sting*.

"Who are you?" Byron asked.

Khalid's expression didn't change, and he said nothing.

"Let me ask you this: when was the last time you saw Ali?"

"You know that, Mr. Johnson. Before he went to Germany."

"Let me tell you what I think. You never saw Ali in your life, isn't that right?"

Khalid calmly looked at Byron. "Why do you say that, Mr. Johnson?"

Byron had spent many years learning not to let people answer his questions with questions of their own. "He doesn't have children, does he?"

"He does."

"What are their names?"

"Are you joking, Mr. Johnson?"

"How much does your brother weigh?"

"He's been in prison for years. He's probably lost weight."

Although Khalid's expression hadn't changed, Byron knew he was swiftly becoming furious. Byron said, "Let the Imam know that I've lost interest in the *Koran*."

"He knows that. What you're giving him, he says, doesn't make any sense anymore. It's garbage."

"What sense were they making before?"

"All the sense in the world, Mr. Johnson."

"Tell me, what messages were the holy man and Ali sending back and forth?"

"Messages of honor, love, and devotion, Mr. Johnson."

"The Imam doesn't strike me as a man of honor, love, and devotion." Byron paused. "And you certainly don't."

"You know, Mr. Johnson, you're our brother now. You have a new family with us."

"No, that's wrong."

"We're brethren, Mr. Johnson."

Even in the afternoon on a work day, Washington Square Park was alive with activity: shrieking kids, street music, dogs barking, and Frisbees floating and flashing. Because of all that activity, sound, and color, Byron didn't notice until the last second the man in a tight-fitting sheath of clothing streak between them on a sleek Italian bicycle.

He slashed Khalid Hussein's face and sped on.

Stunned, Khalid raised his right hand to his face, as if trying to deflect a hand that had already done its damage.

Some of his blood, at high velocity, splattered on Byron. He was terrified. Holding his hands in front of his own face, an instinctive protective gesture, Byron saw the bicyclist disappear through the crowds, a slipstream. Byron then pivoted to glance all around to look for other bicyclists, other men, other sources and signs of damage. He heard himself saying, "Jesus, Jesus, Jesus."

And then he realized Khalid Hussein might himself be a source of danger. Byron faced him, prepared to act if he had to. Blood still flowed from a sabre-like cut on Khalid's cheek.

There was absolute fury in his eyes as he looked at Byron Johnson. He spoke in Arabic before he turned and walked away.

Byron was now completely isolated. Several men and women were watching from a semi-circle that had formed around them as soon as Khalid Hussein was cut. These people had no intention of helping. They were spectators waiting for a spectacle. One of them was even recording the scene on a tiny digital camera, hoping for a scene of mayhem for YouTube.

And Byron ran toward an exit in the iron fence on the western border of the park. For the first time in his life he felt like a fugitive.

# 23

SIMEON BLACK HAD LIVED for more than three decades in a two-bedroom apartment in Greenwich Village, at the quiet corner of Waverly Place and West 10th Street. His second-floor window overlooked the Three Lives Bookstore, an intimate shop into which Simeon had walked at least once each week in all the years he had lived there. A small section of the store's shelves was devoted to his books, including the 1971 book based on his reporting about the secret American invasion of Cambodia, *The Dark War*. As a favor to the owners, he had autographed each copy.

It was rare for Simeon to invite anyone to his apartment. He had been married twice but never had children; the two much younger women with whom he had been involved over the last fifteen years had both left, one thirteen years ago and the other three years ago. He had lived with his two wives and his two live-in lovers in this rent-controlled, low-cost apartment. He had long ago run out of bookshelf space—books were now piled carefully in the corners and along the walls. Long expanses of built-in filing cabinets lined the walls in the hallway; they contained notes and drafts of his articles and books. He had already made arrangements for the Columbia School of Journalism to take the papers after he died. He still wrote every sentence of his first drafts in long-hand, but now that he had become adept with computers, he put his second and final drafts in the deep reservoirs of his hard drive.

Byron Carlos Johnson was one of the few people who regularly visited him. Simeon, like a classic New York psychiatrist working from an office in his apartment, had now spent hours interviewing Byron.

"And what else did he say?" Simeon asked.

"That there was always one man who was in the room with him, no matter where in the world he was."

"Does he know who?"

"Not by name, Sy." Although he was surrounded by computer equipment at his cluttered, old-fashioned rolltop desk, Simeon Black still took notes on the spiral notebooks he had first used when, just out of Harvard where he was an editor at the *Crimson*, he joined the *Washington Post* and started on the night police detail, learning that the first sentence of each article had to convey the name, the place, and the event. "But Ali is a very smart man, and he has described this man so well that I'm certain I've been in the same room with him."

"He's followed him to New York?"

"He's Zelig-like," Byron said, leaning backward in a frayed, overstuffed chair. "If I'm right—and I think I am—he appears in court and in conferences with the judge. Even sometimes on the streets where I'm walking."

Simeon was urbane, and he recognized that Byron Carlos Johnson was as well. He liked to rib Byron. "Sure we're not a little paranoid here, fella?"

"Not a whit," Byron answered. Simeon hadn't heard the word *whit* in a conversation in years.

"What does he look like?"

"Like an older model out of *GQ*. Blue suits, pinstripe gray suits, dress shoes, sometimes even a vest. Mustache. The look of one of those Ivy League CIA agents from the early sixties." Byron paused. "And breath that exudes the smell of Cuban cigars."

Simeon Black looked up from his notebook, glancing over the half-frame of his reader's glasses. "And how do you know what his breath is like?"

"Two days ago, when I was leaving Washington Square Park after Ali's moody brother was slashed, I saw him. Loitering with intent, as they say, just staring at me. I did something simple. I walked over to him, held out my hand, and said, 'I'm Byron Johnson. We seem to bump into each other all the time. You know me, I don't know you.'"

"What did he do?"

"I love his style," Byron said. "He laughed."

Just outside the windows of the second-floor apartment, the upper branches of the London plane trees glittered in the mid-autumn sun. Yellow and orange light swept through the comfortable, book-filled room.

"And then?"

"To my surprise, I've become reasonably accomplished with digital technology. I had my BlackBerry in my hand. I held it up and took his picture."

Simeon lit a cigarette. He was one of those rare people who had smoked for so long that he was able to make a cigarette appear from nowhere and ignite a match so deftly that it was all one motion, like a magician's trick. Simeon lifted his chin, blew out the first smoke from the unfiltered cigarette, and asked, "How did he react?"

"Flat-footed. He was so surprised that he had no change of expression."

"So what you had was basically a mug shot?"

"That's a good way to put it, Sy."

They shared a laugh as the cigarette smoke expanded over Simeon Black's head. The smoke was bright and diaphanous in the leafy light.

"I'll bet he took your camera away."

"Sy, he couldn't pry my BlackBerry out of my cold, dead hand."

Simeon stopped taking notes. "Do you want a drink, Byron?"

"I gave it up for Lent. But I'll have some water. You're making me do all the talking."

Simeon tossed a bottle of water, and Byron, always a quick-handed athlete, caught it firmly. "I have nothing to say, really, Byron. You've got all the information."

"It's interesting: the concept of the source, Deep Throat. I never saw myself as Deep Throat."

"But I need more than Deep Throat," Simeon said, "I need to have what Ali is saying confirmed, or have it made more concrete."

This was a persistent theme for Simeon Black. He preferred verification from one or more other sources of the information Byron Johnson was relaying to him. He made that point several times to Byron, who once chided him, "What is it, Sy, you don't believe me?" Simeon had shrugged. "I'd trust you with my first-born, Byron, but my editors won't."

He liked Byron Johnson, and he knew that liking a source was a problem. Simeon had done his apprenticeship with hard-edged, skeptical, and long-forgotten reporters. *The facts, just the facts, ma'am.* Simeon's mentors never, as far as he knew, developed friendships with anyone they used as sources. They lived lonely lives.

He had relaxed some of that rigidity; he saw it as a sign of age and experience and also a profound change in the world of journalists, who were now chatty and ingratiating. But he still clung to the idea that a story without verified sources was in many ways a fiction. Byron, he felt, was a person he could trust. He was the kind of person Simeon, a scholarship boy from the Bronx, had first encountered in his freshman year at Harvard. Byron was born to the American ruling class, the son of an ambassador who had written a small classic on diplomacy. Byron had received as if by right of birth almost every gift America could bestow: famous parents, elegant homes, private grammar schools, a boarding school (Groton), Princeton, and Harvard Law School. An officer in the Army, a partner at one of the most white-shoe of all the white-shoe law firms in the country. Not to mention the looks that accompanied that kind of pedigree, tall, slender yet powerful, brown hair that he never lost and now was graying just slightly, and a face that had some of the vivid features that a Latin mother could pass along, unexpectedly dark eyebrows, a slightly cleft chin, and an almost imperceptibly aquiline nose.

But now something else had happened to Byron, and it was a something else that made Simeon think twice about finishing and publishing his articles. Byron had passed ever so slightly into the realm of the outcast, the man who could be made to seem paranoid, off, delusional. He had gotten a great deal of bad publicity in conservative, even right-wing newspapers like the *New York Post* and the *Washington Times*.

He had been called, by Kimberly Smith and others, a "lackey for bin Laden" on the Fox network.

Byron said, "I can have something as close to what you need, Sy, as you are ever likely able to get."

Simeon held his cigarette the way men in France in the 1950s had: the butt between his forefinger and middle finger, the lit end pointing away from him, the way Sartre held his cigarettes in pictures taken of him. "What?"

"Next week there will be a hearing in a sealed courtroom on a motion I've made to dismiss the indictment on the basis of what we lawyers like to call prosecutorial abuse. That's a nice expression for really nasty behavior by government agents and lawyers. Justin Goldberg surprised the hell out of me when he read my motion and then issued an order saying he would hold a hearing."

"What kind of hearing? The usual stuff where lawyers get up and argue with each other and there's no testimony from real persons?"

"Not that kind. Ali Hussein will testify. Just as defendants who contend there has been an illegal search and seizure testify."

"The problem is I can't get in there to hear that."

"I know. But I'll be asking the questions and Ali will be speaking under oath."

Simeon exhaled: a billow of smoke refilled the space where the earlier smoke had been suspended in the autumn light from the window. "But it's still the same problem," he said. "It's tough to rely on what you say happened in court. There is too much at stake for me. I need the words from Ali himself. I can't rely on the good graces of my editors any longer that what I'm writing is based in reality."

"I'm going to give you a source that's better even than an interview between you and Ali."

"What's that?"

"The actual transcript of the hearing. My questions, Hal Rana's cross-examination, the judge's questions, and most important, Ali Hussein's answers, under oath."

Simeon Black sipped from the glass of Scotch that had been sitting on his desk for several hours, untouched. He tilted the glass toward Byron, as if saluting him. "How can you do that, Byron?"

"The judge said in that same surprising order that I'm entitled to the videotape and transcript."

Simeon immediately recognized the risk to Byron Johnson. "Isn't it a felony for you to give that to me?"

"Sy, let me worry about that. At this point I have men following me, my phones and my emails are intercepted, I'm watched every second when I'm speaking to Ali Hussein. Not to mention, on the other side, a supposed brother who takes too much interest in my client's religious well-being."

Simeon took another sip of the warm Scotch. He raised his eyebrows, waiting for more.

Byron smiled. "You don't know this, Sy, but you're giving me something I can't get anywhere else. Protection."

"You think I can protect you?"

"At this point, Sy, where else can I go? Barack Obama? The Pope? Costa Rica? There's an old expression I learned in those boring chapel sessions I was forced to attend as an eleven-year-old in cold, cold New England."

"What's that? My parents in the Bronx never let me go to chapel."

"The truth shall set you free."

# 24

"STATE YOUR NAME FOR the record."

He leaned forward slightly, toward a slender, snake-shaped microphone. "Ali Hussein."

"How old are you?" Byron Johnson asked.

"I'm not sure."

"Why aren't you sure?"

"I've been in prison for a very long time."

"How long have you been in prison?"

"I don't know."

"More than five years?"

"For sure."

"Do you know what today's date is?"

"No, not really." Ali sat back slightly from the microphone, waiting for the next question.

To his left, Byron heard but did not see Hal Rana stand. "Judge?"

"What's the objection, Mr. Rana?" On the wall behind Justin Goldberg was an immense seal of the United Sates in bronze, the fierce eagle at the center, its talons gripping symbols of power and peace. Goldberg looked annoyed.

"The United Sates will stipulate that Mr. Hussein is forty-three years old."

"Does that work for you, Mr. Johnson?"

"It does, Judge."

As Hal Rana sat down, Byron looked steadily at Ali Hussein, in prison clothes, an enigmatic expression on his face (fear, contempt, indifference?), and had one of those moments when he was uncertain whether his client was focused, or even aware of the place and time, or cared about the outcome, or simply so nervous that he was losing all sense of direction. "Mr. Hussein," Byron said, "how old were you when you were taken into custody?"

"I was thirty-five."

"Where were you when you were arrested?"

"Bonn, Germany."

"Why were you in Bonn?"

"To work."

"What work did you do?"

"I was an accountant."

"How long had you been in Bonn when you were arrested?"

"Three days."

"How long were you planning to stay?"

"Two more weeks."

Byron adjusted his own slender microphone at the podium where he stood. A loud acoustic noise briefly filled the courtroom. Ali Hussein sat at least thirty feet from him, in the witness box well below and to the right of Judge Goldberg. Ali Hussein was now focused. Byron liked the crisp back-and-forth rhythm of the questions and answers he and Ali had now established.

"When were you arrested in Bonn?"

"July 14, 2003."

"Before you went to Bonn, where were you living?"

"Fort Lee, New Jersey."

"Are you a United States citizen?"

"No."

"What is your immigration status?"

Byron had learned that Ali Hussein sometimes said unexpected things. He leaned forward crisply to the microphone.

"Prisoner, Mr. Johnson, prisoner."

Justin Goldberg glanced at Byron over his half-frame reading glasses. His glance was meant to convey that he expected Byron to control his witness.

"What was your immigration status?"

"Green card."

"How long had you held it?"

"Five years."

"Who was your sponsor?"

"Khalid Hussein."

"Who is he?"

"My brother."

Byron, uneasy with the thought that his client might be lying, asked, "What does your brother do?"

"He owns a warehouse business in New Jersey."

"Where were you born?"

"Syria. I was Syrian."

Byron knew that it would not take long for Justin Goldberg to intervene. And now he did. "Mr. Johnson, it's not my intention to cut you off, but the purpose of this hearing is to give you the opportunity to show, as you've put it in asking for this proceeding, that the government is guilty of gross misconduct—I think you called it *criminal abuse*—that, you believe, has deprived your client of due process of law justifying dismissal of the indictment. I think I have that right, Mr. Johnson, do I?"

Justin Goldberg—acerbic even though soft-spoken—looked at Byron Johnson, expecting an answer.

Not answering, Byron simply stared at Justin Goldberg.

"Given all that, Mr. Johnson, the defendant's pedigree doesn't matter. So let's cut to the chase, sir."

Byron's gaze shifted from the judge to slender Ali Hussein. "Mr. Hussein, how were you arrested?"

"I was driving in a rental car, a Toyota at nine in the morning. I stopped for a light at an intersection. Four men jumped out of a Mercedes SUV stopped next to me. Two of them held up what looked like badges. They pressed them against the side window. Two held guns."

"Did they say anything?"

"Get out of the car. Show me your hands. Get out of the car."

"Did you get out of the car?"

"No."

"Why not?"

"Terrified, Mr. Johnson. I didn't know who they were. They were angry. They were fierce."

"Did you have any reaction when that happened?"

"I did."

"What reaction?"

Without hesitating, he leaned toward the microphone, as if bowing slightly. "I soiled myself." He paused. "I was shaking, Mr. Johnson. I had no control over my body. I thought they were going to shoot me."

"Had you been sick that morning?"

"No. I was a healthy man."

"What happened then?"

"They smashed the window next to me. They opened the door."

"And then?"

"Pulled me out of the car."

"And next?"

"They put a cloth bag over my head."

"Let me ask you this: before the bag was put on you, did you see the faces of the men who took you?"

"Yes, I did, Mr. Johnson."

"Did you ever see any of those men again?"

"One."

"How often?"

"Many times."

"What does many mean?"

"I stopped counting. I was an accountant. I love numbers. I counted thirty-three times, and then I stopped. I saw him many times."

"Do you know his name?"

"His name? He never told me. I gave him a name. *Jesse Ventura.*"

Justin Goldberg touched the edge of his reading glasses, whose lenses flashed like a blade in the light from his desk lamp. "Mr. Johnson, your next question, please."

"Jesse Ventura. Why that name?"

"I had just seen Jesse Ventura on television. He was crazy, this man is crazy."

"When was the last time you saw this man?"

"Last night."

*Last night*: the answer surprised and unsettled Byron. He had spent ten minutes with Ali in his holding cell before the hearing started. He had said nothing about this.

"Did he say anything?"

"He did."

"What?"

"He said I am stupid."

"Anything else?"

"That you're a lousy lawyer."

Byron felt a sudden, uncomfortable flush.

"What else did he say?"

"That my lawyer is *so* stupid that I'm going to end up dead."

"Anything else?"

"He said what he always says."

"And that's what?"

"The money, Ali. Where is the money?"

"Did he *do* anything?"

"Not what he usually does."

"And what does he usually do?"

"Usually he hits me."

"How often has he hit you?"

"Many times, Mr. Johnson. Many times in many countries."

"When did he first hit you?"

"In Bonn, just a few hours after I was picked up. I hadn't yet been moved to another city. It was a hotel room. The shades were drawn. I heard the traffic outside. The European car horns. They took my hood off. There was a painting on the wall. It was an English countryside, horses and dogs and men in eighteenth-century riding clothes. There were dead foxes on the ground. Then this man stepped in front of me. There were a few other men in the room. They wore masks. Zorro masks: over the bridge of the nose, the eyebrows, below the eyes, across the temples. But I could see their eyes."

"And the man who stepped in front of you?"

"No mask. He was big. He wore a suit. He was smoking a cigar. He had an American flag lapel pin on his suit jacket."

"What did he say?"

"That I should be sick of myself. That I smelled like shit."

"What happened?"

"He handed me a towel and told me to clean myself."

"Did you?"

"No. I would have had to touch my soiled pants and my body and private parts in the presence of these men."

"Then what happened?"

"He said they wanted to talk to me in private, and that this room was private. He said he knew I was a wizard with numbers—that all I had to do was spend some time writing down the names of banks and account numbers where the money was kept."

"What else?"

"That as soon as I wrote this down he would give me time to go into the bathroom, shower, and put on fresh clothes."

"Fresh clothes?"

"My clothes. He said he had picked up the suit I had given to the hotel cleaning service the night before and that it was in the bathroom waiting for me."

"Did that surprise you?"

"It did. It scared me. How did they get my clothes? What else did they have? Who were these people? What were they going to do to me?"

"And?"

"He said my underwear, also clean, was in the bathroom, too. He and his friends, he said, had arranged to help me by taking some of my clothes from my room."

"What did you say?"

"I said, *Please leave me alone.*"

"He asked you to write something down, correct?"

"Correct."

"Did you write anything down?"

"No, I didn't know what to write down."

"What next?"

"The men in masks pulled my pants off. They wore plastic gloves. They took off my underwear, and they rubbed my underwear into my face."

"And then?"

"I gagged, Mr. Johnson."

"And then?"

"The man hit the side of my head. *Jesse Ventura.* Just above my right ear."

"And?"

"I fell over."

"And?"

"They dragged me into the bathroom. I was crying. The bathtub was filled with water. Two of the men picked me up. By the wrists and the ankles. The man who had hit me said I was filthy and needed a bath. He pushed my head under the water. I couldn't breathe. I tried to scream. The water rushed into me. And then he pulled me out of the water. They left me on the floor."

Byron Johnson took up a picture from the surface of the lectern. "May I approach the witness, Judge? I have a photograph to show him."

"Show it first to Mr. Rana."

Byron walked to his left. Rana did not stand. Byron put the picture in front of him. Rana rose to his feet. "This is a national security item, Your Honor. We object to its use as an exhibit."

Byron said, "This is simply a picture of a man. It may assist Mr. Hussein in identifying the man who hit him."

Judge Goldberg said, "The man who hit the witness, Mr. Johnson? It is an open question, in my view, that the defendant was hit at all."

"He just testified to it, under oath."

"And I'm sure, Mr. Johnson, that you've advised the defendant of the adverse consequences of perjury?"

"Judge, let me say this: it's not the function of a judge to suggest that a witness is lying."

Justin Goldberg slapped the palm of his hand on the bench. It was the first time that he had fully unleashed his temper, that anger he always concealed under his urbane, skeptical surface. "Mr. Johnson, I won't tolerate contempt."

Byron stared at him. After five seconds, Justin Goldberg disengaged from the stare. He impatiently held up his hand, saying, "Bring that photograph up to me."

One of the marshals took the picture to Goldberg. He glanced at it. Byron, who was certain the judge would never let Ali Hussein look at it, managed to stay impassive when he heard Goldberg brusquely and unexpectedly announce: "I'll admit this. Mark it as defendant's Exhibit 1."

The court reporter—a woman in her forties who had been steadily typing into a computer that instantly created a transcript on the laptop computers in front of the judge and Hal Rana—took the picture and placed an old-fashioned sticker marking it as defendant's Exhibit 1 on the upper left corner of the picture. The marshal handed the picture to Byron, who carried it to Ali Hussein.

"Take a look at the picture marked as Exhibit 1, Mr. Hussein."

It was a reproduction of the picture Byron Johnson had taken with his cell phone of the man just outside the western edge of Washington Square Park.

"Is this the man?"

"It is."

"Is this the man who hit you in Bonn?"

"Yes."

"Is this the man who came to your cell last night?"

"It is."

"Is this the man you know as Jesse Ventura?"

"Yes."

In that pulse of an interval before Byron could ask another question, Justin Goldberg said: "We will go into recess."


Two days later, Byron Johnson stepped out of the number 6 train at the City Hall station. Rainwater dripped from the street-level grating to the concrete subway platform. Above the station, as in all Manhattan, wind-driven, cold gusts of rain had been falling steadily since the night before. Most of the leaves had finally been stripped from the trees. They lay sodden on the pavement.

Byron fastened his raincoat up to his neck and put on his wide-brimmed Barsolino hat. He had carried the Humphrey Bogart–style hat since looking out at the street that morning from his tall bedroom windows. He knew a hat would be more useful because destroyed umbrellas were strewn across the plaza's gray pavement and piled against the ornate railings around the Federalist-era City Hall.

Holding down the soaked brim of his hat, Byron trotted through the noisy congestion of cars, yellow taxis, and trucks that had crossed the Brooklyn Bridge and come to a halt in the narrow maze of streets around Foley Square. Alert, agile and quick, Byron went through the colonnades of the Municipal Building. The passageways were wet, but he was briefly sheltered from the downpour. Even in heavy, windswept rain, people still walked while gazing down at the lit screens of their cell phones.

As soon as he emerged from the colonnades under the Municipal Building, Byron almost sprinted to the nearby entrance of One St. Andrew's Plaza, that Soviet-style building that housed the U.S. Attorney's Office. He made his way through the two security checkpoints that led to the lobby. Several well-dressed men were waiting near the security machines. He sat on a plastic chair in the waiting room. Now dominated by big photographs of Barack Obama and Eric Holder—both with that look of eager, youthful aptitude— the waiting room was a place through which John Gotti, Bernie Madoff, Ivan Boesky, and other legendary criminals had passed, together with their lawyers. There were also forlorn Puerto Rican and black women in the rows of chairs that resembled the sitting areas in bus stations. As he waited, he spent fifteen minutes reading the soaked paperback edition of *Emma* he had carried in the roomy pocket of his raincoat.

It took Byron a second before he recognized the man walking into the waiting room.

It was Jesse Ventura.

Byron stood up.

"Good morning, Mr. Ventura."

"You came for this, Mr. Johnson."

He handed Byron a computer disk that Byron knew contained the video of Ali Hussein's day-long hearing. The man also gave him a handwritten receipt describing the disk Byron had just been given. Byron signed it.

Without speaking, the man gave a hard, deliberately insincere smile as Byron turned away and left the brown lobby.

Waverly Place—tree-lined, orderly, and quietly beautiful—was empty. Rain still fell. Water ran along the old gutters and pooled at each sewer, congested with fallen leaves. The Three Lives Bookstore had just opened for the day. In its warm interior, a young woman with purple hair sat near the cash register, head bowed, reading. There were no customers in the store.

Just inside the front door of the townhouse in which Simeon Black lived, Byron pressed the intercom button. The peremptory buzzer sounded at the door, and Byron quickly pulled it open. Shaking the water off his felt hat, Byron walked up the creaking stairs. The carpeting was worn. The hallway was damp; it smelled of wet wool and soaked newspapers.

The door was unlocked. At the end of the bookshelf-lined hallway, Simeon, at his desk, lifted his right hand and waved Byron in. He was smiling. Byron had grown to feel comfortable in the shabby, scholarly aura of Simeon Black's apartment—it reminded him of the cozy, book-filled, and cluttered apartments of some of his bachelor professors at Princeton. Even though it was the 1960s, those genteel men actually still wore tweedy blazers with elbow patches. They were literate and kind, and they seemed completely at ease in a style of life that would soon end, in fact had already ended without their knowing it.

And now, in Simeon's old-world, immensely attractive apartment, Byron, taking off his raincoat and draping it on a standing hat rack, felt a sudden uneasiness. Those professors at Princeton—all certainly dead by now—had only wished Byron and the other students well. They were intelligent, privileged, and kind. They had no agenda other than to live out their lives in the austere luxury of Princeton, and to accomplish that, all they had to do was teach and, if they could, write books of literary criticism, history, or, in one case, a wildly successful novel about a year at a New England prep school.

But, as Byron knew, Simeon was not a kindly professor, and his mission was not to move Byron safely forward in life. Simeon was a reporter. He had written about Army generals and politicians who had waged a secret war. Simeon had named the killers in his books and articles. He had once uncovered the secret financial life of a House of Representatives Democrat who, not long after Simeon's articles appeared, shot himself in the head in his office. Byron had recently read, because he was now skilled at finding information in the deep recesses of Google, Yahoo, and Bing, that the man's seventeen-year-old daughter had naively begged Simeon not to publish the articles about her father. Byron also knew the old adage about dealing with reporters: *Those who ride the tiger's back might end up in the tiger's stomach.*

Simeon reached over the clutter on his desk and shook Byron's hand. He assumed Byron had come to describe what had happened two days earlier, when Ali Hussein testified at the secret hearings in a sealed courtroom about years of physical and emotional torture, the mind-numbing pain of total isolation, and the persistent demon who had followed him for years. *Jesse Ventura.*

Byron held the gleaming disk. "I want you to make a copy of this, Sy. What's that called? Burn the CD."

"What is it?

"It's the transcript of the hearings, word for word. And the video."

Simeon knew that, as Ali Hussein's lawyer, Byron had a legitimate right to have the disk, but he had no right to give it away.

Byron handed the disk to Simeon. He inserted it into the slot at the side of his computer. They could both hear the whirring hum as it was replicated.

"Is the hearing over?"

"It is."

"When will the judge make his decision?"

"Don't know." Byron smiled. "He may never make it. It's an old trick some judges use. Never ruling. Remember, these federal judges are our modern royalty. They have lifetime appointments. That literally means they stay until they die. And the truth is they can do, or not do, whatever they want. One of those stupid lawyers' jokes is this: 'What's the difference between God and a federal judge? God wants to be a federal judge.' If Goldberg never rules, then I can never appeal."

Simeon smiled. "So, Dr. Johnson, what's your next step?"

"Will you be my Boswell?"

"Of course, I'm already writing *Life of Johnson*."

Rain flowed down the windows just beyond Simeon's desk. All the leaves had been stripped from the London plane trees.

"My next step? I'm going to start insisting that the government turn over to me every videotape, report, note, plane ticket, picture, blood sample, bank record, and DNA sheet that relates in any way to Ali."

"Talk to me about the videotapes of the torture."

"Ali testified that cameras were often running, especially in the times when Jesse Ventura was with him." Byron paused. "Including when he was pushed under water."

"Waterboarded?"

"That's what it's called, although Ali never heard the word, since it started to be used after he was picked up. Waterboarding, it turns out, is being pushed under water. Just like fourteen-year-old boys do in school pools to twelve-year-old boys. But in this case, it's men doing it. And it lasts longer, long after it stops feeling like a prank. A whole different order of magnitude."

The gentle whirring inside the computer had stopped. Simeon stood up, sat on the edge of his desk, and turned the computer screen so that he and Byron could both view it. He deftly hit two keys.

And there on the screen was a scene from the hearing.

An image of Ali Hussein, in mid-sentence, emerged. Simeon Black, his voice with that edge of awe of a man winning a lottery, said, "Lordy, lordy, is that him? Your client?" There were no known pictures of Ali before or after he was taken down.

Arms folded, Byron stood behind Simeon as they both gazed at the screen. "The one and only."

"You know, sightings of these men are rare."

"He's a man, Sy, not an egret."

Simeon grunted. He was excited. He pressed a practiced finger on the volume key, and as if out of nowhere, Ali Hussein's soft and precise voice rose to high volume.

Byron's voice, well-modulated and intelligent, spoke in the background: "And you have no idea where the room was, is that right, Mr. Hussein?"

"It was in a hot place. Far from Germany. The flight from Bonn took two hours."

"Can you describe the room, sir?"

"A hotel room. More like a motel room. The window had a steel plate that covered all of it. There was a double bed. No door between the bedroom and the bathroom. A painting of an oasis nailed to the wall over the bed. No television. No phone. A motel-style desk."

"How do you know it was a hot country?"

"The air conditioning unit blew out warm air. Along the edges of the steel plate on the window there was always a glare from the outside. It must have been very bright outside, always. As if there was a desert out there."

"Did anyone visit you?"

"Visit? Visit means a pleasant thing, Mr. Johnson. I expect visits from friends."

"Did you see anyone else?"

"There were always two men in the room with me. Day and night."

"Did they speak to you?"

"Never. And I never said a word to them."

"They were in the room when you slept?"

"Not the same two men. There were six or eight men. They were there in shifts."

"What else happened?"

"I was naked all the time. No sheets on the bed. I couldn't cover myself, or hide any part of my body. I couldn't take the towels out of the bathroom. I didn't have pillows or a sheet, so I could never cover any part of my body. Exposed. In the middle of the night I shivered, even though the air conditioning was weak. And the men watched me all the time."

"How long were you in that room?

"I don't know. Weeks, I think. I never heard a sound from outside the room. I don't think there was anyone else in the motel."

"Did anyone hit you when you were there?"

"No."

"Did anyone push you under water while you were there?"

"No."

"Did anyone keep you awake all day?"

Simeon pressed a key on the computer, and the image paused. On the frozen screen Ali Hussein appeared calmly attentive. In that image he was gazing directly into the camera.

Simeon said, "Byron, are you sure you want to leave this with me?"

"Why, don't you want it? It's what you've been asking me for."

"I do." Simeon lit a cigarette and inhaled. The smoke almost immediately flowed from his nostrils. "But you have to be worried about what might happen to you."

188 | PAUL BATISTA

"I can't make any prediction about that. In the last couple of months I've learned that every day is a new adventure."

"My editors will want to use these pictures of him. It's proof that he exists."

"Let me also tell you this, Sy. You may want to use this information, or not. Ali is a sweet man. At first he was nervous and suspicious and guarded. When he first met me in Miami, I was the only non-hostile face he had encountered in years, but he didn't trust me. Over time I've learned that he is thoughtful. I look forward to meeting with him."

Simeon took a fresh unfiltered Gauloise from the cellophane-covered package. He pressed the tip of his cigarette he was finishing against the tip of the new one. *The handing of the torch*, Byron thought.

"Let me ask you this," Simeon said. "What did he do?"

"Do you mean is he guilty? Did he launder money? Move millions and millions of dollars around the world so that the bad guys could buy AK47s, M-16s?"

Simeon smiled. "Something like that."

Byron smiled in return. "I don't have a fucking idea."

# 25

CHRISTINA ROSARIO WAS A strong runner. In the months during which she had been Byron Carlos Johnson's lover, she had brought him time and again on long runs in Riverside Park, on the footpath's curving lanes overlooking the Hudson River, in the beautiful arteries of roadways in Central Park, and sometimes as far upriver as the looming George Washington Bridge.

Christina wasn't surprised that Byron quickly evolved into a strong and effortless runner. He had played squash for years in the upper floors of the University Club, that old-world bastion of privilege at the corner of Fifth Avenue and 55th Street, and he had stamina, grace, and strength even though he had never been a dedicated runner.

And the runs with her were fun. Byron often said to her, "Get ahead of me. I love watching your beautiful ass." They had developed a custom of stopping at the Boat House when they ran in Central Park. They would order hot chocolates and take them to the iron chairs on the flagstone plaza overlooking the lake or sit on the massive granite boulder in front of the building as they watched other runners, roller-bladers, cyclists, and walkers moving on the slopes of East Drive.

The November sunlight glinted on the surface of the reservoir. After their stop at the Boat House, they ran on the cinder path that encircled the reservoir. The path was more than a mile long. Byron remembered the reservoir and the cinder path from his early teens, when he had lived for a year with his mother's sister in her Park Avenue apartment while his father was on a mission to Saigon, before the war began its grim escalation.

Byron later learned that his father for that year had been temporarily assigned to the CIA from the State Department and had prepared secret reports that Byron saw for the first time in the late 1990s, when the government had suddenly released all classified material from the Vietnam era. In those meticulously written reports, typed on onion-skin on a Smith-Corona, his father had detailed the assassinations of Vietnamese suspected of working for the Vietminh and the Viet Cong. They were called action reports or after-action reports, depending on whether they described events that had already happened or were planned.

Byron was profoundly disturbed. There were descriptions of South Vietnamese politicians and military officers who were considered "impediments to success of the mission" and details of how they were to be killed. His father had written reports on villages whose populations were to be relocated because the villages were "impaired." There were "scenarios" for the bombing of North Vietnamese targets. At the bottom of each report—each written with the precision and clarity that set the tone for everything his father did and said—his father's signature was unmistakable, even though Byron had wished they were unsigned so that he could deny to himself that his father had prepared them. Byron was a man who understood the logic of evidence: this evidence showed that his father was a murderer just as certainly as a Mafia don who ordered a hit. Byron, after reading those reports, had burned them. But he could only burn and eradicate his own copies. The reports were in the public domain. Recent books on the history of Vietnam mentioned the reports and his father. The reports were described as what they were—"testaments to and plans for murder." Even the generally flattering biography of his father on Wikipedia had been altered to identify him as one of the profoundly misguided "best and brightest" who had callously manufactured and mismanaged that insane, useless war.

But Byron didn't want to think about his father now. All that mayhem and intrigue was decades earlier, and his father was dead. Even on a cold day, the air over the reservoir was warm in the early afternoon sunlight. Above the reservoir three seagulls, widely separated, rose and descended on invisible currents of wind; they were absolutely white against the bluest possible sky.

Byron and Christina stood against the low railing that encircled the reservoir; it had replaced the dreary chain-link fence that had surrounded the reservoir for many years. Suddenly, she said, "Carlos, some guy stopped me today. He asked questions about you."

Byron glanced down from the point in the sky where one of the seagulls floated on extended wings. A speck of dazzling white against absolute blue. He looked into Christina's face. "So tell me about it."

"I'm worried."

"Maybe I'll be, too. But I can't be until I know more."

Runners swept behind them on the cinderblock path. They heard the strained breathing and the pounding of feet. "Let's walk, Carlos."

"Come on, Brighteyes. You sound as though you had a visitation from the golem."

"I was leaving Low Library. Halfway down the steps, a big blond guy said, 'Ms. Rosario.' We were right next to the alma mater statue. I stopped. 'Can I help you?' I said. I used that haughty voice."

"I know that voice." Byron, sensing her anxiety, was trying to put her at ease. But he, too, was anxious.

"He said, 'I need to speak to you about Byron Johnson.' I walked quickly. I said, 'I don't want to talk to you.' He didn't go away. We were walking toward the gates on Broadway. He said you were the target of a grand jury investigation. And that I was a person of interest, a subject. He told me it was very likely you would be indicted."

Even though he showed his instinctive stoicism, Byron sensed that surge of fear and anxiety that made his knees feel as if they had lost their bone structure and muscle: they melted.

"That's crazy," he said. "Who was this guy?"

"A strange name. *Nashatka. Special Agent Nashatka.* He seemed to enjoy the sound of his name. He gave me his card."

To steady himself, he took her hand. They were in the shadow of one of the three stone pump houses, built during the Civil War, that stood at the reservoir's edge. He placed his free hand against the cool, gray, ancient stone blocks. "He must have said something else."

"Sure, that I would have to testify to the grand jury."

"Did he say when?"

"At that point he handed me a grand jury subpoena. I left it at the apartment. Soon. I have to go soon. Next Thursday, I think."

They turned and left the reservoir. As they approached the bridle path, two elegant riders, a man and a woman, galloped by on big horses. Their hooves thundered, the air vibrated as they passed. Huge, intense animals.

"What should I do, Carlos?"

"You're a law student. You know the answer. You have to go."

"Why shouldn't I take the Fifth and not answer?"

He put his arm around her waist. She was still sweating from their run. She was so close to him that he could smell the residue of sweat mixed with the faint scent of perfume. He said, "Because you haven't done anything wrong. You can't take the Fifth unless you have a reason to believe your answer will incriminate you."

She hesitated. "What about the money, Carlos?"

"Money?"

"He asked if you kept large amounts of cash."

"Don't I wish."

"He asked if I could get copies of your bank statements, brokerage accounts, receipts for safe deposit boxes."

He laughed. "I'll pull them together for you so you can give them to him. He'll see I'm fast running out of money."

"Carlos, I'm worried. Nothing like this has ever happened to me."

"And not to me either, Christina."

They left the park at West 86th Street and Central Park West. Streams of yellow taxis flowed uptown and downtown on the avenue, using all four lanes. In front of them, the monumental canyon formed by the rows of apartment buildings on 86th Street ran west to the Hudson. Now that they had left the park, the afternoon air seemed to have turned more chill. The beautiful skin of Christina's right arm was suddenly prickly. Byron rubbed her arm, as if to warm her.

"Let's grab a taxi," Byron said. "It's too far to run back home."

In the loose rear seat of the old taxi, Byron slid close to her. He took her hand, which had been resting on the cracked vinyl of the seat cushion. A bright panel with a television screen was embedded in the back of the front seat, an innovation of the city's corporate mayor that must have earned millions of dollars for whatever company made these devices and installed them. The screen had bright graphics. A local news reporter was talking, a montage of soldiers in Afghanistan behind him. They were American soldiers dressed in what looked to Byron like space suits—goggles, miner's lights on their helmets, bulky bulletproof vests that made them resemble puffed-up action figures, all that technological apparatus.

Ahead of them were the rows of traffic lights leading uptown along Central Park West. There were mothers with their young children on the sidewalks. Runners jogged across the avenue into and out of the park. Bright banners advertising the Museum of Natural History hung from the lamp poles. To their right were the tall walls of granite that underlay the northern reaches of the park. The granite walls were coal-colored.

"Christina, we don't need to stay together. You don't need all this in your life."

The taxi turned left off Central Park West at 96th Street. Just as it completed the sweeping turn, a car decorated with Puerto Rican flags made a U-turn across the four lanes of the street just in front of them. The taxi slowed abruptly, and

Byron instinctively put out his arm to brace his hand against the partition and with his other arm kept Christina from jolting forward. Byron glanced at the taxi driver's license taped to the partition. His name was *Ali Hussein*.

As they settled back into the seat, Christina, without looking at him, said, "I can't do that, Carlos. I love you."

Those words from this beautiful young woman—this woman with whom he could lie awake late into the night talking about books, the day's events, the movies they regularly went to see, and the years he had passed as a boy moving from country to country—caused a rush of hot emotion to course through his body and mind.

"I love you, too."

Christina squeezed his hand. He leaned against her and kissed the salty skin on her shoulder.

# 26

It was Wednesday afternoon, almost winter now. Byron walked on the worn cobblestones in the middle of Greene Street in Soho. Double-parked delivery trucks had brought all traffic on the narrow street to a standstill. Sunlight shone on the smooth stones of the street and threw into etched relief the iron facades on the old industrial buildings on both sides. At street level, each building housed expensive stores, all filled with bright light and mostly bare interiors. The international glitter in what had not long ago been a warehouse district: *Givenchy, Tse, Polo.*

Byron loved these long walks on weekday afternoons through parts of Manhattan in which he had literally never set foot. Several weeks earlier, he had remembered a line from the first chapter of *Moby Dick*, which he had read as a twelve-year-old during a long summer on the coast of Maine with his aunt and uncle; it was early in the first chapter when Ishmael is speaking to the readers and tells them: *Circumambulate the city of a dreamy Sabbath afternoon.* Over the last six weeks he had walked through the streets of Soho—Greene Street, Broome Street, West Broadway; through the wide areas on West Fourteenth Street where there were still trolley car rails embedded in the pavement, as faint as chalk lines; and through the cozy companionable neighborhoods around Christopher Street, Perry Street, and Bank Street in the West Village.

Byron now thought of the years he had spent in Manhattan, and of his life, as carpet-bombing. The weaponry of the bombing was his work. It dominated virtually everything from the day he arrived in Manhattan. From the outset he was vigorous, engaged and driven. For many years he loved the work, and loved the traveling across the country, as well as to Europe and Asia, for clients. He had far more interest in the issues he dealt with and the people—clients, judges, witnesses—he encountered than in the money.

In fact, the money for him was almost invisible. His large income simply flowed by electronic transfer from the firm's bank account into his own bank account. Without his even counting it, the money paid for the Fifth Avenue apartment where he lived with his wife and children, the upkeep on the second house in Maine, and his children's school tuition. For many years he worked six days a week; he relished the quiet Saturday mornings or Sunday afternoons in the office. Each week he played squash on Wednesday afternoon, and this was his regular break from work. And for years he had gone each Thursday night to the opera or symphony in Lincoln Center or Carnegie Hall. In the long years of his marriage, his wife Joan went with him, often in the company of some of the other faculty members who taught with her at NYU.

And finally, in the last six months the long, all-consuming engagement with work was suspended. There was only so much effort he could devote to Ali Hussein's ordeal—a finite amount of time to spend meeting with him, reading background materials, preparing briefs and motions, and handling telephone calls from random people, most of them obvious cranks, who wanted him to believe they had information he vitally needed, or to abuse him. He couldn't spend all of his days with Christina Rosario. She was in class from nine every morning until noon and then, in the afternoon, in the wood-paneled, frayed offices of the law review.

So he took to the streets to fill the extra time he now had. On the three or four days each week when he went on his long walks, he picked the neighborhoods based on the names he had heard for years: Soho, the Meat Packing District, the East Village, and Morningside Heights. He was a prodigious walker. He spent at least three hours crisscrossing each neighborhood, often walking down the same streets several times because Manhattan was, in fact, a small island, and the legendary neighborhoods were even smaller. He stopped at each bookstore, usually the vast, shiny Barnes & Noble stores, where tall posters of famous writers (Twain, Virginia Woolf, Kurt Vonnegut) hung from the ceilings. He drank iced coffee in the Starbucks enclave in each store, surrounded by scruffy kids bent over their laptops. Less often, because there were far fewer of them, he stopped in the small bookstores that had managed to survive. In those stores he made it a point to buy books, which he always arranged to have shipped to either his apartment or Christina's because he didn't want anything to encumber his hands as he continued his free-wheeling walking.

At the congested intersection of Greene and Spring, Byron waited for the light to change in his favor. At first he didn't notice the dark blue Chevy sedan with tinted windows that gradually came to a halt near him. When he focused on it, he guessed, correctly, that the oversize tires without hubcaps meant that it was a government-owned vehicle. As soon as the door opened on the passenger side of the front seat, Byron realized that the man leaving the car was there for him. Another man rose from the back seat. They were both blond. Byron glanced into the car to see if Jesse Ventura was there. He wasn't. The man closest to him had a gold earring in his left ear lobe, in total contrast to the blue sport jacket, white shirt, blue pants, and penny loafers he wore. His head was completely shaven.

"Mr. Johnson."

Byron faced him. He forced himself to look composed. And in that moment he realized he had seen this man before, in the courtroom gallery and in Justin Goldberg's chambers.

"Let me guess," Byron said. "You are Agent Nashatka."

"That's right."

"And where is Jesse Ventura?"

Tom Nashatka was unfazed. His training for this work had taught him that at times the appearance of politeness, restraint, and deference was appropriate. "Why don't we walk toward West Broadway?"

"Why don't we not do that?"

"That's fine, sir; we can talk here."

Young men and women passed by them. This area of the city, Byron knew, belonged to the young.

"Your call," Byron said.

"Fifty-two million dollars came into your bank account yesterday afternoon, by wire. Two hours later, fifty-two million dollars flew away, also by wire."

"You need to say that again. Slowly."

"Mr. Johnson, you need to talk to us. You need to tell us what you know."

"You need to tell me what you know. Don't talk fantasies with me."

"Sure, Mr. Johnson. You have a checking account with the Private Wealth Management Division at Chase. A wire transfer from the Royal Bank of Canada arrived at 7:52 last night. It was there until 9:55. Then it was sent, intact and in full, to the Bank of the Caribbean in the Turks and Caicos. And three hours ago it flowed again to Norde Bank in Iceland. And from there it's vanished."

"You're making this up as you go along."

"You really need to talk to us. Hal Rana wants me to let you know that he's waiting for you."

"Why are you here? Rana knows my number."

"It's procedure, Mr. Johnson, that agents first approach the target."

*Target.* That was a special word, as well defined and dangerous as a stiletto. In the special parlance of federal criminal law, it designated a person who was almost certain to be indicted. There was a simple ranking system, as in the Army, except with fewer levels. Target was the top rank. Below that rank was the subject, a person who had a fifty-fifty chance of indictment. The next rank was person of interest, and below that was the witness. But it was a system that was also like chess—a subject could rise quickly to the rank of target, just as a person of interest could rise to the rank of subject. But the person who was the target rarely fell in rank to a subject. A target was, in essence, a marked person.

Byron had learned from his austere aristocratic father that *compose yourself* was the central message of manhood, as in the Kipling line about never losing your head while all about you are losing theirs and blaming it on you. Byron stood almost chest to chest with Tom Nashatka.

"Why don't you tell me," Byron asked, "anything else you think I should know."

"Sure, Mr. Johnson. We think you've been carrying messages in aid of terrorism."

Byron let slip his anger. "You're a hell of a messenger boy yourself, aren't you?"

"We're trying to help you, Mr. Johnson. That's the basic message Hal Rana wants me to carry to you."

*Compose yourself*, Byron thought again, almost uttering the words. *Steady.* "Thank you," Byron said, turning to walk west on Spring Street. Cold sunlight fell diagonally through the intricate pattern of iron fire escapes attached to the upper surfaces of the old buildings. The intricate grille-work of shadow and light.

Byron Johnson walked into a Starbucks, entered the bathroom, locked the door, and vomited into the sink.

# 27

SIMEON BLACK MAINTAINED WHAT he called a "slush fund" in which he consistently kept at least fifty thousand dollars in cash to cover the expenses of researching and writing his articles. Virtually all of the money in the account came from expenses advanced by the magazines and newspapers and more recently from online publications willing to pay for articles from a legendary Pulitzer Prize winner who had been able to develop and evolve with the times. After the award-winning stories on Vietnam, he had moved on to journalism about the influence of oil companies on the Arab oil embargo in the 1970s, the hostage taking in Iran that ended on the day when the vacuous Reagan was inaugurated, the Iran-Contra episode in the mid-1980s, the murders in Bosnia in the 1990s, and now the wars that had followed the September 11 attacks. Simeon Black was a journalist, not a historian; but he liked hearing himself compared to Thucydides, who wrote about the Peloponnesian War as it happened—in effect, the first journalist.

He had used his fund over the last several months to track and investigate Byron Carlos Johnson and to follow the paths of the information Byron gave him.

His favorite investigator was Duke Churchill, a retired FBI agent who was capable of such routine work as tracking license plates—still essential gumshoe work even in an age of cyberspace—and arranging to extract the entire contents of a personal computer, like a medieval golem seizing a person's soul. Simeon's assignment to Duke was to get the name of the man whose picture Byron had taken on the border of Washington Square Park. The only information Simeon conveyed to Duke was the cell phone picture of the startled man and the name by which Ali Hussein knew him, *Jesse Ventura*. Simeon had his doubts that even Duke could deliver on such slender sources.

It took two hours for Duke to send an email message. "Andrew Hurd, (202) 793-9242. Not clear what agency. Major player. Be careful."

Duke charged only six hundred dollars for that information. Simeon had many thousands left in the fund. He wanted to know more before he placed a call to Andrew Hurd's cell phone and was willing to pay for it. "Follow him around," Simeon told Duke. "Let me know the people he sees, how he spends his time, that kind of thing. Get me some pictures of him and his friends."

Duke admired Simeon, and in turn Simeon, despite his long history of investigating and criticizing generals, politicians, and presidential candidates and uncovering the crimes and frauds of men in power, enjoyed the errant rogue in this former FBI agent. They only rarely met face to face. When they spoke, they used public pay phones, because calls involving pay phones were difficult to intercept or trace. Street-level drug dealers had learned that long ago. As pay phones began finally to vanish from the world—the Superman-style booths were long-lost relics, and even the open-air phones were steadily disappearing—they more and more often used the land lines in their homes, old technology much more accessible to modern forms of interception. It concerned Simeon that land lines were unreliable, but cell phones and email were as easily overheard as shouts on a street.

Just five days later, Simeon's computer emitted the sound of small cymbals that signaled the arrival of an email. At the moment the cymbals chimed, he had his back to the laptop as he edited the close-to-final version of his article for the *Atlantic* magazine on Byron Carlos Johnson, Ali Hussein, and the terror inflicted on Ali Hussein by an elusive American agent known to his victim as *Jesse Ventura*. Although adept and skillful with computers for what he called an "old man," Simeon still clung nostalgically to some of the tools and habits he learned during his early years in journalism: he edited a printed copy of the article with a sharp blue pencil. He used a small, toy-like metal sharpener. He loved the odor of the curling pieces of pencil wood. It was as satisfying for him as tending the garden of his summer house in Columbia County in upstate New York.

So it may have taken ten minutes after hearing the computer's cymbal chime before he rose from the reverie-like trance of his work. He rotated in the wooden swivel chair he had taken with him from his dormitory at Harvard to many apartments over the years until he finally came to rest in his cluttered, companionable apartment on Waverly Place. The chair squeaked. It was a sound that mystified and annoyed people with whom he was speaking on the telephone, particularly on the speaker phone he often used so that his hands could be free to write. An editor once sent him a can of oil.

Simeon opened the email from the screen name *oliver-north@yahoo.com*. It was Duke Churchill's *nom de guerre*. It was also the name of the tough Marine who overmastered the Senate with his unflappable testimony at the Iran-Contra hearings. The email read "See pictures below," and Simeon moved the arrow to the *Download* box, pressed the trackball, and watched as the screen's tiny gloved hand opened a series of pictures.

There were ten pictures. In each of them, the common element was Andrew Hurd. And in each picture there were other people, several of them young women. The pictures had obviously all been taken over the last several days, since they were all set outdoors, and the background in each picture was the weather of late fall, the weather of the last few days: gusty rain.

Simeon recognized one of the young women in the pictures. He had seen the face many times on television. He was not only a devoted daily reader of newspapers and magazines, but he also kept two televisions on constantly in his office, tuned to CNN and Fox. He was a prolific provider of information, and a voracious consumer of it.

It took only seconds for Simeon to conjure up her name. She was the woman, Kimberly Smith, who appeared on CNN, Fox, and other networks. Simeon thought of her as the Ann Coulter of Islamic reporting: with flair and a shake of her blonde hair, she once said that Islamic terrorists were "religious garbage." Kimberly was Sarah Palin with brains, but just as silly and dangerous. The "religious garbage" comment was so odd, so forceful, and so pandering to right-wing audiences that Simeon had even made an entry of it in the notes he made and kept of daily events, references, and quotes.

Like all old-fashioned reporters, Simeon was fearless and direct about his work. As soon as he recognized Kimberly Smith in the vivid pictures that Duke had taken, he went to the Stanford University website and found her email address and telephone number. He intended to ask her why a Stanford professor and network talking head would be walking into a building in Manhattan at some point in the last five days with a man who was a torturer.

Simeon placed the call to Palo Alto. A cultured, British-accented voice said, "This is Dr. Smith's office."

"I'm trying to reach her."

"Who may I say is calling?" she asked.

"Simeon Black."

He was put on hold. It often happened that his name was its own calling card. He was as famous as any print journalist in the world, and he sensed that someone like Kimberly Smith would know who he was.

Kimberly's confident voice came on the line: "Mr. Black, what can I do for you?"

"Professor, thanks for taking my call."

"When the legendary Simeon Black calls, who wouldn't answer?"

"Thanks," he said. "I'm working on a story about enhanced interrogation techniques."

Her bright, strong voice rang out. "Hope you're writing a manual on how to do them."

Simeon, leaning back in his creaking wooden chair, joined in her laugh. There were not many people in the world, Simeon Black thought, who would pull his leg. People either feared him or were eager to please him.

"Actually, I need to ask you about Andrew Hurd."

She had learned from all of her work on live television that there should never be dead time between question and answer. But there was some dead time before she said, "And who is Andrew Hurd?"

"He's a federal agent who was with you four days ago in Manhattan."

"Mr. Black, if you have questions, why not put them in an email?"

And then her side of the call went silent: the technological equivalent of the curtain falling.

Simeon smiled as he pressed the *End* button on his cell phone. He had no intention of writing an email to her. He had her picture. He had this abrupt conversation. For now, that was all he needed.

# 28

BYRON CARLOS JOHNSON TOUCHED Christina's face, amazed as always at her skin's softness.

"Your friend Special Agent Nashatka came to see me."

They were in the Athens coffee shop on West 113th Street and Amsterdam Avenue. The noisy and convivial place was filled with Columbia students. The steamy air was redolent with the odor of hamburgers and french fries and the faint scent of black coffee. Across Amsterdam Avenue was the immense and unfinished mass of the Cathedral Church of St. John the Divine. Against its Gothic front doors, homeless men and women had set up a cardboard village.

"What did he want?"

"To tell me I had become a rich man."

Christina loved his playful moods. In the months they had been together, the reserved Byron—the Byron whose formal tension she had sensed when she approached him in the Central Park Zoo at the SpencerBlake summer party—had evolved into a man who made her laugh.

"How so?"

"It was my Michael Anthony moment."

"Michael who?"

"Michael Anthony. In the 1950s, long before you were born, there was a television series called *The Millionaire*. Every week a very rich man, John Beresford Tipton, would call Michael Anthony into his library and give him the name of a man or woman on whom he wanted to bestow a million dollars, a fortune then. Mr. Tipton, a recluse, would hand a check for the million to Mike. Mike would smile at Mr. Tipton, slip the check into his suit jacket, and go out to find the lucky and totally unsuspecting man or woman who was to become the next millionaire. Mr. Tipton had an almost sadistic interest in seeing how a million dollars would screw up someone's life. And Mike Anthony was the cordial emissary who delivered the check. The lives of the lucky winners never turned out well."

Trying to smile, Christina sipped cold water from a plastic, brown-hued glass. "And so did he give you a million dollars?"

"Fifty-two million."

"Say that again, Byron," she said, "it's a little too noisy in here."

"Fifty-two. Actually, a little bit more."

She blessed him with one of her smiles. At that moment, he was startled, as he often was, by how beautiful she was and how much he loved her.

"Is this a joke?"

"No, that's what he said."

"What did you do?"

"I have only three banks where I keep accounts. I called them. It turns out there are people I've never heard of called relationship managers. My calls got routed to them. I never spoke to any of them before. I never knew I needed a relationship manager."

She paused as a waiter in a white shirt, open at the neck, deftly poured coffee for them. "That must have been awkward," she said. "What did you ask: 'Do I have fifty-two million dollars in my account today? I have some cell phone bills I need to pay.'"

"In all three cases, I was told the accounts had been closed, frozen. Late yesterday. When I asked why, they said I would have to talk to the bank's lawyers. I did. Each of them said the banks had been served with forfeiture orders."

She looked bewildered and concerned. "Forfeiture orders?"

"The accounts were seized. When I asked to see the orders they said they no longer had them. They said agents showed them the orders, waited as they read them, and wouldn't let them make copies. Once they saw the orders they closed down the accounts."

"Did fifty-two million dollars go into one of the accounts?"

"They refused to let me know that."

She leaned forward. Her face was grave. "Carlos, what's going on?"

Voices and the laughter of the young swept the room. These were happy kids, he thought, remembering the austere dining halls of his years as a student at Groton and Princeton. Nothing but men, all in ties, button-down Brooks Brothers shirts, and blue blazers. Everything orderly, subdued, cowed. No gay boys (at least none who acknowledged it), two blacks, few Jews. This was so different. It was so much more vital and vibrant and happy.

"There was once an expression I never used when I was in college, but I think about now. *They're fucking with my head.*"

"We still use that, Carlos. It transcends generations." She paused, sipping more water. He detected an ever-so-slight tremor in her hand. "You need help. You need a lawyer of your own, don't you think? You're in a labyrinth. Everything is twisted. You stay on straight paths. Those straight paths are leading to walls and no exits. You're hitting walls. You need to adapt. You need a guide."

"You mean as in Virgil and Dante?

"Don't joke, Carlos. You're way too cool for your own good."

Byron reached out for her hand. He held it. "You're wrong. I'm scared out of my wits, Christina. Don't you think I understand that I was in a world, just six months ago, in which I was denied nothing, as untouchable as Prince Valiant? Now I wake up every morning in stark raving dread."

She looked straight into his eyes. He thought about the many times he was so close to her face as they made love that he could see in her brown eyes the reflection of his own.

"Is that why you're up at five?"

"If I try to stay in bed, as I did for years knowing I'd drift back to sleep for another peaceful whole hour or so, I get racing, bad thoughts about my future. I get up now as quickly as I can, believing that being awake will ease the fears."

Again, she tried to drink water but only wet her lips. "What fears, Carlos? Talk to me."

"Such as losing everything I have."

"What else?"

"Having yet another hateful news story about me show up in the *Post* and then instantly get etched forever in that great tablet for all ages, the Internet."

"Tell me more."

He hesitated. When he touched the cup of lukewarm coffee, his thumb was shaking. He doubted he could lift the heavy ceramic cup without that shaking becoming obvious to her. He didn't want to let Christina see that. He knew that at this stage in his life, and with this woman, it was pointless to hide his weaknesses. But he still lived by the aristocratic instincts for privacy and surface calmness his father had instilled in him. *Hold it together, son. Hold it together.* It was as though his father, in those few times in Byron's childhood and teenage years when they were actually together, had decided to communicate advice to him derived from the cold-water, bracing ethics of English boarding schools in the nineteenth century. Maybe it was that reserve that had enabled his father to compose thoughtful, perfectly grammatical orders for murder.

Byron was in free-fall, and knew it. He said, "Sure, there is more, Christina. How about being indicted? These visits from Nashatka aren't background checks for my Supreme Court nomination. They're meant to unsettle me, in fact to scare the shit out of me." He smiled. "And you know what? They're working. I've got the message."

"Maybe you're wrong."

"Wrong? I don't think so. I've thought for years that a sense of realism was one of my most useful personal assets. *This is what is.* I built a career out of that one sentence, clients came to me because I had the capacity—at least they and I thought I had it—to see reality. Now very little in the world I live in seems real, but I've got enough connection still to that lifelong sense of reality to recognize what all the signs around me mean."

The same waiter stood near them, raising a glass carafe of steaming coffee, the silent gesture asking, "More?"

"No thanks," Byron said. "Do you want more, sweetie?"

She shook her head.

Byron said, "Check, please, sir."

The hairy-chested Greek waiter took the check out of his shirt pocket and set it upright on the table between a salt shaker and a slender glass vase containing three plastic roses.

She took her scarf from the back of her chair and gracefully draped it over her shoulders. "Look at me, Carlos. In the face."

He did.

"How can I help you?"

His words surprised him, but not her. "Stay with me."

# 29

THE TILED WALLS OF the Astor Place subway station were decorated with murals depicting beavers. Astor Place was named for John Jacob Astor, who had built his early fortune on the trapping of beavers and other wildlife, making an industry out of the sale of animal furs. These murals, Byron thought as he walked over the platform toward the turnstiles, commemorated the slaughter of millions of innocent animals, and now they looked like cute pictures in a children's book. Not the first time, Byron thought, that systematic slaughter had over time become trivialized. Once beyond the turnstile, he trotted up the worn iron steps that led to the wide Astor Place plaza.

He came to street level facing the Cooper Union building. Built with brownstone in the early nineteenth century, it was the place where Abraham Lincoln delivered his anti-slavery speech before he became president. The stone looked porous. A new, all-glass building, itself constructed with cube-shaped walls, stood at the far side of Astor Place on a space long occupied by an outdoor parking lot. On the streets around Byron were hundreds of young people moving quickly in the brisk late autumn air.

Byron walked south on Lafayette Street, passing the Public Theatre building. Long pennants were suspended from the upper floor of the building. One advertised *The Merchant of Venice*. Two stories high, the pennant bore a sketch of the familiar, now aging face of Al Pacino. Years earlier, in the mid-seventies, Byron had brought a date to the Public Theater to see Raul Julia—dynamic, bold-eyed, young—play Macbeth. Joseph Papp was in the small audience, near the stage, as was Al Pacino. Papp's frizzy hair, shaped in an Afro, glowed in the theater lighting. Byron could remember Raul Julia, Joseph Papp, and Al Pacino from that night, but he could not remember the woman he'd brought with him. He did recall crossing Lafayette Street with her after the play, going into the Colonnade Building and having dinner in a restaurant known as Lady Astor. It had a dark and seductive bar and wall coverings that were really velvet theater curtains; they were blood-red and a little frayed. The waiters were aspiring actors. It was one of the few times in his life that Byron got drunk. He remembered the glow of innumerable bottles behind the bar and the reflection of his own handsome face in the mirror behind the rows of bottles.

Now there was a Thai restaurant, Boontang, in the space where Lady Astor had been. The tall windows between the Doric columns of the Colonnade Building were filled with bamboo trees, not the velvet curtains of the long-closed Lady Astor.

Fifteen minutes later, after a fast walk along Eighth Street to the West Village, he entered the quiet precincts of Waverly Place. He pressed the grimy buzzer to Simeon Black's apartment. At the same time, he pushed open the lobby door. The buzzer sounded, but the lock had stopped working years ago. He stepped quickly up the one flight of stairs and opened the door to the apartment.

Early in his relationship with Simeon Black he had decided to just let go of what he knew. He felt that if he shared the information he had with another person, and broke his isolation, he might find some protection in that. He had restrained himself from telling Christina everything. He loved her, he admired her maturity and intelligence (and took delicious pleasure in her body and her presence), but something in his breeding or character or experience in life made him resist the temptation to tell her all he had learned about Ali Hussein, his heavy-faced and heavy-set brother, the judge, the prosecutors, the Imam in the mosque on Raymond Boulevard in Newark, and the passages from the *Koran*. She appeared to find it all exciting, but there were limits to what he wanted to share with her.

Not so with Simeon Black. Byron continued to believe, despite what he had learned about the unpredictability of journalists, that providing Simeon with what he had learned over the last six months gave him some protection in a world he knew was increasingly treating him as some bizarre outcast, a man who had been hijacked by some defect of his own character or by a misguided, or even demented, sense of justice. If he gave Simeon Black the truth, then there might be a credible person to bear witness for him. And so far, the drafts he'd seen of the article Simeon was writing gave Byron confirmation of his own hope. Simeon's working title was *America at War with Itself*.

"Holy shit," Simeon said, smiling, after hearing Byron tell him about the wire transfers, "it's like missing the winning lottery by one number."

"Imagine what we could have done with it. We could have lived out that scene at the end of *Casablanca* where Rick and Captain Reynaud walk into the desert and look forward to a beautiful friendship."

Smiling, Simeon drew one of his unfiltered Gauloises out of its blue cellophane package. After lighting it, he snapped the match downward once and the flame went out.

"Sy, how many of those do you think you've had over the years?"

"Probably fifty-two million dollars' worth."

"We could be rich."

"Who did you say this agent is?"

"He pronounces it Na-Shat-Ka. He didn't spell it for me, I didn't ask. He tried to hand me his card. I didn't take it."

"Was it Jesse Ventura?"

Byron laughed. "Who's on first? Who's on third? No, it wasn't Jesse. This one was younger. But the same type of presence, only younger. The spawn of the devil."

Simeon Black was not as open with Byron as Byron was with him. He needed information from Byron, not Byron's protection. "I had a friend take some pictures of Jesse Ventura this week," he said. He didn't use the name Andrew Hurd.

Intrigued, Byron looked directly at Simeon, who turned the computer screen in his direction. The screen filled with a tableau of ten pictures. In that array—five on top, five under them—not one of the pictures was large enough to be seen clearly. Simeon clicked the trackball on the computer, and the first picture came forward enlarged, filling the screen.

It was Jesse Ventura. "Look at the devil," Byron said, whistling between his teeth.

"Do you see who he's with?"

In the picture, Jesse Ventura was opening the door to a modern office building, so much like the entrance to the Seagram Building that Byron searched the background of the picture to find any familiar object or sign. There was nothing definitive.

"Who is it?" Byron asked.

"Don't you watch TV?"

"No, it's on all the time but I don't watch. I worry I'll see myself. Complete with a turban and the dangling wires of a homemade bomb. House counsel to al-Qaeda."

"It's interesting, the company Jesse keeps. The blonde is a television star. She's created an aura for herself as an anti-Muslim prophet. She's also a professor of Islamic studies at Stanford."

"Maybe Jesse Ventura has charms we can only guess at."

Simeon passed through six more pictures. On the miraculous computer, they began as tiny images and instantly came forward with absolute clarity as they filled the screen.

Simeon said, "And he seems to keep company only with gorgeous women."

Another picture blossomed on the screen. In it, Christina Rosario was leaning forward toward Hurd at a table in a restaurant. Her face had that vital animation that had attracted Byron since that moment at the Central Park Zoo when she had first approached him.

Byron barely flinched. Simeon may have sensed some slight tensing up. Simeon asked, "Who is she?"

"Let's take a look at the next one."

There were no other pictures of her.

In Simeon Black's bathroom were the usual objects of old New York City bathrooms. None of that chrome and marble of modern bathrooms. The toilet, the sink, the bathtub were all made of bloated ceramic with spidery and faint veins and cracks on the surface. There were separate faucets for hot and cold water. The floor had chipped small tiles in a black and white pattern. There was grime between the tiles.

Even in that cold room, Byron was sweating. He bent over the sink and splashed cold water on his face.

And then he let himself slip down to the cool tile on the bathroom floor. "What," he said out loud, "what have I done to my life?"

# 30

Simeon had long ago learned to ignore the twice-daily rumble of sound in the stairwell. Harry and Jack, two sweet gay men who had recently celebrated their fiftieth anniversary together, went up and down the narrow squeaking stairwell at least four times each day, usually to walk their two Shih-Tzus, Wobbie and Oliver. The men—both big blonds from the Midwest—were always together. When they navigated the stairs to their apartment just above Simeon's, they jostled against the walls. Harry, once a stage dancer in Broadway musicals, who wore a cravat around his neck every day of the year, had developed diabetes. Because of the disease, he recently had two toes removed, and he often stumbled. Jack held him up, talking to him at times in an encouraging tone as if he were a parent urging on a child just learning to walk: "Good for you, you can do it."

Simeon looked up from his writing. He had been editing his article with a pencil he had just sharpened. He held the pencil aloft as he waited for the rumble to pass from the landing in front of his apartment. But this time the sound was suspended. Simeon thought that something might have happened to them.

Then the door, always unlocked, burst inward. Two black men in winter street clothes—sagging corduroy pants, puffy winter jackets that made them look like the figure in the Michelin tire commercials, basketball-player sneakers, and those big baseball-style caps too large for their heads—rushed into the apartment and raced toward Simeon from different directions. Simeon instinctively pushed backward in his wooden chair. As the chair toppled over, he shouted, "Please don't hurt me. Please."

# 31

HAL RANA WAS ONE of the few Assistant U.S. Attorneys with a window in his office in the drab 1970s-era building at St. Andrew's Plaza. Most of the other lawyers had interior offices with no windows, no natural light, and no view. He could see the glorious span of the Brooklyn Bridge. In clear sunlight, as on this cold day, the multitude of intricate steel cords that held the bridge in space glinted like millions of bright filaments.

He was surprised when one of the U.S. Marshals at the security barricades in the lobby told him over the house intercom that Byron Carlos Johnson wanted to see him. There was a rule in the office that unscheduled visits weren't allowed. It was called the Wizard of Oz rule: look what happened to the Wizard when he let Dorothy, Toto, the Tin Man, the Scarecrow, and the Cowardly Lion enter his domain without an invitation. The curtain was opened by the dog, and the Wizard was revealed as a fraud.

But Hal Rana was senior enough, and given his size and bearing, potent enough, that these house rules didn't apply to him. When he heard the slow South Carolina drawl of U.S. Marshal Vernon Claridge, a retired Army sergeant, on the security phone saying, "There's a fella here calling himself Mr. Byron Johnson says he wants to see you, sir." Hal responded, "Does he look dangerous to you, Sarge?"

He heard Claridge, a deep-voiced and genial man, say, "Mr. Johnson, are you dangerous?" In the muffled pause, Hal heard Claridge and Johnson laugh. Claridge then said, chuckling, "Says he's Peter Pan."

"Let him through, Sarge."

Another rule of the house was that lawyers never met alone with visitors, even the invited ones. And this was known as the Rule of the Two. None of the meetings inside the U.S. Attorney's Office was ever recorded. Recordings were a mine field. A recording of a conversation could reveal words and intonations of the government lawyers and agents that they didn't want anybody to hear later. Recordings could also capture a suspect's confessions, but if the government wanted to use that confession, it would have to produce the full tape or video, including what the agent and government lawyers themselves said. But with two or more lawyers and agents in the room with the visitor and no recording device operating, it was possible later to correct memories or harmonize and coordinate them. The Rule of the Two was that two memories, particularly those of two or more government agents, trumped one.

But the rule didn't necessarily apply to Hal Rana, any more than the rule against uninvited visitors. He put on his suit jacket, a deep and lustrous blue, as elegant in its own way as his carefully wrapped turban. He took the elevator down the four floors from his office to the lobby, gave a hand signal to indicate that he recognized the visitor (two quick fingers snapped downward, like the signal from a baseball catcher), and said as he shook Byron's hand, "What can I do for you?"

"Let's talk, Mr. Rana."

After silently riding the elevator, he took Byron Johnson through the last security barrier—an ugly steel reinforced door on the fourth floor that led into the warren of offices. The walls were lined with bankers' boxes containing documents. It was obvious that the file rooms were overloaded, so the hallways had been overtaken with case files.

There was one small visitor's chair in the office. Byron sat on it. "You wanted to see me," Byron said. The calm tone of his voice surprised him, for in the two hours since he saw Christina Rosario's picture, his mouth had become parched. He had a thirst that all the bottled water he drank couldn't quench.

"We got your attention, I see, Byron."

"Don't *Byron* me, Mr. Rana. You could have picked up the phone and called me. I don't appreciate having goons walk up to my girlfriend on the Columbia campus and me on a downtown street to pass along messages."

As always, Hal Rana sounded polite, calm, and deliberate. "You know the problem. Telephone calls can leave an unexpected residue, so to speak, and email and letters can live longer than the half-life of nuclear waste. Face-to-face contact is still the best way to operate."

Byron paused. He reached back into his experience to rely on the wisdom of creating silence to let the other person speak. You learned more that way, and, as he reminded himself, he was here to learn more.

Rana said, "We—you and I—have the privilege of working on the most important case in the country. Unless O. J. Simpson goes on trial again."

Even in a folding chair—and even when his feelings were consumed by anxiety, jealousy, fear, and hurt—Byron Johnson looked comfortable. And he continued to wait.

"Let me tell you what's on our mind. We're concerned because we don't know whether you're in deeply over your head, or profoundly naïve and trusting, or whether you know what you're doing is criminal. We don't know whether you recognize that the messages from the *Koran* you have been carrying from and to Hussein are coded to correlate to account numbers of banks in which he controlled funds for al-Qaeda. The money was collected from mosques all over the United States. The funds—and we think there are many, many millions because he was doing this since the first World Trade Center bombing in 1993 and until the time he was taken down in Bonn—have been dormant for the years he's been in detention. Only he knows the secret. He doesn't want to die with it. He wants to get the word out to the people who need to know. But for years he's had a problem: there's no way for him to do that. He's isolated. He's frustrated. The Imam isn't isolated, but he's frustrated. And then you come into Ali's world, the first person he's spoken to in years except for one solo agent, who learned nothing. Your client is a very smart man with an uncanny memory. And dedicated. We think he knows the account numbers. The verses in the *Koran* hold the key."

Byron shifted ever so slightly in his chair, but his expression, attentive and serious, didn't change. *Go on*, he thought, *tell me more.*

And Hal Rana did. "We've learned from other sources that he is very sincere, almost sweet. An appealing person, obedient, respectful. He may have taken you in, or you may have been so taken by his personality that you willingly turned a blind eye—let's call it conscious disregard of the truth—to assist him."

Byron put two fingers to the side of his face, an elegant and thoughtful gesture, a gesture that invited more words from Hal Rana.

"We can't think of any legitimate purpose for your visits to the mosque in Newark. Or for your face-to-face encounters with Khalid Hussein."

This was one of those rare times in his life that Hal Rana was becoming uncomfortable. He turned from Byron's steady gaze. He looked again through the narrow window in his office. The dazzling structure of the Brooklyn Bridge appeared to float above the East River, the river's surface itself on silver fire in the sunlight.

"The issue, Byron, is whether you want to help us. And help yourself. We won't ask you to explain the inexplicable passage of $52 million through your account, and for now we won't ask you where it went. But we will ask you to continue to work with, or on, your client. He trusts you, Byron. The word is that you're a man who inspires trust."

"You realize, Mr. Rana, that you're asking me to violate the element of trust in my relationship with my client."

Still looking through the window at the brilliant scene outside, Hal Rana said, "That can't really matter to you, Byron. Hussein has provided the lifeblood of money to men who bomb innocent people, commit spectacular acts of hatred. He now wants to loosen up the flow of more of that lifeblood. He knows where the money is, and he's using you to lead his brothers to it. It won't be used to fund the producers of *Sesame Street*."

Even for Byron Johnson, the urge to ask a question was irresistible: "What do you want me to do?"

"First, give us the correct verses that you've been scrambling recently. Why did you put out misinformation? The algorithms our people are developing to locate the banks and accounts from the book, chapter, and verse numbers have fallen apart with the new numbers you're sending to the Imam. We assume you got some sense of what was happening and you decided not to pass along information your client gave you, just to test the waters, so to speak, and see what happened. And you did a good job at that. We're out of whack now, and the brothers are suspicious, and the Imam and his friends are growing restive. They're beginning to get agitated."

"And?"

"And spend more time with your client. He devotes his days to looking forward to seeing you. He has developed a passion for you. He believes you. Continue to cultivate that. He thinks you are an honorable man, so honorable he would never suspect that you were doing anything for him other than giving him legal advice and religious solace. Tell him the date for his trial is coming up soon. Lie to him: tell him that once the trial starts you'll be able to see him less often, not more. He'll accelerate the pace of messages he wants you to carry. The more messages, the clearer the picture we get. We think we're not far from striking gold."

"And?"

"And wear a wire. There's likely to be information other than the *Koran* verses in what he says that will be meaningful to us."

Byron couldn't resist the next question: "Why should I do this?"

Hal Rana looked at him. "Why? To save your life, Byron. Your friends in Newark are planning to kill you when they get all the information they need from you, or if they think you're giving them garbage. They may even get the notion that you're trying to use the information for yourself. Think about it: we might not be the only people who know that millions of dollars passed through your account and skipped off somewhere into the world." Hal Rana paused. "Or they may think you are already working for us, on the dark side. Or Khalid Hussein may believe you set him up to slash that face he loves so much."

"What else?"

"If you work with us, we'll protect you."

"And if I don't?"

"We won't protect you. And we'll let the judge know we have a grand jury that is about to indict you for assisting terrorism."

Byron rose from the folding chair. "Let me help you, Mr. Rana. I'm an older guy than you and I've been around in the world for a long time. You need to know something about yourself. You're an asshole."

# 32

WHEN THEY LEFT THE Thalia, the first snow of the season was descending in shimmering curtains through the street lamps at the corner of 95th Street and Broadway. It was crystalline and gorgeous, just enough to barely cover the parked cars and the sidewalks. The snow had brought the children of the neighborhood to the streets. The shriek of young voices. In the adults, the wonder at the renewal of the snow, the coming of winter.

Byron took Christina Rosario's hand, as if to steady her on the glistening sidewalk. They had just finished watching *The Third Man*, the Orson Welles movie Byron had first seen when he was a teenager, in Paris on one of his brief visits to his parents, probably in 1965. Christina had never seen the movie. The opening scenes of cold and steel-gray Vienna, just after the Second World War, and the unforgettable zither music, had brought Byron to watch the movie at least ten times over the years. At the outset of the film, Orson Welles as Harry Lime had staged his own death, assisted by a team of effeminate and evasive Romanians and Hungarians, so that they could continue trafficking in adulterated and deadly vaccines. Joseph Cotton, mourning the lost Harry Lime, continued to believe in him until he saw children in the hospital crippled by the adulterated vaccine Harry distributed. He then discovered that Harry was alive and helped to hunt him down in the Vienna sewer system. In the last scene, the fingers of the shot and dying Harry Lime gripped the rails of a manhole cover on a Viennese *strasse* as he futilely attempted to lift the cover off.

"What a great movie," Christina said. "Thanks for bringing me, Carlos."

"And next week I'll take you to *The Maltese Falcon* downtown."

They walked three blocks west to Riverside Drive and then uptown to Christina's apartment at the familiar corner of Riverside Drive and 116th Street. To their left, the park shone in the darkness as snow fell through the bare branches. Ghostly, seductive. She let go of his hand and held onto his arm, walking as if in an embrace. As the snow created an evanescent veil on her hair, he felt the overwhelming pang of his love for her. He found himself wanting these times he had spent with her to last forever.

They didn't turn on the lights in the apartment. The whiteness outside suffused the rooms with a faint glow. They stood at the windows overlooking the park. The upper branches of the trees were covered with snow. The trunks of the trees and the bare shrubs were etched in black against the snow on the ground. There was less snow on the winding walkways, and there were already footprints in it. The old-fashioned street lamps in the park were surrounded by white halos as the snow swept downward. Further west, two or three barely visible tugboats, their red lights shining steadily, moved on the Hudson River.

Crazy with desire for her, Byron touched her shoulder. He inhaled the chill odor of snow that had freshened her face and hair, and with it the smell of her skin. She kissed him, and then her tongue caressed his tongue. In a swift gesture she shed her shirt. Byron lifted his turtleneck sweater over his head. Skin touching skin, they embraced. Even while they stood at the window, he kissed the upright nipples of her beautiful breasts, holding them in his hands.

In her bedroom—itself very familiar to him (the odors, the placement of furniture, books, and lamps)—he stroked the folds of her vagina first with his fingers and next with his tongue before slipping his finger deep into its luxurious softness. She said, "Oh, Carlos," and shifted her body beneath him, beckoning him. He entered her. He fell into her luxuriousness. Thrusting, he made her move beneath him. Her breasts rose and fell, soft except for the erect nipples.

She signaled him by a slight movement to her left to roll onto his back. They managed to stay connected as she rose to her knees and looked down on him. As always in this position he felt he could not be more deeply buried in her. And her face, her breasts, her shoulders—all exposed to his view—rose above him. She moved her hips.

Then they neared that magic point when they knew they would soon come at the same time. They deftly exchanged positions. Byron rose high above her, accelerating his back-and-forth thrusting. Her moaning escalated to a scream. She squeezed her eyes shut. Her arms were spread out to her sides. Her fists were clenched.

He nailed her to her cross.

At three in the morning, he woke to a room that still shone in a ghostly white as the snow continued to fall. Christina slept deeply. Naked, Byron Johnson got up, found his wallet in his jacket, and went directly to the small room cluttered with books where she kept her computer. Even though he was habitually and deeply protective of other people's privacy, as well as of his own, he had once, for reasons he never understood, written down the lengthy password to her AOL account. He took from his wallet the worn slip of paper with her password. And now he entered the world of her Internet space.

He bypassed the many entries he was sure were the ordinary email traffic of a young woman who was a law student. He scrolled the blue bar down through dozens of entries, most of which were from screen names ending in *columbialaw.edu.*

But, as he sat naked in the glow from the computer screen, he noticed another recurrent suffix on the incoming and outgoing emails: *hotrocks.org.* He began clicking on those that had attachments. Christina kept a diary. It was about him, describing his conversations about his visits with Ali Hussein, the thoughts he expressed about strategy, and the research assignments on legal issues he gave her. There was no personal history about her relationship with him in the entries.

And there were other recurrent entries—every reference to the verses of the *Koran* he had ever written down in his visits to Ali Hussein and to the Imam. Christina had forwarded every one of those references to *fantasy7@hotrocks.com.*

Christina and Byron had active, inquisitive, and thoughtful minds. Byron once told her he had never paid as much attention in college to the subject of religion as he had to history, philosophy, and mathematics—the prevalent fare of colleges in the 1960s. She knew that since he began representing Ali Hussein, he had become a reader of the *Koran*, searching for meaning. He had told her several times that the text frustrated him—what was the divine message of all that language of war, of defending the faith, of the need to kill those who didn't embrace the faith? And what about messages of love, obedience, and rapture? They were elusive. They appeared from time to time as phrases surrounded by language about battle and revenge. Early in their relationship, he had shared his frustration—which he often attributed to the narrow scope of his boarding school and college education—with Christina. She bought and read books on the history of Islam and the messages of the *Koran*. There were times as they lay in bed when she read passages from serious books that dwelled on Islam.

Who was *fantasy7*?

Intrigued, suddenly nervous, he left the computer room—which had once been a utility closet in this big, old West Side apartment—and walked quietly through the long hallway to her bedroom. He checked to make sure she was still sleeping. She was.

Still naked and increasingly chilly but sensing that he had to hurry, Byron didn't even stop at the bathroom to urinate, although the urge was acute. He continued to scroll through Christina's computer, still opening only those entries for *fantasy7* that had an attachment. He went back into her emails to the date when they first began to send messages to each other. He found her first email to him—"So good to hear from you, Byron"—which she wrote at the end of that long week after he had sent his first email to her. He recalled those nights in his apartment in Tribeca when he incessantly glanced at his computer, nervous as he was now, waiting and hoping for a response from her.

Not long after he began the random process of opening the emails from her to *fantasy7@hotrocks.com* and from that address to her, an attachment emerged with an image that was some type of logo depicting a shield. He moved the cursor to the center of the shield and clicked. The new screen opened onto a video and audio recording of a scene in progress. There was a scan of what looked like a motel room, the style of room in which amateur porn videos were filmed. Suddenly there were voices, two men speaking. And then Jesse Ventura appeared, seated on the edge of a perfectly made motel bed. He was in a hot country. He wore a suit with the edge of a carefully shaped handkerchief showing in the jacket's pocket.

Byron heard Jesse Ventura ask a question, his tone almost pleasant, although Byron's mind was racing so fast that he couldn't in fact hear the exact words. The video image widened. Ali Hussein came into view, poised almost daintily on a chair next to a motel desk. He didn't answer. Excited, Byron cruised forward through the disk. At some points, he saw Jesse Ventura slap Hussein. At another point, he saw Hussein, naked, hairy, and frail, being forced into an overflowing bathtub by two men younger than Ventura.

Byron took a clean CD from the stack on Christina's desk. He had learned enough by now to sense that he shouldn't forward the email and its video attachment to his own computer because it would be intercepted. He tapped the side of the laptop, and a tray emerged. He placed the disk on the tray, gently pushed the tray into the magical interior of the machine, and reproduced the video. The muted whirring sound ended in five seconds.

He walked quickly down the hallway to the bedroom, holding the disk close to his body, as if protecting it. He had something he believed to be precious and irreplaceable, like a winning lottery ticket. Hamerindapal Rana had often told Byron, and had said in letters to Judge Goldberg, that the prosecution had no photographs, no records, and no images of Ali Hussein from all of his years in detention. No transcripts, no summaries of interrogations, no videos, no records. And, Rana had proclaimed, no physical assaults, no torture, and no enhanced interrogation techniques. It was as though Ali Hussein had spent years as a cipher with whom no one ever interacted.

Now Byron knew he had the disk that laid bare the lies.

The warm, seductive bedroom was darker than it had been when Byron had left it an hour-and-a-half earlier. The snow had stopped. With dawn only an hour away, the heavy iron radiators began to clang and tick as the heat rose from the furnaces in the basement of the building. It was deeper night outside now that there was no falling snow.

He put the disk carefully into the inner pocket of his jacket. Still asleep, Christina lay on her left side. He lifted the sheets and placed the front of his naked body against the back of her naked body. He draped his arm over her shoulder and put his hand on her right breast. His penis, aroused, rested in the cleft of her beautiful rear.

He wondered what insanity made him still crave her.

# 33

BY THE TIME BYRON came out of the subway station at nine, the snow had melted from the Manhattan streets and sidewalks, but it still clung to tree branches and the roofs of the low buildings in his neighborhood. He walked quickly along the four blocks between the station and his apartment, frequently touching the inner pocket of his coat and always finding the outline of the disk.

As soon as he entered the lobby of his building, Pedro, the engaging and gregarious doorman with diamond studs glistening in the lobes of his ears, pointed to two people seated in the lobby chairs. One was a man, obviously an Irish plainclothes cop, and the other a woman. She was obviously Puerto Rican. They recognized him.

They each displayed New York City detective shields. Byron felt a rush of anger.

The man said, "I'm Detective Garrity."

"Garrity? What a surprise. An Irish cop."

Garrity looked momentarily puzzled. And then he set his expression into a tough game face.

"Sergeant Cruz," the woman said.

Byron didn't acknowledge her.

Garrity said, "Simeon Black is dead."

"Sy Black?" For a moment Byron had that out-of-control feeling that he was going to fall. He took a deep breath. "He's dead?"

"Yeah," Garrity said. "Murdered."

"How do you know that?" Byron hadn't heard a radio or seen a newspaper since he woke in the quiet of Christina's bedroom.

"We just left his place. A nine-one-one call came in at five. Our forensic guys are still there."

"How did this happen?"

"Don't know for sure. Looks like knives."

"Jesus," Byron said. "My God."

Byron turned away from Garrity. He was upset, profoundly weak, and dizzy. He glanced at Pedro, who was all intense attention but who only knew that the people talking to elegant, friendly, generous Byron Carlos Johnson were cops. Byron didn't want to fall and didn't want to dissolve into tears and trembling.

He turned again to Garrity and Cruz. They stared at him. Cruz's face was round; she had small eyes, painted-on eyebrows, and a faint sprinkling of freckles on her dark cheeks. She said, "Let's go up to your apartment to talk."

Byron focused first on the tough-girl Bronx accent and then on her words. "That is not going to happen."

"Why not?" Garrity asked. "Don't you want to help?"

Byron said nothing.

Cruz said, "He was a friend of yours, wasn't he?"

"I knew him. He is a very famous man. Many people knew him. Go see them."

"See, the problem, Mr. Johnson," Garrity said, "is that maybe a million people knew him, but only *you* are on the security camera in the lobby of his building. The way we see it, you were there about the time he died, maybe a little later, maybe a little before."

"I visited him often. I'm probably on that security camera twenty times. There are probably fifteen people on the security camera yesterday."

Garrity said, "Not really, Mr. Johnson. There are the two old gents who live upstairs, and you. And then somebody smashed the camera."

"I don't break security cameras. And I don't harm people."

"So why," Cruz said, "don't you let us come on up? We won't hurt you."

"No."

Garrity asked, "Are you sure?"

"Is the Pope Catholic?"

"It doesn't help to get fresh with us," Cruz said.

"No, you're not coming up. And no, we're not talking any longer."

"We'll come back with a search warrant."

"Go ahead. I'll be here. I'm easy to find. You people seem to know where I am all the time, even in the bathroom. In the meantime, have the exits watched to see if I'm leaving with anything."

"For such a smart man," Garrity said, "it's amazing how stupid you are."


Byron Carlos Johnson was frantic when he reached his apartment. He wanted information about Simeon Black, and at the same time it was harrowing to absorb that the seventy-four-year-old man, whom he had grown to admire, whose apartment had come to feel like a safe refuge to Byron, was dead. Within seconds Byron brought up on his computer screen the online version of the *New York Times*.

Byron didn't have to navigate to the obituary page. The news about Simeon Black's killing was the lead story on the front page, just below an article about chaos in yet another Arab country. The article started with the same *who, what, when, where, and how* rule that Simeon said was the foundation of his business. "Simeon Black, the Pulitzer Prize-winning journalist and author, was murdered yesterday in his Greenwich Village apartment. He was 74."

Byron raced erratically through the long article. There were depictions of Sy's career. *Often ranked with I. F. Stone and David Halberstam as an iconic investigative journalist . . . His classic book on the secret invasion of Cambodia earned the Pulitzer Prize in 1971 . . . Simeon Herschel Black was born in the Bronx . . . He graduated from the Bronx High School of Science and Harvard . . . The first Jewish president of the Harvard Crimson . . . Married and divorced three times . . .*

And there were other passages in Byron's frenzied reading that arrested his attention. *Investigators described the incident as well-planned and not a random break-in . . . Mr. Black's computers and notebooks were taken . . . Several thousand dollars in cash, according to police sources, were left in the apartment . . . A security camera in the lobby, which had been operating during part of the day, was disabled . . .*

There was a sharply etched black-and-white picture of Simeon Black. Taken in the early seventies, it showed Sy with black horn-rimmed glasses, black hair just slightly overgrown and bushy in the style of the time, in a black suit with narrow lapels. Sy Black could never have known, Byron thought, when the picture was taken or at any other time, that this was the way his life would end. And Byron also thought that Sy Black's life had ended as it did because he had become a part of it, the messenger who brought death.

Byron had work to do. He reproduced three copies of the disk he had created at Christina's apartment. He put the three reproduced disks in separate envelopes. He addressed one of the envelopes to himself at his closed house on Monhegan Island in Maine. He addressed another one, with no return address on it, to Judge Justin Goldberg. And he addressed the final envelope to Simeon Black.

# 34

THE NEW FEDERAL OFFICE building at the corner of Broadway and Duane Street in lower Manhattan was five blocks from Ground Zero, now a raw excavation where the World Trade Center had once stood. The office building opened only three months after 9/11. On the building's inaugural day, the unimaginable debris still smoldered.

Andrew Hurd was there for the opening ceremony in December 2001, one of at least eighty agents providing security for President Bush, Mayor Giuliani, and the other clowns Andrew Hurd was convinced could never do what was necessary to exact revenge and make certain that the people responsible for this heinous act would be punished. Hurd, watchful of the crowd, could only glance at the people he was protecting. He was twenty feet from them. In real life, Bush was larger than Hurd had expected but had the self-satisfied look of a sneak, someone who had evaded service in the Army during the war in Vietnam and sipped beer on hot afternoons in the empty stands of a Texas Rangers game when he claimed to own that losing team. And, with his hair plastered over the top of his balding head, Giuliani looked like the comedian Bob Newhart, not a hero and not a commander.

Andrew Hurd had made certain when he scheduled this meeting with Hal Rana that Tom Nashatka was with him. Although Hurd had been required to incorporate Rana into his task force for political reasons, he had never trusted him and would have been more comfortable with another lead Assistant US Attorney. It wasn't so much Rana's silk turban that bothered Hurd. It was the deliberate, Anglicized diction the man maddeningly used and the expensive British suits so unlike the routine warehouse suits worn by other lawyers in the prosecutor's office.

Hurd had often wondered how a forty-year-old foreign-born lawyer earning a government salary of less than $100,000 a year could afford suits that must have cost several thousand dollars each. Hurd had free access to every item of information that the United States government had about Hal Rana and hundreds of thousands of other people living in America and around the world. He pulled up Rana's income tax returns and found that he had income from foreign investments five times larger than his salary. He was born in Sri Lanka, according to his immigration papers. His law school applications described his father as an investor living in London and Geneva. Although he was only forty, he had been married and divorced twice, once to a Jewish woman and once to the daughter of a British major. *Unreal bastard*, Andrew Hurd had often thought about Hal Rana.

He knew Hal Rana was cool to the point of toughness. He had the steady presence of Barack Obama. Hurd was sick of treating him like a holy guru. He was intent on breaking the back of that coolness. He asked, "Has the candy ass gotten back to you?"

"Johnson? No."

"Why do you think that is?"

"If I knew why people did or didn't do things, Mr. Hurd, then I would be in another line of work."

Hurd glanced at Tom Nashatka, who was observant and quiet, as though learning from a master. "Screw other lines of work. Let's talk about the work we're in. Tell me again what you told him."

"That unless he cooperated with us he will be indicted, arrested, and tried. That we believed he was passing messages from Ali Hussein to his Imam and taking messages from the Imam to Hussein. That he might be able to save himself if he persuaded his client, who trusts him, to tell him, or us, what he knows about millions of dollars held in bank accounts around the world."

"That sounds pleasant." Hurd paused. "It sounds like a nice, mannerly law school seminar."

"We're both lawyers."

Andrew Hurd pounded his right hand on the table. The sound was as abrupt as a gunshot. Seated across the heavy table, Hal Rana visibly winced. No one had ever done anything like this to him.

"Listen up, Mr. Rana. Our people finally located one of the accounts at a bank in Canada. Yesterday afternoon I got in touch with the Canadians. Thirty minutes later the money was gone."

"Where?"

"I don't know. Somewhere. You tell me."

Hal Rana said, "What are you saying?"

"You had a chance to squeeze the bastard and scare the shit out of him. You fucked up."

"I'm a lawyer, Mr. Hurd. I did all I could do to make it clear that he was in grave jeopardy. I gave him the option we usually give to people who can help us get information. That if he cooperated with us he would save himself a world of pain."

"World of pain? What bullshit. What really happened in that room?"

"I don't know what you're asking me." His voice was quiet, but for the first time in his life, that voice trembled.

"What am I talking about? What I'm talking about is this. I tell you to meet with him. I tell you to do everything to get information from him. You meet. A few hours later, just as we're about to freeze an account, someone pulls the trigger and the money flies out. You either fucked up or you're as much of a wise guy as Mr. Johnson. Which is it?"

Hal Rana had been flattered months earlier when he was selected to lead the legal team spearheading the prosecution in a civilian court of the first accused terrorist brought to the United States. He was told at the time that President Obama, intrigued by having a Harvard Law graduate who was a Sikh lead the prosecution, personally approved his selection. He had been pleased, too, when he met face to face with the Attorney General to sanction the decision to seek the death penalty for Ali Hussein.

"Now I understand, Mr. Hurd." Despite his nervousness, that unaccustomed tension in the core of his body that made his voice and his hands shake, he stared at Andrew Hurd. It was as if this was the first time in all the hours they had spent together that he actually saw him. Hurd had the steady, unblinking eyes and the solid face of a Marine. As Hal Rana instinctively knew,

Andrew Hurd was excitable, dangerous; there was no end to his hatred and his tenacity.

"I don't care what you understand, Mr. Rana."

"So," Hal Rana said, "if you don't care that I don't understand anything, that I fucked up, as you put it, that I'm not as hardcore as you, why don't I just call the Attorney General and tell him to get me off this case?"

"You know too much, Mr. Rana. I never thought you had what this needed, but I got stuck with you. And now you're stuck with me. You work for me, not Mr. Fucking Attorney General."

"I think I'll leave now, Mr. Hurd. You need a chance to calm down."

Hurd lunged out of his chair and reached a powerful arm across the table. He cut the air just in front of Hal Rana's eyes; it was a figurative, slashing warning. "Don't use that haughty bullshit on me."

Rana glanced at Nashatka, as if believing Nashatka would help him, just as a boy being beaten up on a playground imagines that the other boys who are watching will help him, and no one does.

"I want you to use your smooth Eaton style to get Goldberg to sign a search warrant for the Imam's mosque in Newark."

"A mosque? Goldberg will never let you seize a mosque."

"You will put together affidavits from agents saying we have reason to believe there are either weapons in the mosque or information there as to where the weapons are. And you will tell the judge we need to seize all the mosque's financial records."

"Why would the Imam be so stupid as to have guns and rifles in his mosque?"

"He doesn't."

"So you want me to lie to a federal judge?"

"I want you to do what I tell you to do. There are pieces of information out there, Mr. Rana, that are finally starting to coalesce. Johnson has some of the pieces, I have some of the pieces, the fucking Imam has some of them, and Simeon Black had some of them."

"Simeon Black?"

"The writer, Byron Johnson's old girlfriend."

"What did Black have?"

"Resources. He was a safe-keeper for Byron Johnson's knowledge and Ali Hussein's secrets. Byron whispered sweet nothings to Simeon that he never whispered to Christina Rosario."

"And how do you know this?"

"We took down the two brothers who murdered Mr. Black. They were trying to fence his computers."

"Where are these people now?"

"I have them."

"Where?"

"Never mind where, Mr. Rana." Hurd stood up. "Same place I have you, Mr. Rana."

# 35

KHALID HUSSEIN SAW THE six black Chevy SUVs, all unmarked but somehow unmistakably police vehicles, as they parked at the rear gate of the mosque. Two of the cars blocked the exit to Raymond Boulevard. At least fifteen men stepped out of the vehicles, several of them in blue blazers, others in jackets with the words "Homeland Security" or the letters "FBI" on the back. Other men in Army-style uniforms, wearing vests and carrying rifles, suddenly appeared from the rear door of an unmarked van.

Khalid Hussein turned from the window, started to run down the gleaming hallway toward the Imam's office, and stopped. He simply waited. There was no time to do anything. Within seconds, the men carrying M-16s were in the hallway.

"On the ground. Face down. On the ground. Now. Fast, fast."

Slowly, Khalid Hussein fell to his knees, instinctively raising his hands in front of him to show he had nothing in them.

"*Fast, fast, down, down,*" a single commanding voice shouted.

As soon as he was on the floor, his arms spread out in front of him, he felt the painful push and pressure of boots on his back. Powerful hands reached down to pull his hands backward and lock plastic handcuffs tightly on his wrists.

Tom Nashatka knew from surveillance that, by this time of the morning, the Imam had finished his prayers and was in the windowless inner office. The thickly padded door to that office was locked. Nashatka pounded on the door with the palm of his hand, but the padding absorbed the strikes as though he were punching a mattress.

He signaled to one of the armed agents, a black man with the size and presence of one of Tom's drill sergeants when he was a Navy Seal. Intense and perspiring even on this cold day, the man hit the doorknob with the stock of his M-16 rifle. Struck only once, the doorknob fell off.

As planned, two of the armed men entered the Imam's sanctuary before Tom did. The Imam, smaller and more slender than Nashatka had expected, stood up calmly. In English, he said, "Who are you?"

Nashatka shouted, *"Down, get down, get down. Now."* He and Hurd had decided before this raid that they would treat the Imam just as they would treat anyone else who was in a building during the execution of a search warrant. They would apply shock and awe.

For a moment, the Imam remained on his knees, plainly defiant. Tom pushed him face down. The Imam's glasses fell to his side, and a booted foot crushed them as one of Tom's crew members fastened plastic handcuffs to the man's wrists.

As soon as he learned that only two people were in the mosque, Tom sent a signal to the outside that the building was secure. Armed officers pulled Khalid and the Imam, still handcuffed, to separate rooms; they were forced to sit on the floor. Each was guarded by three armed men.

By that point, more than twenty men and women in windbreakers stamped with "Police" in big lettering fanned out through the entire building. At the apex of the central dome was a curved skylight, and from it stark light filled all the circular hallways. Because of that light, and even though it was early morning, every object in the building was vividly illuminated.

They worked like archaeologists at a new site. Wearing latex gloves, they sifted everything—religious artifacts, teapots, desks, papers. The search warrant Justin Goldberg had signed gave them permission "to seize and take all records, including bank statements, ledgers, and account books, that related in any way to financial transactions." The warrant broadened the scope of records to include all computers and all "devices for the electronic collection and transmission of information." The warrant also gave them authority to seize all weapons of any kind. And the warrant directed them to seize and take all religious texts, defining "texts" to include the *Koran*, the *Upanishads*, the Bible, and handwritten sermons, "among other things," that expansive catch-all that essentially let Nashatka and his agents take anything they wanted.

For Tom Nashatka, the highest, most exciting moments in a search were at the start, the instant of entry, the adrenaline high of not knowing who was just on the other side of the door and what their reaction might be. He loved the sense of danger, as well as the intense solidarity among him and the armed men, and sometimes women, in his crew.

After the entry and lockdown, the rest of the search was, for Tom, a long ritual of watching the agents collect things, write down a shorthand description of each item, place hospital-style plastic identification tags on them, and store them in big cardboard boxes. There were hundreds of boxes, all neatly stacked. From time to time, someone approached Tom with something—a document or an ornament or a piece of clothing—to ask whether it should be taken. Tom's crews liked him. He had a standard joke line whenever they asked the question, "Should we take this?" He always answered, "Falls within the scope of the subpoena. Toilet paper falls within the scope of the subpoena. Put it on the inventory sheet and crate it."

At noon, jackhammers began to destroy the colorful inlaid tile on the floor beneath the towering skylight in the mosque's central hall. Translucent columns of dusty debris rose to the skylight like smoke. Within three minutes, the excavation uncovered the tops of coffin-sized metal containers. They were located exactly where Tom Nashatka had been told to expect them. They were brought to the surface by winches and cataloged by Nashatka himself on the inventory sheet. *Three tin boxes.*

# 36

FOR MONTHS, BYRON CARLOS Johnson had kept on night and day the flat-screen television in the high-ceilinged main room of his apartment. He had rarely watched television over the years. The first television set he ever saw was in the master's room in his dorm at Groton, when he was thirteen; it was a circular Zenith with an unmanageable rabbit-ear antenna. By eight each night, the master was so obliterated by whiskey that Byron and the other boys could watch the set for hours while the lost forty-year-old man slept in the next room. Byron could still recall and hum the theme songs of the television Westerns that so engrossed him—*Johnny Yuma the Rebel* ("He searched this land, this restless land, he was panther quick and leather tough and he figured that he'd been pushed enough, the rebel, Johnny Yuma"), *Have Gun Will Travel* ("Paladin, Paladin, where do you roam?"), *Texas John Slaughter* ("Texas John Slaughter made 'em do what they oughta and if they didn't they died"). Byron now realized that the shows he remembered were the ones in which a brave and lonely man confronted a hostile world.

In the three weeks since Simeon Black's killing, Byron had left his apartment only rarely, for groceries, newspapers, and the unfiltered cigarettes he had resumed smoking because they calmed him and because Simeon had smoked them. He also went out for three visits to the Metropolitan

Detention Center to visit Ali Hussein. He had even spent two nights in Christina Rosario's apartment, where she was wakeful and restless and nervous, limiting Byron's ability to search for more information—computer files, written notes, her law school papers—that might help him. "Carlos," she said on one of the visits, "why the one-night stands? Did you forget who I am?"

"I'm working," he said, "on a major brief for Ali. I think the expression is that I'm about to throw a Hail Mary pass."

"Let me help you with it."

"Later," he answered. "Later. Concentrate on your school-work. That article for the law review must be due, and exams are coming."

Years of practicing law had made Byron Johnson a dedicated writer. Very few lawyers were Perry Mason, who appeared to live in court and never spent time in his office or even at home. The fact was that even for a lawyer like Byron Johnson, long a big firm litigator with many cases going at all times, the real work consisted of meetings, writing letters and legal briefs, and research. It was almost monastic work.

Byron wrote in longhand. At the end of each day—or in the morning when, as often happened, he spent the night writing—he made two copies of each page on the copier in his apartment. He put the copies in separate envelopes. He addressed one of the envelopes to his post office box on Monhegan Island. He took the other to the bank on West Broadway where he had safe deposit boxes. Each day he shredded the original papers. To prevent people from finding anything in his garbage, he dropped the shredded papers like confetti in three or four garbage cans along the way.

Byron thought of his writing as a testament. It was a testament for Simeon Black. It was a testament for himself. It was also a quarry out of which he intended to send information to people at newspapers, magazines, Internet news services, and television networks whose names Simeon had mentioned to him as reporters he admired.

This was Byron's Hail Mary pass. His mother was Catholic; he often heard her say when they were together, *Hail Mary, full of grace . . .*

Byron paused at eight, after three hours of concentrated writing. He had started just as the winter night was falling, darkening the tall windows of his apartment. When his concentration lifted, he walked around the apartment, stretching.

The television in the living room was on. Displayed on the screen was a vivid scene of a building he knew well: the mosque at Raymond Boulevard and Broad Street in Newark. The zipper message on the screen read: *Mosque Raided, Floor Dug Up, Thousands of Documents Seized.*

Byron noticed at the bottom of the screen the name of the woman speaking before he focused on her. *Kimberly Smith, Stanford University, Terrorism Expert.* And instantly, Byron recognized the woman. She was the striking blonde whose pictures Simeon Black had displayed on his computer screen. In one of the pictures, Kimberly Smith was with Christina Rosario. In several of the pictures Kimberly Smith was with Jesse Ventura and with Tom Nashatka in others.

In a strong, articulate voice, Kimberly Smith said: "There is nothing wrong, Bill, with the government investigating terrorists to protect this country. It could have been a church, synagogue, cathedral."

Bill O'Reilly said, "And what about drilling holes in the floor?"

"Look, Bill, nobody drilled holes in anyone's head, although law enforcement could have found more information in minds than in floors."

"What about the ACLU screaming foul?" O'Reilly asked.

"They scream over taking off shoes at security gates. We have dedicated law enforcement men and women. Those are the people who need our protection."

*And you are people*, Byron thought, *who live on fear and hate*.

# 37

"THE ROOM IS SECURE," Justin Goldberg said, "and the court reporter is on the record. Counsel, state your appearances."

"Hamerindapal Rana, for the United States. With me are Helen Gardner and Bart Stone, both Assistant U.S. Attorneys."

"Byron Johnson for defendant Ali Hussein."

Justin Goldberg was, as usual, crisp and business-like. "Let the record reflect that I initiated this conference. I did so because I received from an anonymous source, by mail, in an envelope with no return address and with postage stamps, a disk containing a video. It is that video's content that has caused me to call this conference."

Justin Goldberg held up the disk by its edge. It glinted momentarily. "The video on this disk reflects events involving the defendant."

Justin Goldberg paused, staring at Hal Rana. Byron had long ago learned that it was often more important to watch than it was to act. He waited.

"I'm disturbed. Let me tell the government, to which I will give a copy of this disk, that I want a written explanation of why this video was not disclosed by the United States to the court so that the court could evaluate whether to turn the video over to the defense or treat it as national security material."

Hal Rana made a mistake. He said, "I knew nothing about a video depicting Mr. Hussein."

Curt, icy, and imperious as a god, Justin Goldberg said, "Be careful, Mr. Rana. I will continue to pay careful attention to this. You shouldn't comment on this until the government investigates and provides the explanation I require. Listen carefully. Who other than the defendant is on the video? What were their duties? Where was this taken. When? Why? Who had custody of the video? To whom were copies given?"

Hal Rana made another mistake. "Your Honor, can we ask Mr. Johnson whether he has seen a video with his client in it?"

"No, no, no," Justice Goldberg said. "At the moment Mr. Johnson doesn't concern me. You concern me. Mr. Johnson didn't make the video. You did. If I have issues with Mr. Johnson, I will reach them soon."

Justin Goldberg waved his hand as if brushing lint from his suit. It was a gesture of dismissal. Byron Johnson was the first to stand and first to leave. His heart raced. Almost incredibly, Justin Goldberg was showing independence and courage. He had not just tossed away or ignored the disk Byron had anonymously mailed to him.

For the first time in many weeks, he was happy.

# 38

COLD FOG. THE OLD wood of the rambling house never lost the chill of Maine. The wood—the sea-washed shingles and the broad planks on the outside porches and floors throughout the house—always had the same pine scent as the trees on the island's rocky soil. Foghorns regularly sounded from the points of the island, the recurring resonance of warning and reassurance. Byron had seen only two other houses on the island with lights on as he and Christina had sat, three hours earlier, inside the stripped-down passenger compartment of the old ferry on one of the three passages it made each week in the winter from the mainland.

"My God, Carlos," Christina said. "Why do you ever leave this place?"

"I've been coming here since I was nine. In the summers the island is hot in the day, cool every night. The sky was always clear. High Maine weather. Those were usually the only times each year when we spent fourteen continuous days and nights together. My father's father was still alive then. A poetry-quoting Boston lawyer who, of course, loved to sail. Sailing was an addiction of upper-class Bostonians with summer houses on the coast of Maine. As much of an addiction of that class as the gin martinis. I loved him, and loved sailing. I spent more time with him than with my mom and dad. Out on the sea. Sunlight and sea spray. Even twelve miles out you can still smell the pines."

She embraced him. She wore a sweatshirt with a hood; on the front of the sweatshirt was the word "Bowdoin." She said, "It's wonderful how our paths have crossed. When I was in college we used to drive out to Mere Point and light fires on the boulders, cook, smell the ocean, and look out at the small islands that had only pine trees. The same ocean and the same smells you had."

He kissed her lips. They tasted of salt from the chilly air on the ferry and the short walk from the dock to the house. They had carried their bags on red children's wagons. The house was a half mile from the wooden dock.

The only other person they saw in the three days they spent in the house was Eben Cain, the caretaker of Byron's house and several others for more than forty years. He was one of the two hundred year-round residents of the island, probably the last member of the last generation of a family that had been here since the 1700s. Eben kept the furnaces running year-round because Byron, although he rarely came to the island, usually visited on a day's notice, and Byron's sons also came unexpectedly and intermittently. Eben—a thin, compact man with that terse Maine accent—hadn't seen Byron with his sons since they were young teenagers. Eben made sure there was enough oil in the furnace, hot water in the tank, and wood near the fireplaces.

The nighttime fog dissolved just after dawn each morning, as each gloriously clear day began. They woke early. They hiked in the afternoons. The only snow on the island was lodged on the sides of the immense boulders shielded all day from the sun. From the heights and shore of the island they saw the glittering of the frigid sea. In the distance, the small, uninhabited, pine-covered islands were surrounded with brilliant light. The trees seemed to be on fire, but never burned.

At night they read. There were old books on the shelves that Byron had first seen there in the late fifties and early sixties, in the last years of his grandfather's life—novels and short stories by once-famous and now almost forgotten writers like John O'Hara and James Gould Cozzens. *The Cape Cod Lighter. Morning, Noon, and Night. Advise and Consent.* His grandfather was a meticulous lover of books. Each book had its original dust jacket, on thick paper. The pages were all swollen by the sea air.

Christina studied on a table near the fireplace while Byron read. A small lamp shedding soft light glowed on her gorgeous face. Although he tried to resist, Byron often glanced up at her as she studied. From time to time she caught his eye and smiled a wistful but seductive smile, as if she were saying: *Not now, later, I'll give you the ride of your life.*

The kitchen had not changed since the 1950s. Big white refrigerator, linoleum floor, black stove. There was no dishwasher. Byron rinsed the supper dishes and placed them in a rack next to the sink. Christina was cleaning the table with a sponge.

He said, as he dried his hands on a towel, "Who are you?"

Christina reacted as though Byron was teasing her. Then the moment lasted too long. "What?"

"The only Christina Rosario who ever graduated from Bowdoin died eighteen years ago."

"What are you saying, Carlos?"

"And your apartment on Riverside Drive is leased to a company known as Alpha Sources. Tell me why your father the engineering professor didn't leave a single engineering book in his apartment. And why there's no record of anyone named Rosario who ever taught engineering or anything else at Columbia."

"Carlos, I don't know why you're saying this. It's wrong. Someone is lying to you."

"You're lying to me." His voice was vehement. "You're a liar, a fraud."

"Carlos, please."

"Who is this animal you pal around with? The one with the suit and the mustache?"

"I don't know what you're talking about."

"And who is that blonde girlfriend of yours?"

"Please, Byron."

"Tell me the truth."

"Carlos, I'm Christina Rosario. I'm a law student at Columbia. I'm your lover. I admire you. I love you."

"I have pictures of you with a man who is a torturer. I have pictures of you with a woman who works with the same fucking torturer. She's a fraud, like you."

"What's the matter with you? Please tell me."

"I have the video from your computer. You know the one. The one with your friend beating and drowning Ali Hussein."

Suddenly she placed her hands over her face. She turned from him. He heard her cry.


At first light she put her soft luggage and backpack in one of the red wagons and pulled it behind her as she made her way to the dock. The ferry was scheduled to leave at nine. The door to the small, unheated waiting room was always unlocked.

During her two-hour wait in the cold room, she composed on her BlackBerry a long text message to Byron. *Carlos,* she started, *I want you to know this. I hope when you read what follows you can understand that I became involved in the work I've done because I love this country and want to protect it. I had no idea how crazily it would unravel. Or how dangerous it's all become. And I had no idea how much I would love you. Don't look for me. I'll transform myself again. I've done this before. I'll become someone else.*

She created the message as if in a trance. When she finished, she saw for the first time that the old station room was now flooded with morning light. The wooden planks of the walls and floors glowed; they seemed to radiate slightly with heat.

She gripped the BlackBerry, hesitating to press the *Send* button. She found the only bathroom. Still clutching the BlackBerry, she sat on the toilet, which was clean but had rust-colored stains on the porcelain. She looked at the sleek object in her hand as if it were a bomb; she was afraid of it.

Minutes later, just as she pressed *Send,* she saw the heavy, unwieldy lobster boat ease gradually into the dock's wooden pilings, which had been worn smooth by countless dockings over the years. Surprised, she recognized two of the men standing on the cluttered deck of the boat. When she had last seen them in New York a week earlier, they had looked subdued and weary in the lousy midwinter weather. Today in the brisk morning, they looked bright, athletic, and vigorous.

"We got your message," Tom Nashatka called out. "We came out to get you. The ferry was cancelled."

# 39

BYRON JOHNSON STAYED ON the chilly island for two days after she left. There was no television in the house; there never had been. The only radio was a short wave on which the mechanical, inflectionless voices of the announcers for the national weather bureau gave the regional and maritime weather. Byron loved to hear the names of the geographic landmarks— the weather in the vast expanse of Casco Bay as far north as Nova Scotia and south to Kennebunkport, the readings from Execution Rocks, the conditions at the buoy ninety miles from Monhegan Island.

An ice storm enveloped the island for twenty-four hours. The island closed down completely—isolated, quiet, and intimate. Glistening and ice-burdened branches fell from some of the nearby pine trees.

Christina's long text message had riveted him, and he spent those two days reading and re-reading it. Byron was angry, he was relieved, he was harrowed with fear. He was also repeatedly overwhelmed by pangs of love and the grieving void of loss.

*This is who I am*, she wrote. *I'm multiple women. I change often. You were right about Christina. She died.*

She was a Captain in the Army at the time of 9/11, she wrote. She was fluent in Arabic. She wanted to serve the United States. She joined the new Homeland Security Department. She received stratospheric security clearances.

When she and Andrew Hurd learned that Byron decided to represent a man they believed had been a master of terrorist finance since the *USS Cole* bombing in 2000, they drew together a team of diverse people with the same level of security clearances. Within days, she was transformed into a Columbia Law School student and, through people she called "institutional cooperators," she became a summer associate at SpencerBlake, complete with a transcript from the law school and recommendations from two of its professors. She and her team members had several strategies for "downloading" from Byron the information he would absorb from Ali Hussein, the "banker for al-Qaeda."

Only one of those strategies involved placing Christina Rosario into his life, mind, and soul. They knew Byron had left his marriage unwillingly, that he had brief affairs with other women, and that he had joined an online dating service in which he said little about himself and did not post his picture. So, they knew, he was vulnerable.

They also knew that he was a consummate lawyer, a man with an enormous capacity to extract facts from clients and to inspire confidence in them. Byron was one of those increasingly rare lawyers who looked like what people once viewed as the prototype of a lawyer—handsome, tall, well-mannered, projecting an aura of *noblesse oblige* without any trace of arrogance or haughtiness.

And, finally, they knew he had become restless, irritable, and discontented as he entered and warily moved into his early sixties.

From that gorgeous moment in the dusk at the Central Park Zoo, the Rosario strategy worked. *I not only became your lover,* she wrote in the text message, *I became your alter ego. Like any new lover, you let me roam through your life. I had free access to your notes, your computer and cell phone (although I had to work to haul you into the 21st century), and what I knew to be your soul. I took all of that from you, and gave it to others so that they could sift it all to find money, like those prospectors in the California Gold Rush who screened sand and water for gold.*

*It was because I fell in love with you that Hurd and his minions started a campaign of disinformation and deception. When the $52 million kissed your account and fled, I asked Hurd where the money came from and how it had landed in your account and skipped off like a stone a kid tosses on the surface of the water.*

*"Ask your boyfriend," he told me.*

It was never in the plan and strategy as disclosed to her, she wrote, that Byron's life would be put at such profound risk. She told Hurd it was crazy to suggest that Byron had divined how to locate the funds, move them to himself, and then managed to have the money pass through multiple accounts until it slipped into a black hole somewhere. *If he has it,* Hurd said to her, *then he has a choice: he can give it to me or he will never be able to use it. Unless, of course,* he said, *you've got it, too.*

*And in that moment, Carlos, I knew he had decided I'd betrayed him. He kills people, Byron, for the sport of it. Remember King Lear? "Like flies to wanton boys are we to the gods, they kill us for their sport." Be careful, Carlos. I love you.*

Gazing through the windows at the ice-silvered pine trees and the boulders against which the Atlantic crashed, tossing icy foam into the air, Byron hit the keys on his BlackBerry and forwarded her text message to his own email account. *Life at risk.* It felt as though every muscle, bone, and organ in his body were dissolving. The bathroom was cold. But he felt the overwhelming need to strip off all his clothes. Job's words came to his mind, and he spoke them out loud: *Naked, naked came I into the world, and naked shall I return.*

When the ferry docked at Boothbay Harbor on the mainland, he stopped at the coffee shop on the wharf. He sat at the counter, on a circular stool with no arms or backrest. The new weekly edition of the local newspaper, the *Harbor Express*, was on the countertop. He casually pulled it toward him and spread open the first page on the worn counter as his black coffee and glazed doughnut—known here as a honey-dipped doughnut (a name that to him always had a wonderful sexual resonance)—arrived.

At the top of the front page was a driver's license picture of Christina Rosario: *Frozen Body Found on Beach in Acadia.*

Byron struggled for breath, holding his hand over his mouth. The prematurely old waitress, her face worn by cigarettes and perennial cold weather, asked in that laconic Maine accent as she gestured at the headline, "Isn't that something?"

He glanced at her, overwhelmed by a desire to have her take him to wherever she lived on this isolated coast and protect him. He shook his head. He couldn't speak.

# 40

AS ALWAYS, ALI HUSSEIN appeared to grow younger each time Byron Johnson saw him. Somehow the dark pockets in which his eyes were set—the dominant feature of his face when Byron first saw him in Miami—had noticeably lightened. He had also become more talkative, almost light-hearted. He wanted to know more about news in the outside world, including news about himself. "Was I on CNN this week?" he once asked. He had more questions about his case. He was more interested in Byron. Over time, as Ali became more chatty, Byron admired him less.

And he had stopped giving Byron quotations from the *Koran* and hearing the Imam's guidance for readings from the *Koran*. *He knows*, Byron thought, *that I've been changing them, that now I'm the only one who holds the messages.*

Byron was tense and intense. He leaned toward Ali's ear. "We will be in court tomorrow. I have asked the judge to throw out the charges against you."

"How?"

"I was given a video of Jesse Ventura trying to drown you."

Ali raised his hand to his ear, leaning closer to Byron.

"The government said there were no videos of you. But there is one."

"I told you that, Mr. Johnson."

"And I believed you. And now I have a tape."

"I saw the camera. It was humiliating. I was stripped, I was crying, my body was exposed, I was weak. I thought it was insane that they were filming it."

"Ali, you have to understand that there's no way to know what Goldberg will do."

"Mr. Johnson, he's an animal. His heart is bad."

"You don't want to die?"

"No, I don't."

"There's a way to save yourself without relying on Goldberg. The other side has told me that they want to do a deal with you."

"What kind of deal?"

"They say they know that the passages from the *Koran* you gave me, and the ones the Imam had me bring back to you, were codes. They think they're close to knowing what the codes are, but they don't know enough."

"These people are crazy, Mr. Johnson. I never had money, I never took money, I never gave money to anyone."

"All I can do is convey word for word what their offer is. I have an obligation to do that. You have to decide what you want to do."

"I want to live, I want to leave here, I want to be in the world again."

"They are offering you a deal to let you live."

"And what do they want me to do?"

"To sit and talk with them. To cooperate, by which they mean to tell them everything you knew. People, conversations, money, your relationship with the Imam, names of banks, account numbers."

"If I do all that, then what?"

"Then, after you give them all of that, they decide whether they will do a deal with you."

"You mean the idea is that I give away everything first, and they get to decide later. I give, they take, and they can leave me where I am."

"That's the way it works."

"But I don't know anything, Mr. Johnson."

"Then you have nothing to give them."

"Unless I make things up."

"They would tell me they don't want you to make things up. And I can tell you that won't work."

"They are crazy people, Mr. Johnson."

"They are the only people you can deal with. For us there are no other people in the world."

"There is the judge."

"There is."

"And what if he does what you're asking him to do? He sets me free. Then I don't have these people trying to kill me."

"Don't invest too much in him, Ali. He was made a judge by Mr. Bush. He despises criminal defendants. He despises me. He despises you. He doesn't have an Arab friend."

"And he's a Jew."

Byron paused. In their dozens of conversations, they had never uttered the words "Jew" or "Israel." It had never occurred to Byron to ask Hussein about his political opinions. In fact, Byron had only rarely heard any of his clients over the years speak about politics or public issues, except on those isolated occasions when a corporate executive let slip words like the "sweaty unwashed masses," "Obamacare," or the "newly privileged welfare class." Byron said, "There are many courageous Jewish judges."

"I've seen the man. He is not courageous. Asking him to do anything for me is like slapping water. Futile."

"I can't predict what anyone will do in life, Ali, whether he's Jewish or an Eskimo."

# 41

IT ARRIVED IN A tidy Amazon box as if packaged and sent by Amazon itself. The look of the box, Byron thought, was a miracle of counterfeiting. It appeared to hold two hardcover books.

Byron Johnson was endlessly amazed by the Internet. When he randomly typed in the words "Army Service Pistol" three days earlier, he hadn't anticipated that there would be entry after entry describing the history of the Colt pistol and offering them for sale as if they were books.

It was a gorgeous object. Nestled in a soft foam setting shaped to its contours, the pistol was new. Its surface was highly polished. As if it were a perfectly crafted Swiss watch, he lifted it carefully from the box, turned it, and looked at it from every angle.

He lifted the Styrofoam case in which the Colt had been lodged.

Beneath the pistol-shaped indentation was a shoulder holster. He held the holster in front of him, spreading it out, admiring it. The leather was lustrous and new, as finely made in its own way as the burnished steel of the pistol. The odor of the new leather was rich.

There was a last layer in the box, like those colorful Russian eggs within identical eggs, the sizes steadily diminishing. There were two ammunition clips. Byron locked one of the clips into the Colt.

He put on the holster, draping it around his left shoulder like a surplice. He adjusted the straps. He smelled the leather. As soon as the holster was secure, he slipped the Colt into it. When he put on a suit jacket, he saw as he looked at himself in the mirror that the bulge was obvious, but, he thought, who would know? He tried on his overcoats—the expensive clothes from Paul Stuart on Madison Avenue that were the still-formidable remnants of his former life. The bulge wasn't visible. Nor was it visible under the suede jacket he had worn on the weekends for several winters.

He continued wearing the holster for another hour as he concentrated again on the intense writing that engaged him. It was more of a narrative than a legal brief. He didn't go through the process of inserting citations to decisions and statutes that supported legal writing like studs riveted into the sturdy beams of his arguments. He had realized since Simeon died, and particularly since Christina's body had been found on the icy rocks of the Maine coast, that the legal brief he had written for Justin Goldberg elaborating the reasons Ali Hussein's prosecution should be ended—arguments based on torture, abuse of any concept of due process, the opposing lawyers' lies and deceptions—might never see the light of day. Goldberg had required that it be sealed and not filed on the court's new electronic docket. Unlike the hundreds of thousands of other federal cases around the country, the computerized docket for *United States of America v. Ali Hussein* revealed only the name and docket number of the case, the name of the judge, and the name of the prosecutor. Not even Byron's name. And the grid on the computer screen that was ordinarily filled with consecutive numbers and dates for each filing—and in some cases in which Byron had been involved, there were more than a thousand separate entries—was blank, a modern *tabula rasa*. *National security material.*

No trace of the written record of the case might survive, as though the written words might be submerged forever. "This is my tablet, this is what happened." He intended to write those words on the copies of the story he planned to send to his sons, to reporters at the *New York Times* and the *Washington Post*, and to the immense universe of the Internet.

When he rose up from the desk, he stapled the pages he had written that night. He slipped the pages into a manila envelope. He cut his index finger on the envelope's sharp metal clasp. A faint bloodstain was left on the envelope, which he dropped just behind the door of his apartment so that, in the morning, he could take it to the safe deposit at the bank on Lespenard Street, where the clerks appeared unfazed by his frequent visits; they were either indifferent or discreet. He looked like a courtly, important customer, always well-dressed, always courteous.

Byron knew these things could be taken from the safe deposit box, just as he had learned months ago that all of his diaries, bank statements, and tax returns had been removed from his office, just as his notes on the *Koran* given to him by Ali Hussein and the now-imprisoned Imam in Newark had been taken, just as the world he had created on his computer had been removed, just as the millions of dollars that fleetingly appeared in his bank account had been taken.

And just as the woman he loved had been taken.

And, finally, just as his place in the world had been taken.

As he gazed from his window at the cobblestones of the cold, wind-blown street, deserted except for a few parked cars on a frigid night in winter, he ran through a list of probable takers: Sandy Spencer, who had disappeared from his life as if Byron were a leper; Khalid Hussein, who Byron first believed was a tough but loving brother; the Imam, who looked like a caricature of a Muslim holy man; Jesse Ventura, whose scary intelligence was revealed in his eyes. Or Christina Rosario, whose presence, touch, smell, and energy had made him feel vital and loved.

And Byron Carlos Johnson thought: *What have I stolen from myself?*

When he stepped back from the window, he saw the elegant image of himself in the glass. He saw, too, the dark, disfiguring bulk of the holster and pistol draped like a hump over his shoulder and left chest.

*What the Christ am I thinking?*

He removed the holster and pistol. He put on an overcoat and hat. He went out into the frigid streets with the holster and gun in a knapsack Christina had left in the apartment. As he approached the Hudson River, the wind, bred in Canada and sweeping across the vast country, flowed in an icy torrent from the New Jersey Palisades. It took his breath away.

Byron walked to the end of one of the derelict piers. With the knapsack in his right hand, he turned like an Olympic hammer thrower and sent it into the powerful black waters of the river. He wanted to expose himself naked to the danger he sensed everywhere in his world.

# 42

IT WAS STRANGE AND unsettling to see six U.S. Marshals in combat gear and carrying M-16s standing at each door of the stately courtroom. Ali Hussein, in his baggy green jumpsuit, was visibly shaken as soon as he was brought into the courtroom. As he glanced at each of the armed men, the two female guards in blue blazers who escorted him released him from his handcuffs and took several steps back, as if to be out of earshot of whatever words Byron Johnson and his client spoke.

Byron had learned to judge the meaning of the expressions on Ali's face, and Ali had become an expressive man after those first encounters in Miami, when his look was remote, almost inscrutable. Now, as he sat with Byron at the defense table, his expression was fearful.

"Why this?" he whispered, his voice almost inaudible, his breath with that sour smell that Byron had long ago recognized was the breath of fear.

"I don't know, Ali." He didn't tell Ali that, when he arrived at the entrance to the courthouse, several plainclothes marshals had intercepted him and taken him to the back elevators that were reserved for judges and their staffs.

"Why are we here, Mr. Johnson?"

"I had a call from the judge's law clerk an hour ago to tell me the judge was holding an emergency session. I wasn't told why, I was home, and I'm here."

To Byron's left, Hal Rana leaned backwards, utterly at ease in his wooden chair at the prosecution table. There were three other government lawyers with him, a man and two women whom Byron had never seen. One of them stared at the bronze Great Seal of the United States emblazoned on the wall just above the judge's empty bench. The others pretended to write on notepads.

The large room was utterly still. The windows faced north, overlooking the congested streets of Chinatown, the green dome of an old church, and, further uptown, the layered spire of the Chrysler building glinting in the crisp winter morning light.

At the sound of an invisible hand hitting the inside of the judge's door and the intonation of the words "all rise," the lawyers and Ali Hussein stood. Justin Goldberg, carrying a slim folder, walked briskly to his seat. A clerk announced the words *"United States of America versus Ali Hussein."* Sid Rappoport, the court reporter, was poised above his keyboard like a pianist waiting for the opening cue.

"Good morning," Goldberg said. "State your appearances, counsel."

"Hamerindapal Rana, for the United States. With me are Special Assistant Attorneys Larry Goodman, Christine McGuire, and Dimitri Jones."

"Byron Johnson for Ali Hussein, who is to my right."

Goldberg glanced up. "Mr. Rana, let me start with you."

Hal Rana remained standing, everything about his posture and expression relaxed.

"At the last session in chambers I directed the government to prepare and submit by yesterday a confidential memorandum describing in detail the circumstances under which a video was made of the defendant, apparently as he was being interrogated. The video also depicted the defendant being placed, forcefully, in what appeared to be a bathtub filled with water. I required a description of who the participants were, where the video was filmed, when it was filmed, where the video was kept, how many copies were made, and the identities of the people who received it." Justin Goldberg paused, staring at Hal Rana.

"We have reason to believe Mr. Johnson illegally obtained a copy of the video and distributed it to the media in violation of the court's confidentiality order."

Justin Goldberg's voice was as precise and clear as usual. "Mr. Rana, my order was directed at you, not Mr. Johnson. I will deal with Mr. Johnson at an appropriate time."

"I should alert the court to the fact that a grand jury is currently investigating Mr. Johnson for possible criminal activity in connection with this and other matters."

"Let me say this one more time, Mr. Rana. My order was directed at the government. And I did not receive the report."

Rana didn't skip a beat. "Your Honor, the Office of Special Prosecutions has determined that the preparation of that report would entail the violation of highly sensitive national security directives."

"What exactly does that mean, Mr. Rana?"

"The Justice Department has determined that national security mandates prevent us from providing the report."

Crisply, Justin Goldberg said, "That fact, Mr. Rana, will have consequences."

"It won't have any impact on the evidence the prosecution will present at trial."

"And why is that, Mr. Rana?"

"We never intended to use the tapes at trial."

"And I take it that's why the video was never turned over to the defense, correct?"

"Correct. Even if Mr. Johnson had the tape, it would not help his defense. His client made no statements at all on the video, certainly no statements that could incriminate him."

"Mr. Rana, Mr. Rana," Justin Goldberg said, "I know Mr. Johnson's client made no statements on the video. I've watched it several times. Did you expect him to speak when his head was under water?"

Remaining as still as possible, Byron Johnson began to allow himself the belief that Justin Goldberg—mercurial, disciplined, and a slave to the privileges of rank and power—was capable of courage and independence. But Byron had been in this business long enough to know that people like Justin Goldberg were not selected as federal judges because they had demonstrated in their earlier careers signs of dissent or rebellion or tendencies to do the unexpected, the unpopular, or the unconventional. Justin Goldberg, as Byron knew, had a quick and subtle intelligence and enjoyed fencing with lawyers, and this dressing-down of the stately Hamerindapal Rana might be just a performance.

"Can you explain to me," Goldberg said, "how complying with my order for a description of the source and nature of this video poses national security concerns?"

"A report will likely endanger United States agents."

"How is that? The report is for me, not for Mr. Johnson or for public distribution."

"Judge, I am simply delivering a decision that I've received from the highest levels of the Justice Department and Homeland Security."

"But you're the lawyer in front of me, Mr. Rana, not the Attorney General or the head of Homeland Security. I issued an order, you have told me that order will not be complied with, and I am telling you there will be consequences."

"Again, Judge, national security requirements complicate all cases like these."

"Don't lecture me, Mr. Rana. Let's put aside the brutality of the tape. Mr. Johnson repeatedly asked—and the requests were reasonable—for copies of any videotapes, recordings, or written transcripts in which his client appeared or spoke or gave statements. And *you* repeatedly told him and me there were none."

"I did not know about the video."

"That doesn't matter, Mr. Rana. And don't play games with me. When Mr. Johnson asked for videos, recordings, and transcripts, he wasn't asking *you* personally for them. He was asking the government."

"No one told me about a video."

"Enough of that, Mr. Rana. Let me see if I understand. I directed that the government prepare a written report, I laid out what it should address, and I required that it be delivered to me by a certain date. That date was yesterday. And as of today, I've been informed that the government will not comply with that order. Is that not the status?"

"It is, but the record should be clear that it is not defiance of the order but national security concerns that have brought this about."

"Mr. Rana, at the moment I'm concerned about the status, the objective facts, not the reasons. Order, schedule, noncompliance. One, two, three." He paused, a look of intense annoyance on his face.

Hal Rana said, "In cases like this, there are always going to be complicating factors that don't arise in ordinary criminal cases. One of those factors is national security."

"And another factor, Mr. Rana, is to do justice."

"Certainly, and justice for the United States as well. A jury will need to decide what this defendant did and either convict him or acquit him."

"And what is my function, Mr. Rana? Is it my role to let you present any evidence you want to present, and let you withhold any evidence you don't want to present?"

Byron knew that Hal Rana was a flexible and adept lawyer, and Rana now demonstrated that again. "That certainly is not the case, Judge. You have already taken an active role in charting a course for this unusual and very important case. We believe a means can always be crafted to give the defendant a fair trial and safeguard national security interests."

Byron, impressed by Rana's well-tempered agility, decided to hold back. He was tense. Ali Hussein was even more tense, a taut presence at Byron's side. Byron hadn't looked at Ali; he was entirely riveted to the exchange between Justin Goldberg and Hal Rana.

"I'm not about to engage you in that, Mr. Rana. The correct way to have done this was for the government to have advised me that this video existed. In other words, for the United States to have taken the initiative in disclosing this, and then to have presented in an orderly way the national security concerns that you have."

"Again, it was never our intention to use the video at trial."

"Let me make this clear to you, Mr. Rana, so that you can take it back to your supervisor. There may not be a trial."

"We don't believe Mr. Johnson's client will plead guilty."

Byron felt an almost unbearable anticipation. He stared at Justin Goldberg. He waited for the words that would surely follow Goldberg's pause.

"That's not what I mean, Mr. Rana, and you know it. Whether Mr. Hussein pleads guilty or continues to maintain that he's innocent is up to him. I know nothing about that. What I do know is that I'm considering and will consider appropriate sanctions for the government's failure to disclose the video and failure to comply with the order to produce the report that was due yesterday. You didn't even give me the courtesy, Mr. Rana, of notifying me in writing yesterday that no report would be filed."

"We apologize."

"Don't apologize. Apologies are a waste of time. I'm prepared to give the government two more days to file the report I required, and it can include any national security concerns the government may claim. It may be that the government could avoid the sanctions I'm considering if it takes this last opportunity to obey my orders."

"Sanctions?" Hal Rana asked.

Byron had heard the word *sanctions* invoked so often against him during the long life of the case that for a second he thought Justin Goldberg was now speaking to him.

"Yes," Justin Goldberg said, "sanctions. And what kind of sanctions, Mr. Rana, will depend in part on what your report says, if you take the opportunity I'm giving you. I can't sanction you personally, Mr. Rana. I can, however, sanction the government. One alternative is to preclude the use at trial of some or all of your evidence. Another choice I have is to

dismiss the case for prosecutorial abuse. Or I could just repri-
mand the government."

"We don't think any of that is appropriate."

"Of course you don't. And at this stage I'm warning you.
Not only do I look forward to the report I'm allowing you to
give me two days from now—in other words, Mr. Rana, I'm
offering you a reprieve—but I'm also giving you a week to respond to Mr. Johnson's papers asking for dismissal of the case,
and the release of his client, on the basis of a litany of horrors
he has rehearsed about the deliberate mistreatment of his client over the last seven years."

"Mr. Johnson's papers were just given to us two days ago.
We've only had a short time to review them, but it's clear
to us that Mr. Johnson has put forward a great deal of wild
accusations."

"Has he? I'm not so sure. But that's why I look forward to
your written response."

"It will take us six weeks to respond, Judge."

"It will take you one week. I want your papers next Friday."

By this point, Hal Rana appeared depleted. Byron Johnson
had never before seen him even look tired. Ordinarily his tie,
white shirts, blue and charcoal suits, turban, and hand-made
black shoes were always in place, even in hot weather. That had
changed, almost imperceptibly. Hal Rana verged on weariness.

"I'll report all of this, Your Honor, to people with higher
pay grades than I have."

"Of course you will, Mr. Rana." Justin Goldberg at
last looked at Byron. "Is there anything you want to say,
Mr. Johnson?"

Gracefully, Byron Johnson rose to his feet. "No, Judge."

# 43

SHE WAS A COMELY fifty-year-old with her brown hair swept and enfolded, Katherine Hepburn–style, upward from the nape of her neck. She came to his apartment after responding to a small ad Byron had placed in the classified section of the *Village Voice* advertising for a word-processor to type a book-length manuscript. There must have been something intriguing, he thought, to the world at-large about doing secretarial work for an anonymous writer, since more than eighty people had emailed resumes to the address at the *Voice* that passed the resumes on to him. They may have thought they were sending their resumes to Philip Roth. No wonder writers were legendary for all their sexual opportunities.

Her name was Helen Wilson. She said she was an actress and that she would have to work with him on a flexible schedule since she frequently went to calls and, at times, got assignments. They were local, primarily small roles in television commercials. Byron liked the simplicity of her name. And he appreciated her hair and the striking blue eyes in her pale, well-structured face. She said she had been raised in Iowa, and given her looks he wasn't surprised.

She didn't seem concerned when she saw that the work would be done in his apartment, not an office. It was Byron who appeared awkward, as if wondering about the propriety of a woman having to come to her boss's home to work.

He had numbered each page of the six hundred and three yellow sheets on which he had written. He placed them on the work table in front of her after he had taken them out of the bank vault. Helen flipped through some of the pages, glancing only at the handwriting. It was shapely and clear.

"Are you Catholic?" she asked.

"Catholic?"

"Kids in parochial school learn great penmanship."

"My mother was Catholic," he said. "Mexican."

His volunteering of the word surprised him, not her. "So that's where the *Carlos* comes from. Not from William Carlos Williams?"

"It might. My mother loved poetry."

There was a fine web of gray hair at her temples. "Did she read you the Williams poem about the wheelbarrow and the rain?"

He laughed. "She had a red wheelbarrow that she used on a flowerbed."

She touched the neat stack of yellow paper. "Back to business," she said lightly. "It will take fifteen hours or so to do this."

"Is that all?"

"Perhaps less."

"When can you do the work?"

"Do you really want me to do it here? I could get it back to you quickly if I brought it to my apartment. We could make a copy."

"Helen, it has to stay here. No copies."

"You authors are so protective. My schedule, as I said, is unpredictable. I'll be back and forth. Irregularly."

"Don't worry, I never leave. The door's always open."

She wore very simple clothes—a black sweater, black pants, delicate slip-on shoes, and a red and black scarf draped over her shoulders.

"I know who you are," she said.

He smiled. "So, who am I?"

"You're the lawyer who represents that Arab man."

"I am."

"I see you on television. I read about you in the paper. You're probably all over YouTube and the Internet, although I don't look at those."

"I don't either."


Over the next few days he looked forward to her visits. Helen had a life that belied her settled, attractive, and very pleasing appearance. Sometimes she arrived at seven in the morning. Byron woke every day at five-thirty: "I'm an urban farmer," he told her when she asked whether he was bothered by such an early arrival. On other days she would appear at seven at night, entering with that cold scent of winter.

She told him that she was in rehearsal with a small group in the East Village for *The Cherry Orchard*. They performed one night each week in the auditorium at the Washington Irving public high school on Irving Place. "I play a matron," she said. "You should come by soon. The tickets are five dollars each."

When Helen was in his apartment she worked at his steel-and-glass desk, her half-glasses on the bridge of her small nose, her back completely straight, a former dancer's posture. He never left the apartment when she was there. It was not simply because he liked her presence, but also because he didn't want her to copy his papers and leave with them. He was unsettled about the concept of trust. He brought her coffee and tea and sweet rolls.

She was a determined worker who typed steadily and without any reaction to the substance of the words. She could have been typing an article on farm machinery. He waited for the point where she might express surprise or interest. He knew she was an intelligent, alert, and articulate woman. If she knew who he was—Rush Limbaugh had called him the "loony lawyer"—then she had to know that he was writing a long narrative on the arrest and imprisonment of an Arab facing the death penalty, the alternating tortures of physical abuse and total isolation for years, the recurring appearances of Andrew Hurd and Tom Nashatka in his life and later in Byron Johnson's life, Byron's visits to a well-known Imam, an acerbic and difficult judge, the daily presence of a loved woman in his life, Byron's friendship with Simeon Black, Simeon's killing, and Byron's all-pervasive fear.

During one of her late-night visits, Helen said: "Do you have anything else for me? I've finished."

"You have? So soon?"

"What do you want me to do with this?"

"It's in the hard drive and on disk?"

"Yes. Do you want me to print a copy?"

"Just one."

She turned to the computer. On the screen he saw the title page: *Extraordinary Rendition: A Report on a Prosecution.*

"How many pages did it turn out to be?"

"Two hundred and seventy-three." The only sound in the apartment was the methodical shuffling of the pages sifting out of the printer. "What are you going to do with this?"

He smiled: "'There are such things that I shall do as shall be the terrors of the earth.'"

Without skipping a beat, she said: "*King Lear.*"

"An actress. I should've known you'd recognize that."

In her steady, unaccented, and lucid voice, she said, "Two nights ago, two men began to speak to me at the corner of Spring and West Broadway. I was walking home from here; it was milder than usual. 'Ms. Wilson,' they said, 'are you working for Byron Johnson?' Because of the weather, there were lots of people on the street. I was startled, not afraid."

"Who were they?"

"You know, Byron. One of them was the man on the video. He asked, 'Will you bring us the book?' I said, 'No.' He said they would pay me ten thousand dollars. I said thank you and walked on."

Byron felt a gust of regret. "I'm sorry, I didn't realize you would get tied up in this."

She smiled warmly. "That's all right. It's one more interesting thing in my interesting life."

"No, Helen. These people kill people who don't do what they want. They killed Christina Rosario. They killed Sy Black."

"I know. I read it here."

Helen Wilson lived in one of the old townhouses that had been gutted years earlier and divided into five stories of narrow one-bedroom apartments, a tight warren of living spaces. The building was on East Eighth Street, long known as Saint Mark's Place; the street was still a relic of the 1960s, lined with second-hand clothing stores with tie-died shirts and skirts in the window displays, shops that sold the paraphernalia of drug use, and health food stores. Even on a winter night the street was crowded, filled with the restlessness and vitality of the young, the odor of marijuana.

There was no elevator in Helen's building. Byron followed behind her. He could see beneath the light coat she wore that her rear was shapely. He had let go of the pretense that he was escorting her home for her safety.

The narrow living room was crowded with mismatched furniture, the collection of twenty years of living in one place. But it was neat and orderly. On the walls were reprints of photographs by Georgia O'Keefe: a stem on which symmetrical petals were balanced on either side of a soft, fecund opening. And a photograph of hands delicate enough to be a man's or a woman's.

"Would you like tea?"

"No, thanks, Helen."

"A drink?"

"Not now, thanks." He paused, taking in the womanly sight of her after she removed her coat and the sweater beneath it. "Water?" he asked.

"That's easy."

She turned to the tight kitchen. There were no windows in it. Two people couldn't stand side by side in it. The refrigerator was old, white, and bulky. She handed the glass of water to him. He was thirsty. He drank most of the water.

When he placed the glass on the wicker basket she used as a coffee table, he turned toward her. She was standing close to him. She smiled faintly. He took one of her hands. She continued to smile.

"I think you're beautiful," he said. She embraced him. Her body was full. His hand separated the clothes near the small of her back. Her skin was soft.

Helen whispered, "Follow me." She led Byron Johnson to the bedroom.

# 44

BYRON HAD INVITED TEN reporters to the press conference. Five were from television, and the rest were writers for newspapers, magazines, and online services. Every reporter he had invited came to the room he had rented at the wood-paneled Harvard Club on West 44th Street.

"Thank you all for coming." He stood at the front of the room. To his left were fifteen copies of the report, each held together by a rubber band. "All of what I am about to say, and all that is in the report I'm about to give you, is on the record. And you will all be free to take with you what I call 'the torture video' attached to each report."

There was one cameraman in the room. His CNN shield was suspended on a bright ribbon from his neck. On a pre-arranged signal from Byron, he started the camera. "The man I represent, Ali Hussein, was tortured by United States agents. He was hit time and time again. He was repeatedly forced under water. We have a video that demonstrates all this. It is part of each packet. No one has ever seen even a picture of waterboarding. And the United States has always denied that there was a photo, video, or tape."

Byron stared for several seconds at the reporters. He was utterly calm. "What you will see is far worse than the photos of Abu Ghraib. Far worse than images of a human being near death, screaming and naked. And that isn't all. My client

**289**

was held in complete isolation for years. His only visitor was a brutal United States agent. My client knows him only as Jesse Ventura. When we speak of terrorists, we need to expand the definition. You'll see the conduct of Jesse Ventura—whose real name is Andrew Hurd—and I submit that what you will see is terrorism. From a lawyer's standpoint, it is attempted murder, plain and simple."

A measured voice asked: "How do you know the agent's name?"

"Simeon Black was working on a very detailed, deeply researched article on the arrests, detention, extraordinary rendition, and treatment of men arrested overseas in the war on terror. He learned that 'Jesse Ventura' was an agent named Andrew Hurd. And I've had encounters with Andrew Hurd."

Another voice, this one a woman's: "How did you get the video?"

"An agent who once worked with Hurd gave it to me."

"What agent?"

"I knew her as Christina Rosario. That was not her name. I don't know her name."

"Where is she?"

"She is dead."

"How did she die?"

"She drowned."

"Where?"

"Off the coast of Maine."

"Why did she give you the videotape?"

"She was assigned under cover to shadow me. She left the video in plain view, I believe, for me to take. I took it."

The same woman's persistent voice: "Why did she do it?"

He was surprised to hear himself say, "Conscience."

"How is that?"

"She was disturbed at what the government had done. And disturbed as well that it had lied."

"Who else has the video?"

"The people who filmed it, the United States Attorney's Office, the judge. And Simeon Black had it."

"Where did he get it?"

"From me. I gave it to him. When he was killed the day after I gave it to him, it was missing, stolen."

"Do you know who killed him?"

"The people who wanted to gather up all copies of the video and all of the work and research he was producing."

"Who are those people?"

"Ask Andrew Hurd. Ask Mr. Rana, the prosecutor."

"Where do you stand in all of this?"

"I am only a lawyer advocating for his client. He cannot receive a fair trial. He is a victim, not a terrorist. He should be freed, and the people who did this to him should be prosecuted."

With the camera still trained on him, Byron Johnson stood and handed out the fifteen copies of his report and the disk, as carefully as a priest bestowing a communion wafer.


"The only person likely to be indicted is, in fact, Byron Carlos Johnson." Hamerindapal Rana glanced around the crowd of reporters in the press room at One St. Andrew's Plaza.

"He has been the target of a federal grand jury investigation for two months. He has consistently violated rules that prohibited him from disclosing confidential information. He was ordered by a federal judge to hold in confidence and not disclose that information. He signed confidentiality agreements. He made promises. He has completely violated his promises. He has fabricated information. He has violated the confidential privileges that apply to his relationship with his client. And he may have put the lives of patriotic Americans in danger."

"Who are the people in the video?"

"We are trying to establish that. It may be that the people in the video are actors. The video may have been an exercise in disinformation. We haven't ruled out the possibility that Byron Johnson himself had the video produced."

"What does Ali Hussein look like?"

"The man in the video may not be the defendant we have in custody."

"Why not give us a picture of him?"

"That, too, is classified material."

"Mr. Johnson has publicized a picture of his client which he says was given to him by Hussein's brother. The man in the picture appears to be the same man in the video."

"Ali Hussein doesn't have a brother. And our analysts have determined the picture is at least twelve years old."

"Who is Andrew Hurd?"

"We have never had an agent known as Andrew Hurd."

"Isn't he the man in charge in the video?"

"As far as we know, no one in the video is named Andrew Hurd."

"Johnson's report says that Kimberly Smith, the Stanford professor and television expert on terrorism, has ties to Andrew Hurd."

"All Mr. Johnson has is a picture of the person he calls Andrew Hurd with Kimberly Smith. I'm sure Ms. Smith knows many people, and she has been photographed thousands of times with thousands of people. That is the business she is in. She's surrounded by people."

"Is she a government agent?"

"Absolutely not."

"And who is Christina Rosario?"

"We have no record of anyone named Christina Rosario in any relevant agency. Our investigation so far has shown that the person Byron Johnson calls Christina Rosario had a long-term sexual relationship with Mr. Johnson and was with him in a vacation home owned by Mr. Johnson in the three days before she drowned. Local police are evaluating whether her death was a suicide, an accident, or a deliberate killing."

# 45

THE METROPOLITAN DETENTION CENTER was attached by sealed walkways, floor-by-floor, like conjoined twins, to the United States Attorney's Office at One St. Andrew's Plaza. Both buildings were surrounded by the narrow streets that bristled with concrete barricades, walls, and the steel mechanisms like shark jaws that would shred tires to pieces when they were open.

The entrance to the MDC was grim. Visitors had to pass through four separate stations, each of them with increasing severity. At the first, Byron Johnson had to display two forms of picture identification and surrender them in exchange for a brass chit. Like all other visitors, he had to turn in his cell phone, his watch, and his belt. At the next station, he had to put his briefcase, shoes, keys, coins, and wallet in plastic trays before they moved on a belt through a scanner. Barefoot, he had to walk through an electronic arch. At the last station, a guard passed a wand around his body, including the space under his testicles.

After months of regularly visiting Ali Hussein, Byron was patient through the whole process. The guards knew him. They were courteous. They knew his name. He knew some of their names. For some reason, Byron had always carried a card identifying him as a former captain in the US Army, and word of that had spread to some of the guards. That eased, to some extent, the way they treated him.

Before he could enter the hallways and elevators of the prison, he had to write in an old-fashioned log his own name and the purpose of the visit. *Byron Johnson. Attorney-client visit.* In theory, a lawyer could gain entry to the prison and visit a client any time of the day or night on any day of the year. In practice, if a lawyer made a visit after ordinary daytime hours, he or she could wait in this sign-in area for an hour before a guard appeared to escort him.

After Byron wrote his name and the purpose of his visit, a guard whom Byron had never seen said, "Mr. Johnson, could you step over here with me?"

Byron followed him to a group of unoccupied plastic chairs. In his mid-fifties, well-dressed and overly polite, the man, whose name tag was etched with the name "Medina," said, "Mr. Johnson, I'm afraid you won't be able to see your client."

"What's wrong?" Byron tried to control his voice, but fear had reduced it, like a dried reed, to a rasping sound. For a terrifying moment, Byron was convinced that he was being arrested and that the time had come when he, too, would be taken out of the world and consigned to the fear, isolation, and stress of long-term imprisonment.

"He's no longer in the facility."

"Say that again?"

"He's been removed.

"Who did that?"

"Assigned personnel."

"When?"

"Not long ago, Mr. Johnson."

"Why?"

"I don't have that information, sir."

"Where is he now?"

"I don't have that information either, Mr. Johnson."

"Who do you report to?"

"I can't tell you that, Mr. Johnson. My job was to tell you that this guy is no longer here."

As soon as he reached his apartment, Byron Johnson called Rodney Smith at CNN. Smith was a handsome, hard-working man who, three months earlier, had become the anchor of the CNN news show that ran from three to five in the afternoon. Over the last few weeks, Smith personally—and not one his assistants—had contacted Byron several times. Many of Rod's questions were about Simeon Black. Byron sometimes felt that Rod, who had started his career as a serious print journalist at the *Boston Globe* and the *Washington Post*, was interested in learning details about a journalist he admired and with whom Byron was connected, like a young baseball player asking questions of older managers about Johnny Bench to learn more about the master. Simeon had spent little time with other journalists and writers. He was a worker in the vineyards of information for his articles and never believed he was going to get the facts he needed from other writers. He got facts from people who were witnesses. Byron Johnson was a witness.

But Rodney Smith was also interested in what Byron knew, saw, and heard. He was one of the journalists at Byron's press conference at the Harvard Club. He had CNN run excerpts of the video of Ali Hussein being forced under water in a bathroom in some country somewhere in the world. Other networks, less willing to display brutal conduct by people who were obviously American, broadcast tamer portions of the video.

The full video, which clearly showed Andrew Hurd and Tom Nashatka in the room and managing the men who held and pushed Ali Hussein, had quickly made its way onto You-Tube. It had achieved viral status. So had Byron Johnson. He appeared on the most of the Internet postings with his image and words as filmed when he introduced the video.

Rod had several times invited Byron to appear on his show for an interview. He was impressed by Byron's steadiness, his handsome presence, that attractive combination of a classic WASP face and the black eyes of his Mexican mother. Byron had declined to do the on-camera interviews, but he had given Rod details about Simeon Black's work and his own dealings with Ali Hussein, the man invisible to the outside world, and the hidden process of the criminal case.

Rod Smith, who had given his private cell phone number to Byron, immediately took the call. "Byron, how are you?"

"I have some news for you."

"Yes?"

"Ali Hussein is gone."

"As in?"

"The government has removed him from the country. It's called extraordinary rendition."

"How do you know that?"

"I went to see him. I was told he was no longer there. I called the prosecutor. In fact, I bypassed the people I've been dealing with and contacted the U.S. Attorney himself. And he told me that Ali had been returned to administrative detention."

Rod Smith was an experienced journalist—there was a restrained edge of excitement in his tone. "Does anyone else know this?"

"No."

"Can I get you to come up here?"

"This time, for sure. I am the lawyer for a man who has been made to disappear."

"We can send a car down for you."

"No, I'll take that great limousine in the ground. I need to concentrate my thinking."

"Get here, if you can, Byron, in an hour. You know where we are?"

"I know—Columbus Circle."

"Check in with security. We'll let them know."

"Fair enough."

"Byron, thanks for this."

# 46

WIND-DRIVEN SNOW BLEW and wrapped itself in shawls around the slender, tall statute of Christopher Columbus. Mid-afternoon traffic, mainly yellow taxis, swirled continuously around the circle at the base of the statue. Byron, standing at the floor-to-ceiling window in the green room in the Time-Warner Building, waited calmly for the young intern to take him to the set. A television monitor was attached to the wall. Rod Smith was speaking. There were routine reports about explosions in Iraq, a stolen child in Florida. And a commercial for a credit card in which a strong young woman stood on the top of a very high rock pinnacle in a wasted landscape in the West.

Sipping lukewarm coffee as he waited, Byron recognized that he had traveled a long way since that desperate day, on the steps of the courthouse in Miami, when he had reacted to the live camera and the anxious, unfriendly reporters like the proverbial deer in the headlights, his awkward performance that Sandy Spencer once used to insult him. This morning, as the beautiful snow made New York a gracious postcard, he was assured and focused and at ease.

Another commercial was running when he entered the studio. Rod Smith, remaining seated because he was attached to a tiny microphone, reached out his hand. "Perfect timing," he said.

A young woman placed a microphone with a clip on Byron's lapel and draped a cord with an earpiece behind Byron's shoulder. She fitted the earpiece to his right ear.

"We'll have plenty of time with you," Rod said. "Look into the hole of the camera when the red light glows above it. Don't look at the red light above the hole. I'll introduce you. For the rest of the interview, just look at my face as I ask and you answer. Not into the camera."

Byron heard the count: *five, four, three, two, one, go.* Rod, in his vibrant voice and reading from a script scrolled on the screen of the camera, said, "Welcome back. Over the last six months we've been reporting on the case of Ali Hussein. He's the Syrian national who lived in this country for a decade or so until he was arrested in Bonn not long after the Iraq invasion. He had worked, he said, as an accountant, a skill that made him, according to anti-terrorism officials and federal prosecutors, one of the so-called masters of finance for al-Qaeda. After years in detention, Hussein was brought to the U.S. for prosecution in a civilian court. At the time, the Attorney General said the administration wanted to show the world the integrity of the our justice system. And, to the shock of many, Hussein faces the death penalty."

On a cue, Rod turned from the camera in front of him to face Byron. "Here with me on an exclusive basis is Hussein's lawyer, Byron Carlos Johnson. He's an Army veteran with a long and distinguished career as a trial lawyer. He has volunteered to represent Ali Hussein. Welcome to CNN, Mr. Johnson. We understand there have been some important new developments in the case."

Gazing at Rod's handsome face, Byron said, "There have been. Today I learned that my client has been removed from the prison in New York City where he has spent the last six months and sent out of the country. The prosecution, as I was told after I learned of his removal today, has been terminated on a claim that national security interests were impaired by continued prosecution. It is very disturbing that a defendant, any defendant, who faced a trial at which a jury could find him innocent has been deprived of that opportunity."

"What were the national security concerns?"

"That is a mystery to me. It may be, however, that the video I released a week ago showing the torture—including waterboarding—of Mr. Hussein could require the government to disclose other information it wants to hide."

"Questions have been raised about how authentic that video is."

"There are no legitimate questions about that video. The man who is beaten and interrogated and pushed under water to the point of near death is Ali Hussein. I have seen him dozens of times. One of the other men in the tape is an American agent who has acted under the name Andrew Hurd. That person is a torturer."

"How do you know that, Mr. Johnson?"

"The video tells me—tells us all—that he is. You see him on the tape ordering that unimaginable pain he inflicted on Ali Hussein."

"And how do you know his name is Andrew Hurd?"

"He has confronted me at least once, and given me that name. And I have other pictures of the same person."

"You've suggested that he doesn't work alone."

"Of course not. He's worked with the lead prosecutor, Hal Rana, in order to steal confidential information from me; with Christina Rosario, a covert agent who was secretly assigned to become my assistant in this case; and with the news commentator Kimberly Smith."

"Ms. Smith has appeared on CNN."

"And on Fox and on NBC. I have photographs of her with the man in the video and with the covert agent who succeeded in working for me, gaining access to all the information I had about my client."

"Is that Christina Rosario?"

"Like Andrew Hurd, she apparently had a real name and a fictional name. I never knew the real name. I knew her as Christina Rosario."

"We have reports that she committed suicide."

"I have heard those reports, too, Rod. They're false. She was killed."

"By whom?"

"The same people who killed the Pulitzer Prize–winning journalist Simeon Black. Mr. Black was working on articles about torture, so-called Arab terrorists, and the fate of American justice."

"And why is it that you think the people who killed Simeon Black killed Christina Rosario?"

"Because she told me."

By a slight alteration of his expression, Rod Smith made it clear that he had heard something in his earpiece. He turned to the camera. "Stay with us. After a break we'll return to Byron Johnson, the lawyer for accused terrorist Ali Hussein."

Knowing that there was a lull in the broadcast, Byron settled back slightly in the chair. He glanced at Rod Smith for
some sign of approval or disapproval. But Rod continued to
listen to a voice in his earpiece.

He looked at Byron. "Right at the moment the Attorney
General is starting a news conference in Washington. It's
about your client, and you. We're going to cover it live, and
then come back to you."

"That's fair game," Byron said.

Rod Smith stiffened his upper body when the camera
came on. "Welcome back again. We've just learned that the
Attorney General of the United States, in Washington, has just
started a press briefing on the fate of Ali Hussein, the accused
terrorist whose lawyer has been here with us. We turn now to
Attorney General Royce Gallanter."

Gallanter, a slender black man, stood at a podium that
bore on its front the shield of the United States Department
of Justice. He read from a prepared statement. "Prosecution
of complex cases of terrorism in a civilian court poses unique
difficulties. We knew that when Mr. Hussein was brought
to the United States for trial. This was never a case in which
simple evidence would suffice. This defendant, for example,
was not a driver for terrorist leaders. There were, in effect, no
eyewitnesses. He operated in the shadows, he was in many
ways an international financier. Our case required financial
forensics—complicated patterns of wire transfers, bank account statements, and numbered accounts."

Byron knew he had to call on all of his experiences in life,
and to do so at this moment, on live national television, for
whatever number of short minutes might be given to him after

Royce Gallanter's press conference ended. Byron was not going to let himself stumble for words, or look uncomfortable, or abandon his main themes—that it was sheer abuse to take away Ali Hussein, and that this was a prosecution that had relied on terror, coercion, and murder, and which had long ago abandoned even the appearance of fairness to stage a show trial.

The Attorney General continued: "We knew that secrets in the war on terror might be jeopardized in this case. There was always the possibility that identities of important federal agents might be revealed, and that the ways in which we collect, analyze, and act on financial information might be put on public display."

The Attorney General paused, appearing to focus even more intently on the camera in front of him. Byron had a sense that the next words would be directed at him. "There is another reason why we have had to return Mr. Hussein to overseas detention rather than proceed with the trial here. He was represented by a New York lawyer named Byron Johnson who at every step of the process violated the requirements of confidentiality that he had promised to adhere to and that presidential executive orders require he follow. He has shared with people who were never authorized to receive it confidential details of things that happened in court, before a federal judge. He gave documents to outsiders, including many journalists, that he knew were sensitive and confidential and whose secrecy he was obligated to maintain. He may well have planned this outcome—the impossibility of our effectively trying his client—by shattering his obligations to the court and to our system of justice."

Byron overcame that flash of fear that swept through him as he heard these words. The man who was accusing him in this way, and suggesting that Byron would be punished, was, after all, the Attorney General of the United States. He commanded an army of police officers, FBI agents, and lawyers who would obey any order he might give to take down Byron Johnson. To overcome the fear, Byron reached into that core where his sense of calm and toughness was lodged. In seconds, he knew, the camera would re-focus on him.

Royce Gallanter ordered: "We will not let this case deter us from displaying for the world the American system of justice, which is and always will be a model for the world to emulate. Thank you all."

The Attorney General stepped away from the podium. Just before the scene closed, a reporter's voice rang out, "Where is Ali Hussein?"

"That was Royce Gallanter," Rodney Smith said as he gazed into the black hole of the camera, "the Attorney General of the United States, confirming our exclusive report that Ali Hussein, an accused terrorist facing the death penalty, has been removed from the United States."

Rod turned toward Byron. "We still have with us Byron Carlos Johnson, the lawyer for Ali Hussein. These are harsh words from the Attorney General, Mr. Johnson. Your reaction?"

"The failure of this prosecution was the result of what the Justice Department did, not what I did. The torture depicted on that video was only part of the campaign of terror that the government has used."

"What else?"

"Holding my client in solitary detention for years, during which his only visitor was the agent we see in the video hitting him and orchestrating his waterboarding. Keeping that video hidden, presumably on phony national security grounds, from the defense and even from the federal judge overseeing the case. Recruiting people to extract information from Mr. Hussein when they knew he was represented by me."

"Doesn't the government have a right to investigate crimes?"

"Of course. But it does not have the right to commit crimes and to abuse and torture."

Rod Smith asked, "What about you, Mr. Johnson?"

"Look, Rod. I'm just a lawyer. I represented a client. I learned things as the case moved forward that I believed helped my client. I looked forward to the trial and to having a jury decide his guilt or innocence. Ali Hussein has been deprived of that right."

Rod Smith said, "That's all the time we have, Mr. Johnson, on this fascinating and disturbing story. Thanks for coming in."

Utterly calm, Byron nodded. "Thanks for helping the truth."

# 47

HELEN WILSON, STILL AT irregular and unpredictable hours, brought Byron the newspapers each day. Each time she had to make her way through reporters and cameramen waiting in the wet cold on the sidewalks of Laight Street. On her first visit after the CNN show, she passed by the reporters and cameramen without being asked a single question, as though she was another tenant in the iron-façaded building. Then the doorman told the reporters that the comely woman in her early fifties was a frequent visitor to Byron Johnson. She smiled like a gracious and patient school teacher when she moved through the excited gauntlet of reporters, not even answering the question, "Who are you?"

Byron had taped to a wall in the kitchen the front page of the *Post* that appeared after the CNN interview: *Qaeda Lawyer Queers Trial.* Next to that headline was a doctored picture of Byron's face wearing the headgear of Osama bin Laden. Several long articles appeared in the *Times.* Byron read them carefully, searching for reports on where Ali Hussein was and for anything that would give him a clue as to what steps the government was taking against Byron himself.

There was no hard news about Ali Hussein. One article suggested, based on an anonymous source, that Ali Hussein was in Romania, where there were still "black prisons." Another anonymous source said that Ali was cooperating with the government in the disclosure of "vast reservoirs of hidden funds" at banks in Spain, Syria, and Singapore. And another source said that he was assisting in an ongoing criminal investigation of his former lawyer, Byron Carlos Johnson.

"Do you think that's possible?" Helen asked.

"There's an expression in this business about clients. They're either at your feet or at your throat."

She paused, ignoring the hint of false bravado.

"How do you really feel about all this, Byron?"

"What? That Ali is helping them to put together an indictment of me?"

She nodded slightly, a look of concern and sympathy on her face.

"Of course it makes me anxious. For years I had an easy passage in life. I didn't even have to take the subways. I wanted for nothing."

"That doesn't necessarily remove fear and anxiety from anybody's life."

"It did for me. I'm almost embarrassed to admit that the only shock I had in years was when Joan said she was leaving me. I loved her, I loved the life we had together."

"What happened?"

"She fell in love with somebody else."

"That can't be the whole answer."

"Of course not. But I ran out of time trying to figure out all the other reasons. My father taught me to march forward in life, face what's ahead of you, not what's behind you. That's probably why he moved from assignment to assignment: Mexico, Uganda, Paris, even Vietnam in the early sixties. At the time I was a kid, and I didn't learn he was in Vietnam until he died twenty years ago."

"I have a confession. I looked up your father on Wikipedia. He had one of those lives I associate with WASP aristocrats in the early twentieth century. Fancy-dancy prep school. Princeton, the Foreign Service, Colonel in the Army during World War Two, Ambassador to Mexico, Ambassador to Egypt, editorial board of *Foreign Affairs* magazine."

"Wasn't the world a better place before Google and the Internet? There was once some privacy and mystery in the world."

"You're there, too, on the Internet."

"I know. I stopped looking at it."

"You should. I checked just yesterday. There are articles on how courageous you are. Someone compared you to Daniel Ellsberg, and Ellsberg, now ancient, said the video you released was more powerful than all of the Pentagon Papers."

"And other people are saying that I'm a traitor, that I'm a lawyer for terrorists, that I'm an incompetent fool."

"What do you think you are?"

"I think I have never been more settled and centered and happier in my life."

Helen smiled. "I'm glad I answered that ad in the *Voice*."

"So am I."


Three hours later they left the building. It was dark. Byron held Helen Wilson's hand. On the sidewalk, in the iron-gray cold, a dozen or so people with microphones and cameras suddenly swarmed out of panel trucks and cars in which they had been keeping warm.

"Mr. Johnson. Mr. Johnson. Byron." Multiple voices called out. Wearing only a blue blazer, white shirt open at the collar, gray slacks, and a scarf, Byron was relaxed and smiling. He said nothing. He led Helen to the sidewalk and, as if by a miracle, a taxi pulled up, and they climbed into it, Helen first.

They drove to the East Village. Helen had a role in *The Merry Wives of Windsor*. Byron sat in the small audience, engrossed by her performance.

# 48

*THE SUN IS DAZZLING. The Atlantic is exquisitely blue. In the distance, the small outer islands covered with pine trees seem to be on fire without ever being consumed by the afternoon light. My two grown sons, both in their thirties, in the strength and wonderful vitality of their lives, are tossing a fleet Frisbee across the verdant lawn that leads to rugged shrubbery on the edge of the small cliff and Maine boulders overlooking the ocean.*

*The air is hot and dry. It's filled with the summer fragrance of pine, the sea, and the moss and seaweed on the boulders. My three grandchildren—Hector, Tomas's son, dark like my mother, and Hunter's twins, Foster and Tom, with my father's slim, blond litheness and elegance even though they are only seven—run, screaming happily, back and forth between their fathers, trying to intercept the Frisbee. Here they are, my sons and my grandsons, together for the first time with me.*

*Their wives are in the kitchen behind me. They like each other. I can hear that in their voices. They're at ease in their lives. If divorce and disruption are in their future, I can't detect that. One is a doctor, the other is a lawyer. I don't know them well, but they are without pretense.*

*I've just finished a six-mile run on the winding, traffic-less roads of this island to which I've been coming in the summers all of my life. Helen, who rode on a bicycle beside me while I ran, is in the shower. I'm still sweating, drinking lemonade, and standing*

*on the flagstones of the old patio where my mother and father en-*
*tertained famous people when I was a kid. Their ghosts are here.*
*They seemed to my eyes to be happy, successful people. But who*
*can ever know these things? My parents are dead, and not one of*
*their famous friends is still alive.*

*Those of us here now—my sons, my grandchildren, their vi-*
*brant mothers, Helen, and me—are vital, as were those guests in*
*that long-ago time, in this moment in the high Maine summer.*
*The sun and the clean, bracing air gave them, and now us, that vi-*
*tality, the joy that can sometimes come in the simple act of living.*

*My sons are intelligent men, and they have overcome the hurt*
*feelings I know they bore toward me in the years when they were*
*at school in Manhattan as boys, then in Massachusetts at board-*
*ing school, and then in college. I had become the father for them*
*that my father was for me. Remote, cool, often inaccessible, more*
*of a message-giver than a mentor. Now they have allowed me to*
*become their friend. I ask them for advice. I tell them my truths,*
*I've asked for their forgiveness. I feel they are giving it to me, and*
*I want to be worthy of it and of them.*

*For the last several days I've honored my sons' need to know*
*what I've done, where I stand now, and what the future will likely*
*be for me. Just before I left New York, I hired Vito Calabrese, a*
*criminal defense lawyer whose name I'd heard for years. As I*
*explained to my sons, he had represented Mafia dons, indicted*
*Congressmen, investment bankers, and even Elaine, the woman*
*who owned Elaine's, the celebrity restaurant on Second Avenue.*
*She'd scratched the face of a customer early on a Sunday morn-*
*ing. Vito, a friend of the police commissioner and Rudy Giuliani,*
*got the charges dismissed. When I left New York two months ago,*
*I left with the settled sense I was in the right hands. Vito may be*

*flamboyant—he could get rid of the colorful matching ties and pocket squares—but he is steady, intelligent, and realistic.*

*Hal Rana has moved to Washington to become an Assistant Attorney General, a significant promotion. Justin Goldberg has issued a one-sentence order dismissing all charges against Ali Hussein. The Imam and Khalid Hussein were released from custody without being indicted. The government has refused to apologize to the Muslim community in Newark for the seizure of the mosque.*

*And Ali Hussein is somewhere in the world.*

*"And what about you, Dad?" Tomas asked.*

*"Vito says the grand jury has been disbanded. Since Jesse Ventura disappeared—since, as the government says, he never existed—Vito says that any evidence that Jesse gave the grand jury would be zeroed out. Vito has a way with words. But he also said that they can put together another grand jury. Something can happen, or nothing."*

*"How do you feel, Dad?"*

*"Completely at peace. Blessed to be here with you, your wives, and your kids."*

*I haven't told them about the one-page note Eben Cain, the man who watched over this house in the lonely winters, handed me yesterday. Slow-speaking and deliberate, Eben said it had been months since he looked into the old mail slot in the waiting room at the island's dock, where for years his family's mail was left. In his one concession to the modern world, Eben had a shiny new mailbox in the post office in Boothbay Harbor. He went there once every two weeks.*

*"Sometimes," Eben told me, "I take a gander in the old slot. This was in it."*

*Eben handed me an envelope on which Christina's writing appeared. "For Eben Cain, To Be Given to Mr. Johnson." I opened the envelope. In it was a single sheet of paper. "Carlos, if you wish to follow the money, there's an account in Banco Popular de Venezuela in Bogota. Anyone who has the numbers I've written here can get full access to the money in that account." At the bottom of the page was a line of fourteen numbers and below that were the words: "All my love, Brighteyes."*

*Tonight we'll have a bonfire on the beach. We've already assembled the stones and the wood and the seaweed for the fire. I'll show my grandchildren how to bake lobster in the seaweed and stones as my own grandfather taught me.*

*And I'll let Christina's note float momentarily over the fire and then dissolve as the ashes disperse into the night air.*

*Now I hear the screen door open. At different times in my life, I've seen my grandfather, my mother, my father, my wife, my boys when they were children, and Christina Rosario walk through that door. And now, in this place and time, I see Helen.*

*"Helen," I say. "Come here. Let me hold you."*